Miss Mephistopheles

Miss Mephistopheles

A Novel

Fergus Hume

MINT EDITIONS

Miss Mephistopheles: A Novel was first published in 1880.

This edition published by Mint Editions 2020.

ISBN 9781513278353 | E-ISBN 9781513278810

Published by Mint Editions®

 MINT
EDITIONS

minteditionbooks.com

Publishing Director: Jennifer Newens
Design & Production: Rachel Lopez Metzger
Project Manager: Micaela Clark
Typesetting: Westchester Publishing Services

Contents

I

Faces in the Fire

A wet Sunday—dreary, dismal, and infinitely sloppy. Even the bells ringing the people into evening service seemed to feel the depressing influence of the weather, and their brazen voices sounded hoarse and grumbling, as if they rang under protest. Cold, too!—not a brisk sharp frost—for here in Melbourne frost and snow are unknown; but a persevering, insinuating, gnawing cold, just disagreeable enough to make one shiver and shake with anxiety to get home to a bright fire and dry clothes. Overhead a leaden-coloured sky, with great masses of black clouds, from out whose sombre bosoms poured the steady rain, splashing noisily on the shining roofs, and swelling the gutters in the streets to miniature torrents.

And then the wind,—a gusty, chilly wind,—that came along unexpectedly, and drove the unwilling rain against the umbrellas of struggling pedestrians, or else took a mean advantage of its power, and turned their umbrellas inside out, with a shrill whistle of triumph. The steady light streamed out from the painted church windows, and the dull, blurred glare of the street lamps was reflected in the wet pavements. Ugh! a night not fit for a dog to be out in, and yet there were a good many people hurrying along to the church, in answer to the clamorous voices of the bells.

Some folk, however—wise in their generation—preferred staying at home to sitting in church, with damp boots and a general sense of stickiness about their clothes, and though possibly their souls suffered from such an omission, their bodies were certainly more comfortable. Among these godless people, who thus preferred comfort to religion, were two young men occupying a room on a first floor, the windows of which looked across to the church, now full of damp and steaming worshippers.

A room in a boarding-house—especially one where boarders only pay twenty-five shillings a week—is not generally a very luxurious apartment, and this special room was certainly no exception to the rule. It was square, with a fairly lofty ceiling, and the walls were covered with a dull red paper, which, being mellowed by time, had assumed a somewhat rusty hue.

It was rapidly growing dark outside, and there was no light in the room, save that which came from a roaring coal fire blazing brightly up the chimney, and illuminating the apartment in a curiously fantastic manner. It sent out red shafts of light into dark corners, as if to find out what was hidden there, and then being disappointed, would sink back into a dull, sulky glow, only to fall into a chaotic mass, and blaze merrily up once more.

The apartment wherein the fire played these elfish tricks was furnished comfortably, but the furniture had a somewhat dingy look. The carpet was threadbare, except under the table, where there could be traced some vestiges of its original pattern. A cottage piano was pushed into a corner slanting ways, and beside it was a great untidy pile of music. At one end of the room, a desk covered with papers, and immediately above it a shelf containing a small array of well-worn books. Near the desk stood an aggravatingly bright sideboard, whereon were some glasses, a jug of water, and a half-empty bottle of whisky. Four or five lounging chairs of wicker-work were scattered about, covered with rugs of wallaby fur, whilst the walls and mantelpiece were almost covered with photographs, mostly of women, but here and there a male face, showing the well-known features of Beethoven, Chopin, and other famous musicians.

This somewhat incongruous apartment was a private sitting-room in an East Melbourne boarding-house, and was at present in the occupation of Ezra Lazarus, journalist. Ezra Lazarus himself was seated at the piano playing snatches of music, while on the hearth-rug, smoking a pipe, lay a man propped up on his elbow, with his head resting on his hand, staring into the burning coals, and listening to his friend playing.

Ezra Lazarus was a young man of medium height, with a slender figure, a pale face, rather dreamy, dark eyes, and black hair and beard carefully trimmed. He dressed neatly, and, in contrast to most of his race, wore no jewellery. Why he had become a journalist no one knew,—himself least of all,—as his tastes did not lie in the direction of newspaper work, for having all the Hebraic love of music, he was an accomplished pianist. As for the rest—staid in his demeanour, soft-spoken in his language, and much given to solitary wanderings. Yet he was no misanthrope, and those who knew him intimately found him a most charming companion, full of quaint ideas and bookish lore, but he was essentially a man of ideality, and shrank from contact with the work-a-day world. For such a nature as this a journalistic sphere was most unsuitable, and he felt it to be so, but having drifted into such a position, he lacked the energy to extricate himself from his uncongenial employment, and accepted his fate with oriental apathy, recompensing himself in some measure by giving every spare moment to the study of music.

The man lying before the fire was the direct opposite of Ezra, both in appearance and temperament. A tall, sinewy-figured young fellow of six-and-twenty, with restless keen grey eyes under strongly-marked eyebrows, and a sensitive mouth, almost hidden by a small fair moustache. His nose was thin and straight, with delicately-cut nostrils, and his head was well set on his broad shoulders, albeit he had a trick of throwing it back which gave him a somewhat haughty carriage. He had a fair complexion, with that reddish-brown hue which comes from constantly living in the open air, and altogether looked like a man addicted to sport rather than to study.

This was Keith Stewart, who, having passed most of his life in Gippsland, and in wandering about Australia generally, had a year previously come down to Melbourne with the laudable intention of devoting himself to literature. That he was poor might be surmised from his shabby, well-brushed clothes, and his face constantly wore that expression of watchfulness habitual to those who have to fight the world in their youth and be on their guard against everyone.

That two such dissimilar natures as these could find any reciprocity appears strange, but curiously enough some undercurrent of sympathy had drawn them together from the first time they met. Jew and Gentile, musician and student, different nationalities, different trains of thought, yet the mere fact that they could both live in an ideal world of their own creation, heedless of the restless life which seethed around, seemed to form a bond of concord between them, and their mutual isolation drew them almost imperceptibly together.

Keith had only been boarding in the house a week, consequently Ezra knew nothing about his friend's life, beyond the fact that he was poor and ambitious. As Stewart never volunteered any information about himself, Ezra, with the delicacy of a sensitive nature, shrank from forcing himself on his confidence. The inexhaustible subjects of books and music, a walk by the banks of the Yarra, or an occasional visit to the theatre, had been, so far, the limit of their social companionship. Their inner selves were still unknown to each other. To all, however, there comes a moment when the desire to unburden the mind to a sympathetic nature is strong, and it was in such a moment that Ezra Lazarus first learned the past life of Stewart.

On this dreary Sunday night Ezra let his fingers wander over the piano, vaguely following his thoughts, and the result was a queer mingling of melodies—now a bizarre polonaise of Chopin, with its fantastic blending of patriotic joy and despairing pain, then a rush of stormy chords, preluding a Spanish dance, instinct with the amorous languor and fierce passion of the south. Outside, the shrill wind could be heard sweeping past, a sheet of rain would lash wildly against the windows, and at intervals the musical thunder of the organ sounded from the adjacent church.

Keith smoked away steadily and listened drowsily to the pleasant mingling of sounds, until Ezra began to play the Traviata music, with its feverish brilliancy and undercurrent of sadness. Then he suddenly started, clenched his hand, and taking his pipe from his mouth, heaved an impatient sigh, upon hearing which, Lazarus stopped playing, and turned slowly round.

"A link of memory?" he said, in his soft voice, referring to the music.

Stewart replaced his pipe, blew a thick wreath of smoke, and sighed again.

"Yes," he replied, after a pause; "it recalls to me—a woman."

Ezra laughed half sadly, half mockingly.

"Always the Eternal feminine of George Sand."

Keith sat up cross-legged in front of the fire and shrugged his shoulders.

"Don't be cynical old chap," he said, glancing round; "I'm sick of hearing the incessant railing against women—good heavens! are we men so pure ourselves, that we can afford to cast stones against the sex to which our mothers and sisters belong."

"I did not mean to be cynical," replied Ezra, clasping his hands round one of his knees, "I only quoted Sand, because when a man is thinking, it is generally—a woman.

"Or a debt—or a crime—or a sorrow," interposed the other quickly; "we can ring the changes on all of them."

"Who is cynical now?" asked the Jew, with a smile.

"Not I," denied Keith, emphatically, drawing hard at his pipe; "or if I am, it is only that thin veneer of cynicism, under which we hide our natural feelings now-a-days; but the music took me back to the time when 'Plancus was consul'—exactly twelve months ago."

"Bah! Plancus is consul still; don't be downhearted, my friend; you are still in the pleasant city of Prague."

"Pleasant? that is as it may be. I think it a very disagreeable city without money. Bohemianism is charming in novels, but in real life it is generally a hunt after what Murger calls that voracious animal, the half-crown."

"And after women!"

"Ah, bah! Lais and Phryne; both charming, but slightly improper, not to say expensive."

"Take the other side of the shield," said the Jew gently.

"Lucretia, and—and—by Jove, I can't recollect the name of any other virtuous woman."

"Who is the lady of the music?"

"My affianced wife," retorted Stewart curtly.

"Ah!" said Ezra thoughtfully, "then we have a feeling in common, I am also engaged."

Stewart laughed gaily.

"And we both think our lady-loves perfect," he said lightly. "'Dulcinea is the fairest woman in the world,'—poor Don Quixote."

"Mine is to me," said Ezra emphatically.

"Of course," answered Stewart, with a smile. "I can picture her, tall, dark, and stately, an imperial daughter of Judah, with the beauty of Bathsheba and the majesty of Esther."

"Entirely wrong," replied Lazarus dryly, "she is neither tall, dark, nor stately, but—"

"The exact opposite—I take your meaning," said Keith composedly; "well, my Dulcinea is like the sketch I have given—beautiful, clever, poor, and—a governess."

"And you haven't seen her for a year?"

"No—a whole twelvemonth—she is up Sandhurst way trying to hammer dates and the rule of three into the thick heads of five small brats, and I—well I'm an unsuccessful literary man, doing what is vulgarly known as 'a perish.'"

"What made you take up writing?" asked Lazarus.

"What made me take up writing?" repeated Stewart, staring vaguely into the fire. "Lord knows—destiny, I suppose—I've had a queer sort of life altogether. I was born of poor but honest parents, quite the orthodox style of thing, isn't it?"

"Are your parents alive?"

"Dead!" laconically.

There was a pause of a few moments, during which time Keith was evidently deep in thought.

"According to Sir Walter Scott," he observed at length, "every Scotchman has a pedigree. I've got one as long as the tail of a kite, only not so useful. I'd sell all my ancestors, as readily as Charles Surface did his, for a few pounds. My people claim to be connected with the royal Stewarts."

"Your name is spelt differently."

"It's spelt correctly," retorted Keith coolly, "in the good old Scottish fashion; as for the other, it's the French method acclimatised by Mary Stuart when she married the Dauphin of France."

"Well, now I know your pedigree, what is the story of your life?"

"My life?—oh! I'm like Canning's knife-grinder. 'Story, I've got none to tell.' My father and mother found royal descent was not bread and butter, so they sold the paternal acres and came out to Australia, where I was born. The gold fever was raging then, but I suppose they inherited the bad luck of the Stewarts, for they did not make a penny; then they started a farm in Gippsland and ruined themselves. My father died of a broken heart, and my mother soon followed, so I was left an orphan with next to nothing. I wandered all over Australia, and did anything that turned up. Suppressing the family pride, I took a situation in a Sandhurst store, kept by a man called Proggins, and there I met Eugénie Rainsford, who, as I told you, taught the juvenile Progginses. I had a desultory sort of education from my father, and having read a good deal, I determined to take to literature, inspired, I suppose, by the poetic melancholy of the Australian bush. I wrote poetry with the usual success; I then went on the stage, and found I wasn't a heaven-born genius by any means, so I became a member of the staff of a small country paper, wrote brilliant articles about the weather and crops, varied by paste-and-scissors' work. Burned the midnight oil, and wrote some articles, which were accepted in Melbourne, so, with the usual prudence of genius, I threw up my billet and came down here to set the Thames, or rather the Yarra, on fire. Needless to remark, I didn't succeed or I shouldn't be here, so there is my history in a nutshell."

"And Miss Rainsford?"

"Oh, I engaged myself to her before I left Sandhurst," said Keith, his face growing tender, "bless her—the letters she has written me have been my bulwark against despair—ah! what a poor devil a man is in this world without a good woman's love to comfort him."

"Are you doing anything now?" said Ezra thoughtfully.

"Nothing. I'm leading a hand-to-mouth, here-to-day-gone-to-morrow existence. I'm a vagabond on the face of the earth, a modern Cain, Bonnie Prince Charlie in exile—the infernal luck of my royal ancestors still sticks to me, but, ah, bah!" shrugging his shoulders, "don't let's talk any more, old chap, we can resume the subject to-morrow, meanwhile play me something. I'm in a poetic mood, and would like to build castles in the air."

Ezra laughed, and, turning to the piano, began to play one of Henselt's morceaux, a pathetic, dreamy melody, which came stealing softly through the room, and filled the soul of the young man with vague yearnings.

Staring idly into the heart of the burning coals, he saw amid the bluish flames and red glimmer of the fire a vision of the dear dead days of long ago—shadows appeared, the shadows of last year.

A glowing sunset, bathing a wide plain in delicate crimson hues; a white gate leading to a garden bright with flowers, and over the gate the shadow of a beautiful woman stood talking to the shadow of a man—himself. Mnenosyne—saddest of deities—waved her wand, and the shadows talked.

"And when will you come back, Keith?" asked the girl shadow.

"When I am a great man," replied the other shadow proudly. "I am riding forth like Poe's knight in search of El Dorado."

"El Dorado is far away," returned the sweet voice of the girl; "it is the Holy Grail of wealth, and can never be discovered."

"I will find it," replied the man shadow hopefully. "Meanwhile, you will wait and hope."

"I will wait and hope," replied the girl, smiling sadly; and the shadows parted.

The rain beat steadily against the panes, the soft music stole through the room, and Stewart, with idle gaze, stared into the burning heart of the fire, as if he expected to find there the El Dorado of his dreams.

II

KEITH MEETS WITH AN ADVENTURE

After a storm comes a calm; so next morning the sun was shining brightly in the blue sky, and the earth had that clean, wholesome appearance always to be seen after heavy rains. The high wind had dried the streets, the drenched foliage of the trees in the Fitzroy Gardens looked fresh and green, and there was a slight chilliness in the atmosphere which was highly invigorating. Indeed, it was like a spring morning, mildly inspiriting; whilst all around there seemed to be a pleasant sense of new-born gladness quickening both animal and vegetable life.

After breakfast, Ezra, who was going to the office of *The Penny Whistle*, the paper for which he worked, asked Keith to walk into town with him, and, as the young man had nothing particular to do, he gladly assented. They strolled slowly through the gardens, admiring the glistening green of the trees, the white statues sharply accentuated against their emerald back-ground, and the vivid dashes of bright colour given by the few flowers then in bloom.

Stewart appeared to have quite recovered from his megrims of the previous night, and strolled gaily along, every now and then inhaling a long breath of the keen air. Ezra, who was watching him closely, saw from his actions his intense appreciation of his surroundings, and was satisfied that the young man possessed in a high degree that poetical instinct which has such an affinity with the joyousness or gloom of Nature.

"Ah! this is a morning when it is good to live," said Keith brightly. "I always envied the satyrs and dryades of heathendom, with their intense animal enjoyment of Nature—not sensuality, but exuberant capability of enjoying a simple life."

"Like that with which Hawthorn endowed Donatallo?" suggested Ezra.

"Poor Donatallo!" said Stewart, with a sigh; "he is a delightful illustration of the proverb, 'Where ignorance is bliss'—he was happy till he loved—so was Undine till she obtained a soul."

"You seem to have read a great deal?" observed Lazarus, looking at him.

"Oh, faith; my reading has been somewhat desultory," replied Stewart carelessly. "All is fish that comes to my net, and the result is a queer jumble of information; but let us leave this pleasant gossiping, and come down to this matter-of-fact world. How do you think I can better my position?"

"I hardly know as yet," replied the Jew, thoughtfully caressing his beard; "but if you want immediate work, I can put you in the way of obtaining employment."

"Literary work?"

"Unfortunately no—a clerkship in a—a—well, an office."

"Ugh! I hate the idea of being cribbed and confined in an office; it's such an artificial existence. However, beggars can't be choosers, so tell me all about it."

"My father wants a clerk," said Ezra deliberately, "and if I recommended you I think you could get the position."

"Humph! And what is your father's occupation?"

"Not a very aristocratic one,—a pawnbroker."

Keith stopped short, and looked at his companion in surprise.

"I can't imagine you being the son of a pawnbroker," he said in a puzzled tone.

"Why not?" asked Ezra serenely. "I must be the son of some one."

"Yes; but a pawnbroker, it's so horribly un-poetical. Your father ought to have been a man of letters—of vague speculations and abstruse theories—a modern Rabbi Judah holding disputations about the Talmud."

Lazarus shrugged his shoulders, and walked slowly onward, followed by his companion.

"My dear lad, the days of Maimonides are past, and we are essentially a money-making race. The curse which Jehovah pronounced on the Jews was the same as that of Midas—they turn everything they touch into gold."

"A pleasant enough punishment."

"Midas did not find it so; but to resume—my father, Jacob Lazarus, has his shop in Russell Street, so I will speak to him to-day, and if he is agreeable, I will take you with me to-morrow. I've no doubt you'll get the billet, but the wages will be small."

"At all events, they will keep body and soul together till I find my El Dorado."

"You refer to literary fame, I suppose. How did you first take to writing?"

"I think you asked me that question last night," said Keith, smiling, "and I told you I couldn't explain. Like Pope, I lisped in numbers, and the numbers came. I've no doubt they were sufficiently bad. I'm sure I don't know why all authors begin with verse; perhaps it's because rhymes are so easy—fountain suggests mountain, and dove is invariably followed by love."

"Have you had any articles accepted since your arrival in Melbourne?"

"One or two, but generally speaking, no one acknowledges that a possible Shakespeare or Dickens is embodied in me. I've sent plays to managers, which have been declined on the plea that all plays come from London. I have seen editors, and have been told there was no room on the press—publishers have seen me, and pointed out that a colonial novel means ruination—encouraging for the future brainworkers of Australia, isn't it?"

"We must all serve our apprenticeship," answered Lazarus quietly. "The longest lane has a turning."

"No doubt; but my particular lane seems devilish long."

Ezra laughed, and they walked down Collins Street, watching the crowd of people hurrying along to business, the cabs darting here and there, and the cable tramcars sliding smoothly along. Pausing a moment near the Scotch Church, they heard a street organ playing a bright melody.

"What tune is that?" asked Keith, as they resumed their walk. "Sounds awfully pretty."

"Song from 'Prince Carnival,'" replied Ezra, referring to an opera then running at the Bon-Bon Theatre. "Caprice sings it."

"Oh, Caprice. I'd like to see that opera," said Keith. "You might take me to the theatre to-night to see it."

"Very well," assented Ezra. "You will like Caprice—she is very charming."

"And if rumour speaks truly, very wicked."

"Added to which, she is the best-hearted woman in the world," finished the Jew dryly.

"What a contradiction," laughed Stewart.

"Women are always contradictory—'tis a privilege of the sex."

"And one they take full advantage of."

This airy badinage came to an end somewhat abruptly, for just as they arrived near the Victoria Coffee Palace, they were startled by the shriek of a woman.

On the other side of the street a gaudily-dressed girl was crying and wringing her hands, while a child of about seven years of age was standing paralysed with fear directly in the way of a tram-car that came rushing down the incline. The two men stood horror-struck at what seemed to be the inevitable death of the child, for, though the driver put on the brakes, the speed was too great, and destruction appeared inevitable. Suddenly Keith seemed to recover the use of his limbs, and, with a sudden spring, bounded forward and tore the child off the fatal track, himself falling together with the child to the ground. He was not a moment too soon, for hardly had he fallen before the car at a slower speed rolled past, and ultimately came to a standstill at the foot of the incline.

Stewart arose to his feet considerably shaken, his clothes torn and covered with mud, and a painful feeling in the arm, on which he had fallen. Ezra crossed over to him, and the rescued child was standing on the footpath in the grasp of the gaudily-dressed girl who spoke volubly, regardless of the crowd of people standing by.

The conductor of the car came to inquire into the affair, and having found that no one was hurt, retired, and the tram was soon sliding down the street. The crowd dispersed gradually, until only the child, Ezra, Keith, and the shrill-voiced girl were left.

"Oh! gracious, good 'eavens!" said this young lady, who appeared to be a nursemaid, and spoke rapidly, without any stops; "to think as you should have bin nearly squashed by that ingine, and all comin' of runnin' out into the road, an' taking no notice of me as was postin' a letter in the pillar-box, not seeing anythin', thro' want of eyes at the back of me 'ead."

The child, a quaint, thin-faced little girl, with dark eyes and glorious reddish-coloured hair, took no notice of this outburst, but pulled Keith's coat to attract his attention.

"Thank you, man," she said, in a thin, reedy voice; "I will tell mumsey, and she will say nice things to you, and I will give you a kiss."

Keith was touched in his soft heart by this naïve appeal, and, bending down, kissed the pale little face presented to him, much to the alarm of the nursemaid, who lifted up her hands in horror.

"Oh! gracious, good 'eavens!" she piped shrilly, "as to what your mar will say, Miss Megs, I don't know, a-kissin' strange gents in the h'open street; not but what he don't deserve it, a-dragin' you from under the ingine, as oughtn't to be let run to spile—"

"Hold your tongue, Bliggings," said Ezra sharply; "you ought to look more carefully after Meg, or she'll be killed some day."

"Oh! gracious and good 'eavens!" cried Bliggings sniffing, "if it ain't Mr. Lazarhouse; and, beggin' your pardon, sir, it ain't my fault, as is well known to you as children will 'ookit unbeknown't to the most wary."

"There, there," said Lazarus, bending down to kiss Meg; "least said, soonest mended; thanks to my friend here, it's no worse."

"Which he ought to git a meddler," asserted Miss Bliggings, on whose feminine heart Keith's handsome face had made an impression. "But, gracious and good 'eavens, they only gives 'em for drowndin', though I never lets Miss Megs go near water, ingines bein' unexpected in their actions, and not to be counted on in their movin's."

"Good-bye, Meg," said Lazarus, cutting short Bliggings in despair. "Tell your mamma I'll call and see her about this."

"And bring the man," said Meg, glancing at Keith.

"Yes, and bring the man," repeated Ezra, upon which Meg, being satisfied, made a quaint-like curtsey to both men, and was going away, when she suddenly came back, and pulling Keith's coat till he bent down, put her arms round his neck and kissed him.

"Mumsey will be nice," she murmured, and then trotted quietly off with Bliggings, who kept expressing her opinion that, "Oh! gracious, good 'eavens! she was red up to her eyes at such conduct," a somewhat unnecessary assertion, seeing her complexion was permanently the colour of beetroot.

"Come into Lane's Hotel and have a glass of brandy," said Ezra, when Meg and her attendant had disappeared; "you need it after the shaking you have had."

"What is the child's name?" asked Keith, as he went into the bar. "You seem to know her."

Ezra laughed softly, and ordered a glass of brandy for his friend.

"A curious way Fate has of working," he said, rather irrelevantly. "She has played into your hands to-day, for that child is Kitty Marchurst's, better known as 'Caprice.'"

"I didn't know she had a child," said Keith. "Who is the father? Is she married?"

"No, she is not married. As to the father, it's a long story; I'll tell you all about it some day. Meanwhile, you have done her a service she will never forget."

"Much good it will be to me," said Keith disbelievingly

"You've exactly hit it," replied Ezra composedly. "She can do you a great deal of good, seeing that she is the reigning favourite of the stage at present. I will introduce you to her to-night, and then—"

"Well?"

Ezra shrugged his shoulders, and replied slowly,—

"The best friend an ambitious man can have is a clever woman; a wiser man than I made that remark."

III

Prince Carnival

The "Bon-Bon" was the smallest, prettiest, and most luxurious theatre in Melbourne, and was exclusively devoted to farcical comedy, burlesque, and opera-bouffe, the latter class of entertainment being now the attraction. There was no pit, the circle and boxes being raised but little above the level of the stalls. The decorations were pink, white, and gold, the seats being covered with pale, rose-coloured plush, with curtains and hangings to match, while the electric lights, shining through pink globes, gave quite a warm glow to the theatre. The dome was decorated with allegorical figures representing Momus, the God of laughter, and Apollo, the God of music, while all round the walls were exquisitely-painted medallions of scenes from celebrated operas and burlesques. The proscenium was a broad frame of dullish gold, the curtain of roseate plush, and on either side of the stage were life-size statues of Offenbach and Planché in white marble. Altogether, a charming theatre, more like a cosy drawing-room than a place of public entertainment.

At the entrance was a high flight of white marble stairs, leading to a wide corridor, the walls of which were hidden by enormous mirrors, and at intervals stood white marble statues of the Greek divinities, holding aloft electric lights. On the one side was the smoking-room,—a luxurious lounge,—and on the other a refreshment bar, all glass and glitter, which was crowded between the acts by the thirsty patrons of the play.

Ezra and Keith arrived about nine o'clock, just as the first act of "Prince Carnival" was over, and finding the *salon* tolerably full, Lazarus sat down near one of the small, marble-topped tables, and lighting his cigarette, proceeded to point out to Keith all the notabilities present.

The first to whom he called Stewart's attention was a group of three. One, a tall, portly-looking man, with a red, clean-shaven face and black hair, was irreproachably attired in evening dress, and chatted to a fair-haired youth with a supercilious smile, and a short, bald-headed old gentleman.

"You see those three?" said Ezra, indicating the group. "The dark man of the ponderous Samuel Johnson type is Ted Mortimer, the lessee of the theatre; the idiot with the eyeglass is Lord Santon, who has come out from London to see us barbarians, and the apoplectic party with the bald head is no less a personage than Mr. Columbus Wilks, the great globe-trotter, who is going to write a book about Australia and New Zealand."

"That will take him some time," observed Keith, with a smile.

"Not at all," said Lazarus coolly. "He will run through the whole of Australasia in a few weeks, be the guest of the governors of the different colonies, and then give his impressions of our government, politics, trade, amusements, and scenery in a series of brilliant articles, whose truth and accuracy will be quite in accordance with the time which he has taken to collect his materials."

"But he cannot judge of things so rapidly."

"Of course not; but he will view everything through the rose-coloured spectacles of champagne and adulation, so his book will depict our land as a kind of nineteenth-century Utopia."

"And Lord Santon?"

"An hereditary legislator, who is being *fêted* for his title, and will go back to his ancestral halls with the firm conviction that we are a kind-hearted race of—savages."

"You are severe," said Keith, in an amused tone; "you ought to give a lecture, entitled 'Men I have noticed;' it would certainly draw."

"Yes, all the women, not the men; they don't care for hearing remarks about themselves; but there is the bell for the rising of the curtain, so we had better go to our seats."

They left the now empty salon, and went into the dress circle, which holds the same rank in the colonies as the stalls do in the London theatres. Though the house was crowded, they succeeded in getting excellent seats, being, in fact, those always reserved for the critics of *The Penny Whistle*. The orchestra played a lively waltz, to which the gods in the gallery kept time, and then the curtain drew up on a charming scene, representing a square in Rome.

"Prince Carnival" was one of those frivolous French operas with a slightly naughty plot, witty dialogue, brilliant music, and plenty of opportunity for gay dresses and picturesque scenery. The principals and chorus consisted mostly of girls, with just a sprinkling of men, so that their deeper voices might balance the shrillness of those of the women. Of the plot, the least said the better, as it was merely a string of intrigues, connected by piquant couplets and sparkling choruses, with occasional ballets intervening.

As far as Keith could gather, it had something to do with the adventures of the quack Cagliostra in Rome, who was the comic man of the play, and figured in various disguises, the most successful being that of a prominent politician. Cagliostra tries to gain the affections of a young girl beloved by a mountebank called Prince Carnival, who thwarts him all through the play. The second act was the carnival at Rome, and a crowd of masquers were singing a riotous chorus and pelting one another with flowers. Suddenly, during a lull in this fantastic medley, a high, clear voice was heard executing a brilliant shake, and immediately afterwards Caprice bounded gaily on to the stage, singing a melodious waltz song, to which the masquers moved in measured time.

She was dressed in a harlequin costume, a mask on her face, a fool's baton in her hand, and innumerable silver bells hanging from her cap and dress, which jingled incessantly as she danced. But what attracted Keith's attention were the diamonds she wore—several stars and a necklace. She seemed one splendid blaze of jewels, and his eyes ached watching their flash and glitter during the rapid gyrations of her restless figure.

"Are those paste jewels?" he asked Ezra, in a whisper.

"Paste!" echoed that young man, with a soft, satirical laugh. "Caprice wear paste jewels! Ask the men she's ruined where all their thousands went—where all their lands, horses, shares, salaries, disappeared to! Paste! Bah! my dear fellow, you don't know the number of ruined homes and broken hearts those diamonds represent."

The act proceeded; the dialogue scintillating with wit, and the choruses becoming more riotous. Intrigue followed after intrigue, and situation after situation, in all of which Caprice was the central figure, until the climax was reached, in a wild bizarre chorus, in which she danced a vigorous cancan with Cagliostra, and finished by bounding on his shoulders to form the tableau as the curtain fell, amid the enthusiastic applause of the audience.

Ezra and Stewart went out into the smoking-room to light their cigarettes, and heard on all sides eulogies of Caprice.

"She'd make her fortune on the London stage," said Santon to Mortimer. "Got such a lot of the devil in her—eh?—by Jove! Why the deuce don't she show in town?"

"Aha!" replied Mortimer shrewdly, "I'm not going to let her go if I can help it. Don't tempt away my only ewe lamb, when you've got so many flocks of your own."

"She doesn't look much like a lamb," said Columbus Wilks dryly.

"Then she doesn't belie her looks," retorted Mortimer coolly. "My dear sir, she's got the temper of a fiend, but she's such a favourite, that I put up with her tantrums for the sake of the cash."

While this conversation was going on, Ezra and his friend were smoking quietly in a corner of the room chatting about the opera, when the Jew suddenly drew Keith's attention to a tall man talking to a friend in a confidential manner. He had a thin, sharp-looking face, keen blue eyes, and fair hair and beard.

"That gentleman," said Lazarus, "could probably tell you something about those diamonds, he is an American called Hiram Jackson Fenton, manager of the 'Never-say-die Life Insurance Company.' Rumour—which is true in this case, contrary to its usual custom—says he is Caprice's latest fancy."

"He must have a lot of money to satisfy her whims," said Keith, looking at the American.

"Money!" Ezra shrugged his shoulders. "He hasn't much actual cash, for he lives far above his income. However, with a little judicious dabbling in the share market, and an occasional help from the children of Israel, he manages to get along all right. Our friend Caprice will ruin him shortly, and then he'll return to the Great Republic, I presume—good riddance of bad rubbish for Australia."

"And who is that colourless-looking little man who has just come up?"

"He is rather washed out, isn't he?" said Ezra critically. "That is his assistant manager, Evan Malton. For some inexplicable reason they are inseparable."

"Oh, and is Mr. Malton also smitten with Caprice."

"Very badly—more shame to him, as he's only been married for twelve months—he neglects his young wife, and dances attendance at the heels of his divinity."

"Doesn't Hiram J—what's his name, object?"

"Not at all. You see they're both mixed up in speculation, and work together for their mutual benefit. Malton is the Lazarus—I don't mean myself—who picks up the crumbs of love that fall from Mr. Dives Fenton's table."

"It can't last long," said Keith in disgust.

"It will last till Malton gets rid of Fenton, or Fenton gets the better of Malton—then there'll be a row, and the weakest will go to the wall. Tell me, whom do you think will win?"

"I should say Fenton," replied Keith, glancing from the effeminate countenance of Malton to the shrewd, powerful face of the American.

"Exactly; he is, I fancy, the stronger villain of the two."

"Villain?"

"Yes; I call any man a villain who neglects his wife for the sake of a light-o'-love. As for Fenton, he is the most unscrupulous man I know."

"You seem to be pretty well acquainted with the scandal of Melbourne society," said Stewart as they went back to their seats.

"Of course, it is my duty; the press is ubiquitous. But tell me your opinion of Caprice?"

"Judging by her acting to-night, she's a devil."

"Wait till the end of this act, and you'll swear she's an angel."

"Which will be correct?"

"Both—she's a mixture!"

The curtain again drew up, amid the shuffling of the audience settling themselves in their places, and represented a *fête* in the gardens of Cagliostra's palace, brilliant with coloured lights and fantastically-dressed people. According to the story, Cagliostra has obtained possession of his prize, and woos her successfully, when Prince Carnival enters and sings a ballad, "So Long Ago," in the hope of touching the heart of his false love.

Caprice, dressed in a tight-fitting costume of silk and velvet, which showed off her beautiful figure to perfection, stood in the centre of the stage with a sad smile, and sang the waltz-refrain of the song with great feeling.

> *"For it was long ago, love,*
> *That time of joy and woe, love!*
> *Yet still that heart of thine*
> *Is mine, dear love, is mine!"*

She gave to the jingling words a touch of pathos which was exquisitely beautiful.

"I believe she feels what she sings," whispered Keith.

"If you knew her story you would scarcely wonder at that," said Ezra bitterly.

The song was redemanded, but Caprice refused to respond, and, the clamour still continuing, she shrugged her shoulders and walked coolly up the stage.

"She's in a temper to-night," said Mortimer to Santon. "They can applaud till they're black in the face, but devil an answer they'll get from her, the jade! She isn't called Caprice for nothing."

And so it happened, for the audience, finding she would not gratify them, subsided into a sulky silence, and Caprice went coolly on with the dialogue. Cagliostra, repentant, surrenders the girl to Prince Carnival, and the opera ended with a repetition of the galop chorus, wherein Keith saw the sad-eyed woman of a few moments before once more a mocking jibing fiend, dancing and singing with a reckless *abandon* that half-fascinated and half-disgusted him.

"What a contradiction," said Keith, as they left the theatre; "one moment all tears, the next all laughter!"

"With a spice of the devil in both," replied Ezra cynically. "She is the Sphinx woman of Heine—her lips caress while her claws wound."

They had a drink and a smoke together, after which they went round to the stage-door, as Ezra, in pursuance of improving Keith's fortunes, was anxious to introduce him to Caprice. Lazarus appeared to be well-known to the door-keeper, for, after a few words with him, they were admitted to the mysterious region behind the scenes. Caprice, wrapped up in a heavy fur cloak, was standing on the stage talking to Fenton. All around was comparatively quiet, as the scene-shifters having ended their duties for the night had left the theatre. Stewart could hardly believe that the little golden-haired woman he saw before him was the brilliant being of the previous hour, she looked so pale and weary. But soon another side of her versatile nature showed itself, for Fenton, saying something to displease her, she rebuked him sharply, and turned her back on the discomfited American. In doing so she caught sight of Lazarus, and ran quickly towards him with outstretched hand.

"My dear Mr. Lazarus," she said rapidly, "I'm so glad to see you! Meg told me all about her accident to-day, and how narrowly she escaped death. Good God, if I had lost her! But the gentleman who saved her— where is he?"

"He is here," said Lazarus, indicating Keith, who stood blushing and confused before this divinity of the stage.

In another moment, with a sudden impulse, she was by his side, holding his two hands in her own.

"You have done what I can never repay," she said rapidly, in a low voice. "Saved my child's life, and you will not find me ungrateful. Words are idle, but if actions can prove gratitude, you may command me."

"I hope the young lady is all right," stammered Keith, as she dropped his hands.

"Oh, yes; rather shaken, but quite well," answered Caprice, in a relieved tone. "Dear me, how careless I am; let me introduce you to these gentlemen—Mr. Fenton, Mr. Malton, and last, but not least, Mr. Mortimer."

The three gentlemen bowed coldly, Fenton in particular, eyeing Keith in a supercilious manner, which made him blush with rage, as he thought it was owing to his shabby clothes.

"Is my carriage there?" said Caprice, in reply to a speech of Malton's. "Oh, then, I may as well go. Good-night, everybody. Mr. Stewart, will you give me your arm?" and she walked off with the delighted Keith, leaving Fenton and Malton transfixed with rage, while Mortimer and Ezra looked on chuckling.

Caprice talked brightly to her new friend till he placed her in her brougham, then suddenly became grave.

"Come down and have supper with me on Sunday fortnight," she said, leaning out of the window. "Mr. Lazarus will be your guide. Good-bye at present," giving him her gloved hand. "God bless you for saving my child."

The carriage drove off, but not before Keith had seen that tears were falling down her face, whereat he marvelled at this strange nature, and stood looking after the carriage.

"She's not as bad as they say," he said aloud.

Ezra, who was just behind him, laughed aloud.

"I knew you'd say she was an angel."

IV

Lazarus

It was a very little shop of squat appearance, as if the upper storey had gradually crushed down the lower. Three gilt balls dangling in mid-air over the wide door indicated the calling of the owner, and, in order that there should be no mistake, the dusty, rain-streaked windows displayed the legend, "Lazarus, Pawnbroker," in blistered golden letters. There were three windows in the upper storey, and these being innocent of blinds or curtains, with the addition of one or two panes being broken, gave the top of the house a somewhat dismantled look. The lower windows, however, made up for the blankness of the upper ones, being full of marvels, and behind their dingy glass could be seen innumerable articles, representing the battered wrecks of former prosperity.

Gold and silver watches, with little parchment labels attached, setting forth their value, displayed themselves in a tempting row, and their chains were gracefully festooned between them, intermixed with strings of red coral, old-fashioned lockets, and bracelets of jet and amber. Worn-out silver teapots were placed dismally at the back in company with cracked cups and saucers of apparently rare old Worcester and Sèvres china. Dingy velvet trays, containing innumerable coins and medals of every description, antique jewellery of a mode long since out of date, were incongruously mingled with revolvers, guns, spoons, cruets, and japanned trays, decorated with sprawling golden dragons; richly-chased Indian daggers, tarnished silver mugs, in company with deadly-looking American bowie knives; bank-notes of long since insolvent banks were displayed as curiosities, while a child's rattle lay next to a Book of Beauty, from out whose pages looked forth simpering faces of the time of D'Orsay and Lady Blessington. And over all this queer heterogeneous mixture the dust lay thick and grey, as if trying for very pity to hide these remnants of past splendours and ruined lives.

The shop was broad, low-roofed, and shallow, with a choky atmosphere of dust, through which the golden sunlight slanted in heavy, solid-looking beams. On the one side there was a row of little partitions like bathing-boxes, designed to secure secrecy to those who transacted business with Mr. Lazarus, and, on the other, long rows of old clothes were hanging up against the wall, looking like the phantoms of their former owners. At the back, a door, covered with faded green baize, and decorated with brass-headed nails, gave admittance to the private office of the presiding genius of the place. The whole appearance of the shop was gloomy in the extreme, and the floor, being covered with boxes and bundles, with a little clearing here and there, it was naturally rather embarrassing to strangers (especially as the bright sunlight outside prevented them seeing an inch before their noses) when they first entered the dismal den wherein Mr. Lazarus sat like a spider waiting for unwary flies.

In one of the bathing machines aforesaid, a large red-faced woman, with a gruff voice and a strong odour of gin, was trying to conclude a bargain with a small, white-faced Jewish youth whose black beady eyes were scornfully examining a dilapidated teapot, which the gruff lady asserted was silver, and which the Jewish youth emphatically declared was not. The gruff female, who answered to the name of Tibsey, grew wrathful at this opposition, and prepared to do battle.

"Old 'uns knows more nor youngers," she growled in an angry tone. "'Tain't by the sauce of babes and sucklers as I'm goin' to be teached."

"'Old your row," squeaked Isaiah, that being the shrill boy's name. "Five bob, and dear at that."

Mrs. Tibsey snorted, and her garments—a tartan shawl and a brown wincey—shook with wrath.

"Lor a mussy, 'ear the brat," she said, lifting up her fat hands; "why, five poun' wouldn't buy it noo; don't be 'ard on me, my lovey—me as 'ave popped everythink with you, includin' four silver spoons, a kittle, a girdiron, an' a coal-scuttle; don't be 'ard, ducky; say ten an' a tizy."

"Five bob," returned the immovable Isaiah.

"You Jewesis is the cuss of hus hall," cried Mrs. Tibsey, whacking the counter with a woefully ragged umbrella. "You cheats an' you swindles like wipers, an' I 'ates the sight of your 'ook noses, I do."

"You'll 'ave the boss out," said Isaiah, in a high voice, like a steam whistle, to which Mrs. Tibsey replied in a rolling bass, a duet which grew wilder and wilder till the sudden opening of the green baize door reduced them both to silence.

An old man appeared—such a little old man—very much bent, and dressed in a greasy old ulster which covered him right down to his ragged carpet slippers. He had white hair and beard, piercing black eyes under shaggy white eyebrows, sharply-cut features, and a complexion like dirty parchment, seared all over with innumerable lines.

"You again?" he said, in a feeble Jewish voice. "Oh, you devil!—you—you—" here a fit of coughing seized him, and he contented himself with glaring at Mrs. Tibsey, upon which he was immediately confronted by that indomitable female, who seized the teapot and shook it in his face.

"Five bob!" she shrieked; "five bob for this!"

"Too much—far too much," said Lazarus in dismay; "say four, my dear, four."

"Ten; I want ten," said Mrs. Tibsey.

"No, no; four; you say ten, but you mean four."

"Say six."

"Four."

"Then take it," said Mrs. Tibsey, clashing it down in wrath, "and the devil take you."

"All in good time—all in good time," chuckled the old man, and disappeared through the door.

"You see, you oughter 'ave taken the five," sniggered Isaiah, making out the pawnticket. "There's four bob, don't spend it in drink."

"Me drink, you hugly himp," said the lady, sweeping the money into her capacious pocket, where it reposed in company with an empty gin bottle; "me drink, as takes in washin' and goes hout nussin', an' was quite the lady afore I fell into the company of wipers: me dr—well," and, language failing her, Mrs. Tibsey sailed majestically out of the shop, coming into collision with Ezra and Keith, who were just entering.

"A whirlwind in petticoats," said Keith, startled by this ragged apparition.

"Askin' your parding, gents both," said Mrs. Tibsey, dropping a very shaky curtsey, "but a young limb h'insides bin puttin' my back hup like the wrigglin' heel 'e h'are, and if you're goin' to pop anythink, don't let it be a silver teapot, 'cause old Sating h'inside is the cuss of orphens and widders," and, having relieved her mind, Mrs. Tibsey flounced indignantly away to refresh herself with her favourite beverage.

"Complimentary to your parent," observed Keith, as they entered the shop.

"Oh, they're much worse sometimes," said Ezra complacently. "Isaiah, where's my father?"

"In 'is room," replied Isaiah, resuming the reading of a sporting newspaper.

Ezra opened the green baize door without knocking, and entered, followed by Keith. A small square room, even dingier than the shop.

At one side a truckle bed pushed up against the wall, and next to it a large iron safe. A rusty grate, with a starved-looking fire, had an old battered kettle simmering on its hob. At the back a square dirty-paned window, through which the light fell on a small table covered with greasy green cloth, and piled up with papers. At this table sat old Lazarus, mumbling over some figures. He looked up suddenly when the young men entered, and cackled a greeting to his son, after which effort he was seized with a violent fit of coughing, which seemed to shake him to pieces. The paroxysm having passed, he began to talk in his feeble, Jewish voice.

"He, he! my dear," looking sharply at Keith, "is this the young man you spoke of? Well, well—too good-looking, my dear—the women—ah, the women, devil take 'em, they'll be turning his head."

"That's his own business, not yours," said Ezra curtly.

"He, he! but it is my business—they'll love him, and love means presents—that means money—my money—I can't trust him."

"That's rather severe, isn't it?" said Keith, speaking for the first time. "You can't tell a man's character altogether by his face—good looks do not invariably mean libertine principles."

"Ah! I know, I know!" muttered Lazarus, rubbing his hands together; "well, well, can you keep books?"

"Yes, I have been accustomed to do so."

"Are you honest?"

Keith laughed.

"I'm generally considered so."

"He, he! that's not saying much. What wages do you want?"

"Three pounds a week," said Stewart modestly.

"Oh, my dear, my dear, what a large sum; say two, my dear, two pounds, or forty shillings, it's very large; you can save out of two pounds."

"I'm glad you think so," said Keith dryly. "I've got my doubts on the subject; however, beggars must not be choosers, so I agree."

"On trial, mind on trial," muttered the old man cautiously.

"I'm quite agreeable," replied Keith complacently, hoping that by the time his trial is over he would be on the staff of some paper. "What are the hours?"

"Nine, my dear," said Lazarus, stroking his beard, "nine till six, with half-an-hour for something to eat in the day—a bun and a cup of coffee—don't be extravagant."

"I can't very well be, on such a salary," replied Stewart. "Well, Mr. Lazarus, as it's all settled, I'll come at nine o'clock to-morrow morning."

"Yes! yes! quite right; but no horse-racing, no gambling, no women—they're the devil, my dear, the devil."

"You're rather hard on the sex, father," said Ezra satirically, "considering how useful they are to you."

"Aha! quite right, quite right," chuckled the old man. "Oh, I know fine ladies; they come to old Lazarus for money—to sell diamonds—ah, my dear, there's lots of diamonds in that safe, he, he!"

"I wonder you're not afraid of being robbed," said Keith.

The old man looked up with a sudden gleam of suspicion in his eyes.

"No, no; I keep the keys under my pillow, and I've got a pistol. I can fire it, oh, yes, I can fire it, then the neighbours, my dear, all round; oh, I'm quite safe—yes, yes, quite safe; no one would hurt old Lazarus. How's Esther, my dear?" turning suddenly to his son.

Esther was the girl to whom Ezra was engaged.

"Oh, she's all right," he replied. "I took her the other night to see Caprice."

"Aha!" cried old Lazarus, lifting up his hands. "Oh, dear, dear, what a woman. I know her, oh, I know her."

"Personally?" asked Keith, whereupon Mr. Lazarus suddenly became deaf.

"Yes, yes, a fine woman; ruins everybody, ruins 'em body and soul, and laughs at 'em, like the fiend she is."

Ezra looked at his paternal relative in disgust, and took Keith's arm. "Come along," he said, "I've got an engagement."

"Good boy, good boy," muttered his parent, nodding his head, "make money, my dear, make—" here another fit of coughing interrupted him, and Ezra hurried Keith away.

"Faugh!" said Ezra, lifting up his hat when they were in the street; "how I hate the miasma of that place. It's like the upas tree, and kills all who come within its circle."

"Do you think your father knows Caprice?" asked Keith, as they walked down Bourke Street.

"Can't tell you," answered Lazarus coolly; "I shouldn't be surprised—he knows half the women in Melbourne. When a spendthrift wants money, he goes to my father; when a woman is in trouble, she goes there also; in spite of her lovers, Caprice is such an extravagant woman, that I've no doubt she's had dealings with my father. If the secret life of Lazarus the pawnbroker were only written, it would be very interesting, I assure you."

"I'm glad I got the place," said Keith thoughtfully; "it isn't much, but will keep me alive till I get on my feet."

"You are sure to drop into a newspaper appointment," replied Ezra, "and of course I will do my best for you."

"You're very good," answered Keith gratefully; "ha, ha, what queer tricks the jade Fortune plays us. I come to Melbourne full of poetic dreams, and find my fate in a pawnbroker's office—it isn't romantic, but it's bread and butter."

"You're not the first poet who has gone to the pawnbroker."

"I expect I'm the first that ever went on such good terms," retorted Keith shrewdly.

V

A Woman's Appeal

According to some writer, "Human beings are moulded by circumstances," and truly Kitty Marchurst, better known as Caprice, was an excellent illustration of this remark.

The daughter of a Ballarat clergyman, she was a charming and pure-minded girl, and would doubtless have married and become a happy woman, but for the intervention of circumstances in the form of M. Gaston Vandeloup. This gentleman, an ex-convict, and a brilliant and fascinating scoundrel, ruined the simple, confiding girl, and left her to starve in the streets of Melbourne. From this terrible fate, however, she was rescued by Mrs. Villiers, who had known her as a child, and it seemed as though she would once more be happy, when circumstances again intervened, and through her connection with a poisoning case, she was again thrown on the world. Weary of existence, she was about to drown herself in the Yarra, when Vandeloup met her, and tried to push her in. With a sudden craving for life, she struggled with him, and he, being weak for want of food, fell in and was drowned, while the unhappy girl fled away, she knew not whither.

A blind instinct led her to "The Home for Fallen Women," founded by a Miss Rawlins, who had herself been an unfortunate, and here for a time the weary, broken-hearted woman found rest. A child, of which Vandeloup was the father, came to cheer her loneliness, and she called the little one Margaret, hoping it would comfort her in the future. But the seeds of evil implanted in her breast by Vandeloup began to bear fruit, and with returning health came a craving; for excitement. She grew weary of the narrow, ascetic life she was leading—for young blood bounded through her veins—and she was still beautiful and brilliant. So, much against the wishes of the matron of the institution, she left the place and returned to the stage.

The Wopples family, with whom she had previously acted, had gone to America, and she was alone in the world, without a single friend. She called herself Caprice, for her real name and history were too notorious for such a public career as she had chosen. All avoided her, and this worked her ruin. Had one door been open to her—had one kind hand been stretched forth to save her—she might have redeemed the past; but the self-righteous Pharisees of the world condemned her, and in despair she determined to defy the world by giving it back scorn for scorn.

It was a terribly hard and dreary life she led at first—no friends, very little money, and a child to support. The future looked black enough before her; but she determined to succeed, and Fortune at length favoured her.

She was playing a minor part in a Christmas burlesque, when the lady who acted the principal character suddenly fell ill, and Kitty had to take her place at a very short notice. She, however, acquitted herself so well that, with one bound, she became a popular favourite, and the star still continuing ill for the rest of the run of the piece, she was able to consolidate the favourable impression she had made. She awoke to find herself famous, and played part after part in burlesque and modern comedy, always with great success. In a word, she became the fashion, and found herself both rich and famous.

Ted Mortimer, the manager of the Bon-Bon Theatre, persuaded her to try opera-bouffe, and she made her first appearance in the Grand Duchess with complete success. She followed up her triumph by playing the title *rôles* in Giroflé Girofla, La Perichole, and Boccaccio, scoring brilliantly each time; and now she had created the part of Prince Carnival, which proved to be her greatest success. Night after night the Bon-Bon was crowded, and the opera had a long and successful run, while Kitty, now at the height of her fame, set herself to work to accomplish her revenge on the world.

She hated women for the way they had scorned her, and she detested men for the free and easy manner in which they approached her; so she made up her mind to ruin all she could, and succeeded admirably. One after another, not only the gilded youth of Melbourne, but staid, sober men became entangled in her meshes, and many a man lived to curse the hour he first met Kitty Marchurst.

Her house at Toorak was furnished like a palace, and her dresses, jewels, horses, and extravagances formed a fruitful topic of conversation in clubs and drawing-rooms. She flung away thousands of pounds in the most reckless manner, and as soon as she had ruined one man, took up with another, and turned her back on the poor one with a cynical sneer. Her greatest delight was to take away other women's husbands, and many happy homes had she broken up by her wiles and fascinations. Consequently, she was hated and feared by all the women in Melbourne,

　　　　　　　　　　　　　　　　FERGUS HUME

and was wrathfully denounced as a base adventuress, without one redeeming feature. They were wrong: she loved her child.

Kitty simply idolised Meg, and was always in terror lest she should lose her. Consequently, when she heard how Keith had rescued her child from a terrible death, her gratitude knew no bounds. She heard of the young man's ambitions from Ezra, and determined to help him as far as it lay in her power. Thus, for the first time for many years, her conduct was actuated by a kindly feeling.

The drawing-room in Kitty's house at Toorak was a large, lofty apartment, furnished in a most luxurious style. Rich carpets, low lounging chairs, innumerable rugs and heavy velvet curtains. A magnificent grand piano, great masses of tropical foliage in fantastically-coloured jars, priceless cabinets of china, and costly, well-selected pictures. One of her lovers, a rich squatter, had furnished it for her. When he had lost all his money, and found her cold and cruel, he went off to the wilds of South America to try and forget her.

There were three French windows at the end of the room, which led out on to a broad verandah, and beyond was the lawn, girdled by laurels. Kitty sat at a writing-desk reading letters, and the morning sun shining through the window made a halo round her golden head. No one who saw her beautiful, childish face, and sad blue eyes, would have dreamed how cruel and relentless a soul lay beneath that fair exterior.

At her feet sat Meg, dressed in a sage-green frock, with her auburn curls falling over her face, playing with a box of bricks, and every now and then her mother would steal an affectionate glance at her.

Curiously enough, Kitty was reading a letter from the very man who had given her the house, and who was now dying in a pauper hospital in San Francisco.

"I forgive you freely," he wrote; "but, ah, Kitty, you might have feigned a love you did not feel, if only to spare me the degradation of dying a pauper, alone and without friends!"

The woman's face grew dark as she read these pitiful words, and, crushing up the letter in her hands, she threw it into the waste-paper basket with a cynical sneer.

"Bah!" she muttered contemptuously, "does he think to impose on me with such tricks? Feign a love! Yes, kiss and caress him to gratify his vanity. Did I not give him fair warning of the end? And now he whimpers about mercy—mercy from me to him—pshaw! let him die and go to his pauper grave, I'll not shed a tear!"

And she laughed harshly.

At this moment Meg, who had been building two edifices of bricks, began to talk to herself.

"This," said Meg, putting the top brick on one building, "is the House of Good, but the other is the House of Sin. Mumsey," raising her eyes, "which house would you like to live in?"

"In the House of Good, dear," said Kitty in a tremulous voice, touched by the artless question of the child. "Come to mumsey, darling, and tell her what you have been doing."

Meg, nothing loath, accepted this invitation, and, climbing up on her mother's knee, threw her arms round Kitty's neck.

"I had some bread and milk," she said confidentially; "then I went and saw my Guinea pigs. Dotty—you know, mumsey, the one with the long hair—oh, he squeaked—he did squeak! I think he was hungry."

"Have you been a good little girl?"

"Good?" echoed Meg doubtfully. "Well, not very good. I was cross with Bliggings. She put soap into my eyes."

"It's naughty to be cross, darling," said her mother, smoothing the child's hair. "What makes you naughty?"

"Mother," said Meg, nodding her head sagely, "it's the wicked spirit."

Kitty laughed, and, kissing the child, drew her closer to her.

"Mumsey!"

"Yes, darling?"

"I should like to give the man who stopped the wheels a present."

"What would you like to give him, my precious?"

This took some consideration, and Meg puckered up her small face into a frown.

"I think," she decided at length, "the man would like a knife."

"A knife cuts love, Meg."

"Not if you get a penny for it," asserted Meg wisely. "Bliggings told me; let me get a knife for the man, mumsey."

"Very well, dear," said Kitty smiling; "the man will then know my little daughter has a kind heart."

"Meg is a very good girl," asserted that small personage gravely; and, climbing down off her mother's knee, she began to play with the bricks, while Kitty went on with her correspondence.

The next letter evidently did not give Kitty much satisfaction, judging by the frown on her face. She had written to Hiram J. Fenton asking for some money, and he had curtly refused to give her any more.

She tore up the letter, threw it into the waste-paper basket, and smiled sardonically.

"You won't, won't you?" she muttered angrily. "Very well, my friend, there are plenty of others to give me money if you won't."

At this moment there came a ring at the door, and shortly after the servant entered with a card. Kitty took it carelessly, and then started.

"Mrs. Malton," she muttered, in a puzzled tone. "Evan Malton's wife! what does she want, I wonder? I thought I was too wicked for virtue to call on me—it appears I'm not."

She glanced at the card again, then made up her mind.

"Show the lady in," she said calmly; and, when the servant disappeared, she called Meg. "Mumsey's sweetheart must go away for a few minutes."

"What for?" asked mumsey's sweetheart, setting her small mouth.

"Mumsey has to see a lady on business." Meg collected the bricks in a pinafore, and walked off to the French window, when she turned.

"Meg will play outside," she said, shaking her curls, "and will come in when mumsey calls."

Scarcely had Meg vanished when the servant threw open the door and announced,—

"Mrs. Malton."

A tall, slender girl entered the room quickly, and, as the door closed behind, paused a moment and looked steadily at Kitty through her thick veil.

"Mrs. Malton?" said Kitty interrogatively.

The visitor bowed, and, throwing back her veil, displayed a face of great beauty; but she had a restless, pitiful look in her eyes, and occasionally she moistened her dry lips with her tongue.

"Will you take a seat?" said the actress politely, taking in at a glance the beautiful, tired face and quiet, dark costume of her visitor.

"Thank you," replied Mrs. Malton, in a low, clear voice, and sat down in the chair indicated by her hostess, nervously clasping and unclasping her hands over the ivory handle of her umbrella. She glanced at Kitty again in a shrinking kind of manner, then, with a sudden effort, burst out quickly,—

"I have called—I have called to see you about my—my husband."

Kitty's lip curled, and she resumed her seat with an enigmatical smile.

"Yes; what about him?"

"Cannot you guess?" said Mrs. Malton imploringly.

Kitty shook her head in a supercilious manner.

"I am at a loss to understand the reason of your visit," she said, in a cold, measured manner.

"I am Evan Malton's wife," said the other rapidly. "We have only been married a year—and—and we have one child."

"I presume you did not call to inform me of your domestic affairs," replied Kitty mercilessly.

"He was so fond of me—we loved one another devotedly till—till—"

"Till he met me, I suppose," said Kitty coolly, throwing herself back with an amused laugh. "I've heard that complaint before—you wives never seem to know how to retain your husbands' affections."

"Give him back to me—oh give him back to me," cried the young wife, clasping her hands. "You have many richer and better than he. I love my husband, and you have parted us—oh, do—do—give him back to me."

"My dear Mrs. Malton," replied the actress coldly, "I do not encourage him, I assure you. He's a bore, and I detest bores."

"But he loves you—he loves you—he worships the ground you tread on."

"A waste of good material; for his devotion will never be rewarded."

"Then you don't love him?" said Mrs. Malton breathlessly.

Kitty rose to her feet, and laughed bitterly.

"Love him—love any one," she muttered, with a choking cry. "I hate the whole lot of them. Do you think I care for their flattery, their kisses, their protestations—bah! I know the value of such things. Love—I hate the word."

"Yet my husband comes here," said the other timidly.

Kitty turned on her fiercely.

"Can I help that? Is it the candle's fault that the moths are attracted? I don't ask your husband to come; if he finds in me what he misses in you, it is your fault, not mine—your errand is useless, I cannot help you."

She turned to go, but the young woman sprang forward and caught her dress.

"You shall not go—you shall not!" she almost shrieked. "You and Fenton are dragging us both to perdition; he has ruined himself for your sake, and his friend—God help him—his friend has insulted me with words of love."

"Am I the guardian of your virtue?" said Kitty pitilessly.

Mrs. Malton stood wringing her hands.

"Oh, God, have you no pity? I am a woman like yourself—my husband should protect me, but he leaves me for you—and," in a whisper, "you don't know all—he has given you presents, rich presents, and to do so has committed a crime."

"A crime!"

"Hush! hush!" glancing fearfully around, "not so loud—not so loud—yes, he has embezzled money, thousands of pounds, for your sake."

Kitty gave a cry, and grasped at a chair for support.

"I—I—did not—not ask him for his presents."

"No; but it was for your sake—your sake. You must help him."

"I," laughed Kitty mockingly, "help him? Help him!—help any man! My good woman, if he went into the prisoner's dock to-morrow, I would not lift one finger to save him."

Mrs. Malton fell on her knees.

"Oh, my God, don't talk like that!" she cried wildly. "You will ruin him—you will ruin him."

Kitty swept round with a cold glitter, like steel, in her eyes.

"Yes! it is my business to ruin men. When I was poor, and anxious to lead a good life, any outstretched hand might have saved me; but no, I was a pariah and outcast—they closed their doors against me. I asked for bread, they gave me a stone—they made of me a scourge for their own evil doing—this is the time for my revenge; fallen and degraded though I be, I can wring their hearts and ruin their homes through their nearest and dearest, and you come to ask me to relent—you, who, if you saw me to-morrow on the streets, would draw your skirts aside from the moral leper!"

"No, no!" moaned the other, beating her breasts with her hands. "Have mercy, have mercy!"

"What do you want me to do?"

"You know the manager of the company, Mr. Fenton; he is your lover—he can refuse you nothing. Speak to him, and see if anything can be done."

"No!"

"For God's sake!"

"No!"

"You have a child?"

"What is my child to you?"

"Everything. You are a mother—so am I: you love your child—I love mine; yet you would make my innocent child suffer for its father's crime.

Oh, if you have any feelings of a mother, spare the father for the sake of the child."

Kitty stood irresolute, while the woman at her feet burst into wild and passionate weeping.

At this moment Meg entered the room by the window, and paused for a moment.

"Mumsey," she said, "why does the lady cry?"

Kitty would have interposed, but Mrs. Malton stretched out her hands to Meg with a quiet in-drawing of her breath.

"I am crying for my little girl."

"Is she dead?" asked Meg, coming to the kneeling woman, and touching her shoulder. "Poor lady—poor, poor lady!"

Kitty could contain herself no longer. With a sudden impulse, she bent down and raised the weeping woman.

"I will do what I can," she said huskily, and sank into a chair.

"Thank God!" cried Mrs. Malton, advancing, but Kitty waved her off, while Meg stood looking from one to the other in amazement.

"Go, go!"

Mrs. Malton bent down and kissed her hand.

"May God be merciful to you, as you have been to me," and, without another word, she departed.

"Mumsey," said Meg, trying to take her mother's hands from her face, "were you cross to the lady?"

"No, darling, no!" replied Kitty, drawing Meg close to her. "Mother was kind to the lady because of her little girl."

"Good mumsey, dear mumsey; Meg loves you," and she put her arms round Kitty's neck, while the poor woman leaned her aching head against the innocent breast of her child, and burst into tears.

VI

The Annoyance of Hiram J. Fenton

It is a curious fact that Melbourne has, in its social and business aspects, a strong leaven of Americanism, and visitors from the great Republic find themselves quite at home in the Metropolis of the South. There are the same bold, speculative qualities, the same restless pursuit of pleasure, and the same rapidity and promptness of action which characterises the citizen of San Francisco or New York. Consequently, there are many Americans to be found in a city so congenial to their tastes, and of these Hiram J. Fenton was one.

He had come over from the States as the agent of a dry-goods firm, and, travelling all through the Australasian colonies, soon saw the enormous capabilities of wealth that lay before him. Gifted with a ready tongue and a persuasive manner, he interested several opulent Victorians in a scheme for floating a Life Insurance Company. A prospectus was drawn up, which promised incalculable wealth to those who would take shares, and, by means of Mr. Fenton's brilliant command of words, and skilful manipulation of figures, The Never-say-die Insurance Company soon became an accomplished fact. A handsome suite of offices was taken in Collins' Street, a large staff of clerks engaged, a genial medical man, whose smile itself was a recommendation, remained on the premises to examine intending policy-holders, and the emissaries of the company went to the four quarters of the globe to trumpet forth the praises of the affair, and persuade people to insure their lives. The company prospered, a handsome dividend was soon declared, and, thanks to his Yankee sharpness, Mr. Fenton now found himself occupying the enviable position of manager with a large salary.

He was a handsome man in a bold, sensual way, with a certain dash and swagger about him which impressed strangers favourably, but a physiognomist would have mistrusted his too ready tongue and the keen glance of his eye. There is no greater mistake than to suppose a villain cannot meet an honest eye, for, as a matter of fact, a successful villain having his nerves under admirable control can stare any one out of countenance, and the keen, rapid glance can take in at once the weak points of a stranger.

Mr. Fenton occupied pleasant apartments, went into society a great deal, and altogether was a very popular man. Cold, calculating, and far-seeing as he was, he had yet a weak spot in his character, and this was extreme partiality for the female sex. Any woman, provided she was pretty, could twist him round her finger; and as Kitty Marchurst now had him in her toils, she took full advantage of his infatuation. There was a certain amount of notoriety in being the lover of the now famous Caprice; but Fenton had to pay pretty dearly for his position. Kitty spent his money like water, and when he ventured to remonstrate, laughed in his face, and told him he could go if he liked, an intimation which only made him resolve to stick closer to her. Nevertheless, about this time relations were rather strained between them, and any one knowing the facts of the case would have seen that the end was not far off.

As to Evan Malton, he was Fenton's assistant manager, and was the moon to the astute American's sun. Weak, irresolute, and foolish, he was, nevertheless, by some strange contradiction, a capital business man. This arose from his long training in office work; he could do nothing by himself, but guided by Fenton, he made an admirable subordinate, and was amenable to his superior in every way. He admired Fenton greatly, copied him in his dress and mannerisms, affected a rakish demeanour towards his friend's mistress, and thoroughly neglected his poor wife, a neglect of which Fenton tried to take advantage. Had Malton known this, it would doubtless have changed his feelings towards the American, for though he thought he was justified in leading a fast life, he strongly objected to his wife showing any liking for any one but himself. Fenton, however, believing in no woman's virtue, did not despair, but protected Kitty openly, to delude Malton into a false security, and made love to Mrs. Malton *sub rosâ*.

It was quite warm out of doors in spite of the season, and out on Kitty's lawn were a group of people laughing and talking together. Kitty, in a comfortable chair, was chatting to Keith and Ezra, who had just arrived, and there were several other ladies present, including Milly Maxwell, who was the second lady at the Bon-Bon—dark-browed, majestic, and passionate; Dora Avenant, who looked like a doll and had the brains of one; and Mrs. Wadby, who wrote scandal and dresses for *The Penny Whistle* under the *nom de plume* of "Baby."

As to the gentlemen, there were present Ted Mortimer, bland and smiling; Slingsby, the parliamentary reporter; Delp, the theatrical critic; Toltby, the low comedian at the Bon-Bon, and about half-a-dozen others, who were more or less connected with the stage and the press. The men were smoking, chatting, or drinking, according to their various tastes, whilst the ladies were sipping their afternoon tea; and, of course, the conversation was mostly about theatrical matters.

In the drawing-room, however, close to the window, sat Meg, buried in a big armchair, reading a fairy tale, and a pretty picture she made with her little loose white dress, and her glorious hair falling about her pale face.

"And the beautiful Princess," read Meg in ecstasy, "fell asleep in the Magic Castle for one hundred years—oh!" breaking off suddenly, "how hungry she must have been when she woke up."

Meg shook her head over this problem and resumed the story.

"And a great forest grew round the castle, which could not be got through till the handsome Prince arrived." Here the drawing-room door opened, and Meg looked up, half expecting to see the handsome prince.

It was only Fenton, however, and he disliked Meg intensely, a dislike which that young person was by no means backward in returning, so she went calmly on reading her book.

"Well, where's mother?" asked Fenton, in his slightly nasal voice, looking at the little figure with a frown.

"Mumsey's in the garden," replied Meg with great dignity, flinging back her curls.

"Just where you ought to be," said Fenton ill-naturedly, "getting fresh air."

"I'm reading a fairy tale," explained Meg, closing her book; "mumsey said I could do what I liked."

"Your mother don't rear you well," retorted the American, and he walked away, when a peal of laughter made him turn round.

"What funny faces you make," said the child; "I feel quite laughy."

"I'd like to spank you," observed Fenton, with no very amiable expression of countenance.

"You're a bad man," said Meg indignantly; "I don't know a badder—not a bit like my Mr. Keith."

"Oh," sneered Fenton, "and who is Mr. Keith?"

"He is a very nice gentleman," replied Meg, pursing up her lips; "he stopped the wheels going over me."

"I wish he hadn't," muttered Fenton vindictively. "Meg, go and tell mother I want her right away."

"I sha'n't," retorted Meg obstinately; "you're a rude man."

"I'll make you smart," said Fenton, catching her arm.

"Oh, mumsey," cried the child, in a tone of relief, and Fenton turned just to see Kitty looking at him like an enraged tigress.

"You lay a finger on my child," she said viciously, "and I'll kill you!"

The American released his hold on Meg with an awkward laugh, and took a seat.

"Why don't you teach her manners," he growled.

"That's my business," flashed out Kitty haughtily. "And now you are here, I wish to speak with you. Meg, my treasure, run out and say mumsey won't be long."

"Mumsey's going to be cross with you now," said Meg consolingly to Fenton, and then ran out laughing, the man looking angrily after her.

Left alone, Kitty sat down near Fenton and began to talk.

"I asked you for five hundred," she said coldly.

"Yes—and I refused," sulkily.

"So I saw by your letter. What is your reason?"

"That's my business."

"Mine also. Why did you refuse?" she reiterated.

"I'm sick of your extravagance."

Caprice laughed in a sneering way that brought the blush to his cheek.

"Do you think I'm dependent on you for money?" she said, with scorn. "I know fifty better men than you who would give me the money if I asked them."

"Then go and ask them," he returned brutally.

Kitty sprang to her feet.

"Of course I will; that means your dismissal."

Fenton caught at her dress in genuine alarm.

"No, no! don't go; you know I love you—"

"So well," she interrupted, "that you refuse me a paltry five hundred pounds."

"I would give it to you, but I haven't got it."

"Then get it," she said coolly.

"I'm nearly ruined," he cried desperately.

"Then retire, and make room for better men."

"You're a devil!" hissed Fenton.

"No doubt. I told you what to expect when I first met you."

"Do you mean to say you will throw me over because I've no money left?" he said fiercely, grasping her wrist.

"Like an old glove," she retorted.

"I'll kill you first."

"Bah! you are melodramatic."

"Oh, Kitty, Kitty!" with a sudden change to tenderness.

"Don't call me by that name," said the woman, in a low, harsh voice. "Kitty Marchurst is dead; she died when she went on the stage, and all womanly pity died with her. You are speaking to Caprice, the most notorious woman in Melbourne."

Fenton sat sullenly silent, glancing every now and then at her beautiful, scornful face.

"If you won't give me money," she said at length, mindful of her promise to Mrs. Malton, "you can do something else."

"What's that?" eagerly.

"Mrs. Malton was here—"

"Mrs. Malton!" he interrupted, springing to his feet. "What did she say?"

"Several unpleasant things about your love for her," said Kitty coolly.

"It's a lie," he began, but Kitty shrugged her shoulders.

"Bah! I'm not jealous; I only care for your money, not for you. But about this visit; her husband has embezzled money in your office."

Fenton turned a little pale, and looked steadily at her.

"Embezzled money, the scoundrel!" he said furiously.

"Yes, isn't he?" said Kitty derisively. "Not a noble, upright gentleman like Hiram Fenton."

He turned from her with an oath.

"I've been a good friend to him right along," he said in an angry tone. "He was fixed up for life, if he'd only behaved himself; now I'll put him in prison."

"So that you can make love to his wife," retorted Kitty coolly.

"I don't care two straws about his wife," replied Fenton, with a scowl. "You are the only woman I love."

"Then promise me to help this unhappy man?"

"Certainly not; you are asking me to compound a felony."

"I'm not a lawyer," she said coldly, "and don't understand legal terms. I am only asking you to save him from gaol for his wife's sake."

"You don't love him?" jealously.

"Bah! do I love any one except myself?"

"And your child," with a sneer.

"Let my child be. Will you help Evan Malton?"

"No; the law must take its course."

"Then I'll help him myself."

"But how?"

"That's my business—the money must be replaced—find out how much is missing, and let me know."

"What's the good? you've not got the cash."

"Do what I ask!"

"Very well!" sulkily. "I can't pay the money myself; but I'll give him time to repay it."

"You will?"

"Yes; and Kitty," shamefacedly, "I'll let you have that five hundred.'

"Good boy," said Kitty approvingly, and laughed. She had gained both her points, so could afford to do so. At this moment Meg entered the room from the garden, followed by Keith, on seeing whom Fenton's face darkened.

"Mumsey!" said Meg, bounding up to Kitty, "I've given him the knife, and he says it's lovely—don't you," turning to Keith.

"Words fail me to express my appreciation," said Stewart, with a smile, looking at the large—very large ivory-handled knife, "and it's got an inscription, 'From Meg,'—beautiful."

"It will cut love, Mr. Stewart," said Kitty, with a laugh.

"Oh, no," interposed Meg, "he's given me a lucky sixpence. He says we're engaged now, and when I grow up, mumsey, I'm going to marry him."

"Is this true?" asks Kitty gaily. "Are you going to rob me of my daughter? This is dreadful! What do you say, Mr. Fenton?"

Mr. Fenton smiled in a ghastly manner, then hurried away muttering under his breath.

"It's bad temper," observed Stewart, looking after him.

"No, my dear," said Kitty airily, "it's jealousy."

VII

Mirth and Laughter

Kitty's supper parties were always delightful, though slightly godless. The guests were usually men and women of the world, connected with art, literature, and the drama, so a general tone of brilliancy permeated the atmosphere. The hostess herself was an admirable conversationalist, and what with the wine, the laughter, and the influence of the midnight hour, the excitement seemed contagious. Every one was amusing, and witty stories, caustic remarks, and sarcastic epigrams followed one after the other in reckless profusion.

Very pretty the supper-table looked, though, it must be confessed, rather disorderly. It was not a very large table, but accommodated the present company admirably, and under the soft light of the tapers, with which the room was illuminated, the silver and glass sparked brilliantly. Half-filled glasses of champagne and burgundy, crumbs on the white table-cloth, and a general array of disorderly plates, showed that supper was over. The guests had pushed away their chairs, and were smoking and chatting, while a light breeze came in through the open French window, and somewhat cooled the temperature of the room. The smoky atmosphere, the flashing of the light on the bare shoulders of the women, gay feminine, laughter, and the general air of unconventionality, fascinated Keith as he sat beside his hostess, listening to the desultory conversation, and occasionally joining in. Slingsby was speaking about a new book which had come out, and this gave rise to a brilliant rattle of pungent wit.

"It's called 'Connie's Crime,' a mixture of blood and atheism."

"Yes, so they say; a hash-up of the Newgate Calendar and Queen Mab, with a dash of realism to render it attractive."

"Awfully bad for the public."

"Bah! they read worse in papers. *The Penny Whistle* was bewailing the prevalence of criminal literature, yet you can't take up a night's issue without finding a divorce case or a murder—the pot calling the kettle black with a vengeance."

"Don't suppose either it or shilling shockers have much to do with the morals of the public—we're all going to the deuce."

"Pessimistic!"

"But true. It's a game of follow my leader, with Father Adam at the head."

"Gad, he ought to have arrived at his destination by this time!"

"Oh! we'll all find that out when we get there."

"But' you forget we start in this new country with all the old-world civilisation."

"Yes, and all the old-world vices."

"Which are a natural concomitant of aforesaid civilisation."

"How abusive you all are," said Kitty, shrugging her shoulders; "people are not so bad as you make out."

"No, they're worse," said Delp lightly. "Put on your diamonds and go through Victoria like that young person in Moore's song, 'Rich and rare were the gems she wore,' you won't be treated as well, I promise you."

"I'm afraid I'm very careless of my diamonds," laughed Kitty; "I certainly take them home from the theatre every night, but I generally put the case safely away in the drawer of my looking-glass."

"A very safe place," observed Lazarus approvingly; "for illustration see Poe's story of 'The Purloined Letter.'"

"All the same, I wouldn't trust to fiction for suggestions," said Fenton gaily; "some night you'll be minus your jewels."

"I'll take the risk," retorted Kitty rising. "I'm going into the drawing-room. Mr. Lazarus, you come also. I have got the score of that new opera-bouffé 'Eblis,' and I want you to try it."

"Bah! a failure in town," growled Mortimer.

"That doesn't necessarily mean a failure in Melbourne," replied Kitty, and with this parting shot she went away, followed by the ladies and Ezra Lazarus. Keith remained behind, and, lighting a fresh cigarette, listened to the conversation, which was now slightly horsey.

"I know what's going to win the cup.

"Never knew a man who didn't."

"This is true, 'Devil-may-care.'"

"An outsider."

"They generally win, but don't prophesy too soon."

"No, or like Casandra, your prophecies won't be believed."

"Who is Casandra—another dark 'un?"

"No—a woman."

"Talking about women, I wish you'd get more chorus girls, Mortimer."

"Got quite enough."

"Of course—quantity, not quality."

"They've been snubbing you?"

"Wrong again; they never snub any one who can give them diamonds."

"Which you can't."

"No, by Jove. I wish I had some myself—say Caprice's."

"Don't grudge them to her, dear boy—the savings of years."

Every one grinned.

Meanwhile, Keith grew tired of this scintillating talk, and leaving Ezra rattling away at a gallop in the drawing-room, he arose and went out into the hall. Glancing carelessly up the stairs, he saw a little figure in white coming down.

"Why, Meg," said Keith, going to the foot of the stairs to receive her, "what are you doing at this hour of the night?"

"Meg wants mumsey," said the child, putting her arms round his neck.

"Mumsey's busy," replied Keith, lifting her up. "I'll take you back to bed, dear."

"Don't want to go to bed," said the child, though she could hardly keep her eyes open.

Keith laughed, and rocked her slowly to and fro in his arms for a few minutes, humming softly till Meg grew tired.

"Will Meg go to bed now?" he whispered, seeing she had closed her eyes.

"Yes! Meg's sleepy."

Keith went upstairs with the quiet little figure in his arms, and seeing an open door leading to a room in which there was a subdued light, caused by the lowering of the gas, he went in, and finding Meg's cot, placed her in it, and tucked her carefully in.

"Good-night, dear," he whispered, kissing her.

"Good-night, mumsey; good-night, God," murmured Meg, thinking she was saying her prayers, and fell fast asleep.

Keith went downstairs again, and met Fenton in the hall.

"Say!" exclaimed that gentleman, "where have you been?"

"Putting Meg to bed," replied Stewart, laughing. "I found her wandering about like an unquiet spirit," and having no desire for a conversation with Fenton, he strolled off to the drawing-room leaving the American looking after him with an angry frown.

No one was in the drawing-room but Ezra and the ladies—the former being seated at the piano playing over the music of "Eblis," while

Kitty Marchurst stood beside him, looking over his shoulder. Lazarus had just finished a valse, which was not by any means original, being made out of reminiscences of other music.

"There's only one decent thing in the whole opera," said Kitty impatiently—"this," and she hummed a few bars; "it's called, 'Woman's Deceit.'"

"Disagreeable title," said Keith idly.

"But a capital song," retorted Kitty "Eblis sings it—that's the principal character."

"You seem anxious to play the devil," said Stewart, with a smile.

"What do you mean?"

Keith shrugged his shoulders.

"Eblis is the Oriental name for the Devil."

"Oh, I understand." Kitty's quick perception seized the idea at once. "Yes, there would be some fun in playing such a character."

"Then give myself and Lazarus a commission to write you a part. I am anxious to make a start, and I think Lazarus would write charming music. I'll be librettist, and, of course, can write the character to suit you."

Kitty glanced critically at him.

"Can you compose music," she asked Lazarus.

In answer, he played a charming gavotte, bright and crisp, with a quaint rhythm.

"Very pretty," said Kitty critically, "but not my style. Play something with a little more 'go' in it."

"Like this?" He brought his hands down on the ivory keys with a tremendous crash, and plunged into a wild fantastic galop that made everybody long to dance. Kitty clapped her hands, and her whole face lighted up with enthusiasm as the brilliancy and dash of the melody carried her away.

"Bravo!" she cried, when he finished. "That's what I want; write me music like that, and I'll engage to have it produced. You'll do. Now, sir," turning to Keith, "what's your idea?"

"Rather a burlesque than opera-bouffe," he answered; "what would you say to 'Faust Upset?'"

"Ah, bah! we've had so many burlesques on Faust."

"Not such a one as I propose to write. I intend to twist the whole legend round; make Miss Faust a Girton girl who has grown old, and longs for love, invokes the Power of Evil, enter Caprice as Miss Mephistopheles, a female demon, rejuvenates Miss Faust by paint and powder, takes her to see Mr. Marguerite, who is a young athlete, and so throughout the whole legend; to conclude with Miss Mephistopheles falling in love with Mr. Marguerite, and disputing possession with Miss Faust."

"Ha! ha!" laughed Kitty, "what a capital idea. It will be new, at all events; but I won't decide till I see the first act complete; if it's as good as it promises, I'll get Mortimer to stage it after 'Prince Carnival.'"

Keith was delighted, as now he seemed to have obtained a chance of seeing what he could do. Ezra smiled, and nodded to Stewart.

"I told you she'd be a good friend," he said.

The gentlemen all came into the room, and in a short time there was a perfect babel of voices talking about everything and everyone. Suddenly Fenton, with a half-smoked cigar in his hand, entered the room and crossed over to Kitty.

"There's a rough-looking man outside who wants to see you," he said quietly.

"What's his name?"

"Villiers."

Kitty turned a little pale.

"The husband of Madame Midas," she said, in an annoyed tone. "Where is he?"

"Walking up and down in front of the dining-room."

"Remain here; I'll see him," she said, in a decided tone, and, without being noticed, left the room.

On entering the dining-room, she found Mr. Villiers seated at the supper-table drinking champagne from a half-empty bottle, having entered through the window.

"What do you want?" she asked, coming down to him.

Mr. Villiers was in his usual condition of intoxication, and began to weep.

"It's Kitty, dear little Kitty," he said, in a maudlin tone, "the friend of my dear wife."

"Your dear wife," said Kitty scornfully; "the woman you deceived so shamefully; she was well quit of you when she went to live in England."

"She left me to die alone," wept Villiers, filling his glass again, "and only lets me have a hundred pounds a year, and she's rolling in money."

"Quite enough for you to get drunk on," retorted Kitty. "What do you want?"

"Money."

"You sha'n't get a penny."

"Yes I shall. You talk about me treating my wife badly; what about you—eh?"

Kitty clenched her hands.

"I did treat her badly," she said, with a cry. "God help me, I've repented it often enough since!"

"You were a nice girl till you met Vandeloup," said Villiers. "Ah, that confounded Frenchman, how he made me suffer!"

"Leave Vandeloup alone; he's dead, and it will do no good you reviling him now. At all events, he was a man, not a drunkard."

"She loves him still, blow me!" hiccupped Mr. Villiers rising—"loves him still."

"Here's a sovereign," said Kitty, thrusting some money into his hand. "Now, go away at once."

"I want more."

"You won't get more. Get away, or I'll order my servants to turn you out."

Villiers staggered up to her.

"Will you, indeed? Who are you to talk to me like this? I'll go now, but I'll come back, my beauty! Don't try your fine airs on me. I'll get money from you when I want it; if I don't, I'll make you repent it."

Kitty stood looking at him like a statue of marble, and pointed to the open window.

"I spare you for your wife's sake," she said coldly. "Go!"

Villiers lurched towards the window, then, turning round, shook his fist at her.

"I've not done with you yet, my fine madam," he said thickly. "You'll be sorry for these fine airs, you—"

He staggered out without saying the vile word, and disappeared in the darkness.

A vile word, and yet what was that Mrs. Malton said about her child blushing for her father? God help her, would Meg live to blush for her mother? Kitty put out her hands with a sob, when a burst of laughter from the next room sounded in her ears. The momentary fit of tenderness was over, and, with a harsh laugh, she poured out a glass of champagne and drank it off.

"My world is there," she muttered. "I must part with the child for her own good, and she will lead that virtuous, happy life which a miserable wretch like myself can never hope to reach."

VIII

A Mysterious Affair

The Penny Whistle was a purely sensational newspaper, and all those who liked spicy articles and exaggerated details purchased it, in order to gratify their tastes. Its circulation was enormous, and its sale increased still more when the following article appeared in its columns on the Tuesday after Kitty's supper party:—

"Burglary at the House of a well-known Actress.

"We often hear accounts of great jewel robberies having taken place in London, but nothing of the kind, at least in any noticeable degree, has been perpetrated in the colonies until last Sunday night, or, to speak more exactly, Monday morning, when the house of Caprice, the well-known actress, was entered, and jewels to the amount of £5000 were stolen. The house in question is situated in Toorak, almost immediately on the banks of the Yarra-Yarra, and, as far as we can learn, the following are the circumstances connected with the affair:—

"On Sunday night Caprice entertained a number of friends at a supper party, and the servants all being downstairs attending to the guests, the upper part of the house was left entirely uninhabited. It is at this time, probably between twelve and one o'clock, that the burglary is supposed to have been perpetrated. The company departed about three o'clock, and on going up to her room, Caprice found the window wide open. Knowing that it had been closed, she suspected something was wrong, and went to the place where she kept her diamonds, only to find them gone. She sent at once for her servants, and an examination was made. It was found that the house had evidently been entered from the outside, as the window was not very far from the ground, and some ivy growing on the wall made a kind of natural ladder, which any man of ordinary agility could scale. Curiously enough Caprice's child, aged seven, was asleep in the room, but appears to have heard nothing. Next morning another examination was made, and it was found that the ivy was broken in several places, showing clearly the mode of entrance. The window had not been latched, as no chance of a burglary was apprehended, the house always having been looked upon as a remarkably safe one. The diamonds were usually kept in a small safe, but on returning from the theatre on Saturday night they had been placed in the drawer of the looking-glass, where they were judged to be safe, as it was not thought likely any thief would look in so unlikely a place for valuable jewellery. Below will be found a plan of the house and grounds as furnished by our special reporter, and the probable track of the burglars indicated."

"It will be seen from this plan that the drawing-room and dining-room, in both of which the guests were assembled, are in the front of the house, so that the most likely thing is that the burglar or burglars entered the grounds by the gate, or along the banks of the river, and climbed up into the house by the window C shown on the plan.

"After securing the plunder, two modes of exit were available, either as indicated by the dotted line which would take the thief out of the gate into the road, from whence it would be easy to escape, or along the banks of the river, as shown by the other lines. In either case escape was perfectly easy. Of course the danger lay in detection while in the house, but this was considerably guarded against by the fact that the noise and laughter going on below effectually drowned all sounds of any one entering the house.

"The thief must have known that the diamonds were in the bedroom, and that a number of people would be present on Sunday night, therefore he chose a time when he would be most likely to escape detection. We believe that a detective has gone down to Toorak to make inquiries, and we have no doubt that the thief will soon be secured, as it would be impossible for such valuable jewels to be disposed of in Melbourne or other colonial cities without arousing suspicion."

It was Fenton who insisted upon a detective being employed to investigate the robbery, as, for some extraordinary reason, Kitty seemed unwilling to allow the matter to be inquired into.

The detective who accompanied Fenton to Kitty's house was known by the name of Naball, and on the retirement of Kilsip had taken his place. He was only of the age of thirty, but remarkably clever, and had already distinguished himself in several difficult cases. Detective work was a positive mania with him, and he was never so happy as when engaged on a difficult case—it had for him the same fascination as an abstruse mathematical problem would have for an enthusiastic student.

To Kilsip belonged the proud honour of having discovered this genius, and it seemed as though the pupil would soon surpass the master in his wonderful instinct for unravelling criminal puzzles. Mr. Naball was an ordinary-looking young man, who always dressed fashionably, and had very little to say for himself, so that few guessed the keen astute brain that was hidden under this somewhat foppish exterior. He listened to everything said to him, and rarely ventured an opinion, but the thieves of Melbourne well knew that when "The Toff," as they called Naball, was on their track, there was very little chance of escape from punishment.

On this day when they were on their way to Toorak, Fenton was excited over the matter, and ventured all kinds of theories on the subject, while Mr. Naball smoked a cigarette, and admired the fit of his gloves.

"Do you think the thief will try and dispose of them in Melbourne?" he asked.

"Possibly," returned Naball, "if he's a born fool."

"I'm certain I know the thief," said Fenton quietly. "I told you that the man Villiers was seen about the place on the night of the robbery."

"By whom?"

"Myself and Caprice."

"Who saw him last?"

"Caprice."

"Oh," said Naball imperturbably, "then she's the best person to see on the subject."

"He's a bad lot," said Fenton; "he was mixed up in that poisoning case eight years ago."

"The Midas case?"

"Yes. Caprice, or rather Kitty Marchurst, was concerned in it also."

"So I believe," replied Naball; "every one was innocent except Jarper and Vandeloup—one was hanged, the other committed suicide. I don't see what it has to do with the present case."

"Simply this," said Fenton sharply, annoyed at the other's tone, "Villiers is a scoundrel, and wouldn't stop at robbery if he could make some money over it."

"He knew Caprice had diamonds worth five thousand?"

"Of course; every one in Melbourne knows that."

"Did he know where they were kept?"

"There's a safe in the room, and a thief, of course—"

"Would go there first—precisely—but you forget the diamonds were taken out of the drawer of her looking-glass—a most unlikely place for a thief to examine. The man who stole the jewels must have known where they were kept."

"Oh," said Fenton, and looked astonished, as he was quite unable to explain this. He was about to reply, when the train having arrived at its destination, they got out, and walked to Kitty's house.

She was in the drawing-room writing letters and looked pale and haggard, her eyes having dark circles beneath them, which told of a sleepless night. When the two men entered the room she welcomed them gracefully, and then resumed her seat as they began to talk.

"I have brought you Mr. Naball to look after this affair," said Fenton, looking at her.

"You are very kind," she replied coldly; "but, the fact is, I have not yet decided about placing it in the hands of the police."

"But the diamonds?"—began Fenton in amazement.

"Were mine," finished Kitty coolly; "and as the loss is mine, not yours, I will act as I think fit in the matter."

Then, turning her back on the discomfited Fenton, she addressed herself to the detective.

"I should like your opinion on the subject," she said graciously, "and then I will see if the case can be gone on with."

Naball, who had been keeping his keen eyes on her face the whole time, bowed.

"Tell me all the details of the robbery," he observed cautiously.

"They are simple enough," replied Kitty, folding her hands. "I bring them home from the theatre every night, and usually put them in the safe, which is in my room. On Saturday night, however, I was tired, and, I must confess, rather careless, and as the case was on my dressing-table, I placed it in the drawer of my looking-glass, to save me the trouble of going to the safe. I gave a supper party on Sunday night, and when every one had gone away, I went upstairs to bed, and found the window open; recollecting where I had put the diamonds, I opened the drawer and found them gone. My servants examined the ground beneath the window, and found footmarks on the mould of the flower-bed, so I suppose the thief must have entered by the window, stolen the jewels, and made off with them."

When she had finished, Naball remained silent for a minute, but just as Fenton was about to speak, he interposed.

"I will ask you a few questions, madame," he said thoughtfully. "When did you see the diamonds last?"

"About six o'clock on Sunday night. I opened the drawer to get something, and saw the case."

"Not the diamonds?"

"They were in the case."

"Are you sure?"

"Where else would they be?"

"Some one might have stolen them previously, and left the case there to avert suspicion."

Kitty shook her head.

"Impossible. The case is also gone besides, I locked the case on Saturday night, and had the key with me. No other key could have opened it, and had the case been forced, I would have seen it at once. See," lifting up her arm, "I always wear this bracelet, and the key is attached to it by a chain."

Naball glanced carelessly at it, and went on with his questions.

"You generally kept the diamonds in the safe?"

"Yes."

"And it was quite an oversight not placing them in there on Saturday?"

"Quite."

"No one knew they were in the drawer of your looking-glass on that particular night?"

"No one."

Here Fenton interposed.

"You get along too fast," he said quickly. "Everyone at the supper-table knew you kept them there; you said it to them yourself."

Naball glanced sharply at Kitty.

"I know I did," she replied quietly; "but I spoke as if the diamonds were always kept there, which they were not. I did not say they were in the drawer on that particular night."

"You mentioned it generally?" said Naball tranquilly.

"Yes. All the people present were my guests, and I hardly think any of them would rob me of my diamonds."

"Were any of the servants in the room when you made the remark?" said the detective slowly.

"No, none; and the door was closed."

Naball paused a moment.

"I tell you what," he said slowly, "the diamonds were stolen between six o'clock and the time you went to bed."

"About three o'clock," said Kitty.

"Precisely. You saw the diamonds last at six; they were gone by three; you mentioned where you kept them at the supper-table; now, the thief must have overheard you."

"You—you suspect my guests, sir," cried Kitty angrily.

"Certainly not," said the detective quietly; "but I suspect Villiers."

"Villiers!"

"Yes. Mr. Fenton tells me you saw him on that night."

Kitty flashed a look of anger on the American, who bore it unmoved.

"Yes, he was outside, and wanted to see me. I saw him, gave him some money, and he left."

"Then I tell you he overheard you say where you kept the diamonds, because he was hiding outside the window; so, after seeing you, he committed the robbery."

"That's what I think," said Fenton.

"You!" cried Kitty. "What have you got to do with it? I don't believe he stole them, and, whether he did or not, I'm not going to continue this case."

"You'll lose your diamonds," cried Fenton.

"That's my business," she returned, rising haughtily; "at all events, I have decided to let the matter rest, so Mr. Naball will have all his trouble for nothing. Should I desire to reopen the affair, I will let you both know. At present, good morning," and, with a sweeping bow, she turned and left the room.

Fenton stared after her in blank amazement.

"Good God! what a fool!" he cried, rising. "What's to be done now?"

Naball shrugged his shoulders.

"Nothing," he replied, "since she declines to give me power to investigate. I must throw the affair up. But," also rising, and putting on his hat, "I'd like to have a look at the ground beneath the window."

They both went out, Naball silent, and Fenton in great wrath, talking of Kitty's conduct.

"What an idiot she is!" he cried. "What is she going on in this way for?"

"I don't know."

"She must have some motive."

"Women don't require a motive for anything," said Naball, imperturbably proceeding to examine the ground under the window, through which the thief had made his exit. The flower-bed was filled with tall hollyhocks, and some of these were broken as if some heavy body had fallen from above.

"He clambered down by the ivy," murmured Naball to himself, as he bent down. "The ivy is broken here and there; the flowers are also broken, so he fell on them in a heap—probably having missed his footing. Humph! Clever man, as he did not step again on the flower-bed, but jumped from where he fell on to the grass. Humph! grass hard and rather dry; no chance of footmarks. Question is, which way did he go?"

"By the gate, of course," said Fenton impatiently.

The detective walked across the lawn to the gate, but could find no trace of footmarks, as the lawn was dry, and the footpath, leading out into the pavement of the street was asphalted.

"No; he did not go by the gate, as a man in such rags as Villiers would have been sure to be seen coming out of a private house. That would be suspicious; besides, he would have been afraid."

"Of the police?"

"Exactly; he's been in prison two or three times since his connection with the Midas case, and has got a wholesome dread of the law. No; he did not go by the gate, but by the river."

"The river!" repeated Fenton, in amazement.

Naball did not answer, but walked back to the window, then along the side of the house, turned the corner, and went down the sloping green bank which led to the river. Still he could see no footmarks. The grass ended at an iron fence, and beyond was the uncultivated vegetation, rank and unwholesome, that clothed the banks of the river. Between this and the grass, however, there was a strip of black earth, and this Naball examined carefully, but could find nothing. If Villiers had come this way, he could only have climbed the fence by first standing on this earth in order to get near enough, but apparently he had not done so.

"He did not come this way," he said, as they walked back.

"But how could he have left the place?" asked Fenton.

"By the gate."

"The gate? You said he would be afraid of the police."

"So he would, had he been doing anything wrong. Had he stolen the diamonds, he would have gone down by the bank of the river rather than chance meeting a policeman on the street."

"But what does this prove?"

"That, had he met a policeman, he could have explained everything, and referred him to Caprice as to his interview, and right to come out of the house. In a word, it proves he did not steal the diamonds."

"Then who, in Heaven's name, did?"

"I don't give an opinion unless I'm certain," said Naball deliberately; "but I'll tell you what I think. You heard Caprice say she won't go on with the case?

"Yes; I can't understand her reason."

"I can; she stole the diamonds herself."

IX

AN UNKNOWN BENEFACTOR

Everyone was greatly excited over the great jewel robbery, especially as it had taken place at the house of so celebrated a person as Caprice, and numerous were the conjectures as to the discovery of the thieves. When, however, it became known that the lady in question declined to allow an investigation to be made, and was apparently contented to lose five thousand pounds' worth of diamonds, the excitement grew intense. What was her motive for acting in such a strange way? All Melbourne asked itself this question, but without obtaining a satisfactory answer. Reference was made to Kitty's antecedents in connection with the Midas poisoning case, and the public were quite prepared to hear any evil of her, particularly as her career since then had been anything but pure.

The name of Villiers was mentioned, and then it transpired that Villiers had been seen outside her house on the night of the robbery It was curious that another crime should have happened where these two, formerly implicated in a murder case, should have come together, and disagreeable rumours began to circulate. Then, by some unexplained means, the opinion of Naball became known regarding his assertion that Caprice had stolen the diamonds herself. Here was another mystery. Why on earth should she steal her own jewels? One theory was that she required money, and had sold them for this purpose, pretending that they were stolen, in order to satisfy the lovers who gave them to her. This was clearly absurd, as Caprice cared nothing for the opinion of her lovers, and, moreover, the donors of the diamonds were long since dead or ruined, so the idea of the detective was unanimously laughed at. But then the fact remained, she would not allow an investigation to be made; and how was this to be accounted for? One idea was mooted, that Villiers had stolen the diamonds, and she would not prosecute him because he was the husband of the woman who had been kind to her. In this case, however, she would have easily got back her jewels by a threat of prosecution, whereas they were still missing. Other solutions of the problem were offered, but they were unsatisfactory, and Melbourne settled itself down to the opinion that the whole affair was a mystery which would never be solved.

Keith and Ezra had both been puzzled over the affair, and offered Kitty their services to unravel the mystery, but she curtly dismissed them with the remark that she wished the affair left alone, so they had to obey her, and remain in ignorance like the rest of the public. Affairs thus went on as usual, and the weeks slipped by with no further information being forthcoming.

Meanwhile, "Prince Carnival" was still running to crowded houses, and Kitty appeared nightly, being now a still greater attraction on account of the robbery of which she was the heroine. She had fulfilled her promise to Keith, in seeing Mortimer about the chances of production for "Faust Upset." The manager was doubtful about the success of the experiment of trying Colonial work, and told Kitty plainly he could not afford to lose money on such a speculation.

"It's all stuff," he said to her when she urged him to give the young men a chance; "I can get operas from London whose success is already assured, and I don't see why I should waste money on the crude production of two unknown Colonials."

"That's all very true," retorted Caprice, "and, from a business point of view, correct; but considering you make your money out of Colonial audiences, I don't see why you shouldn't give at least one chance to see what Colonial brains can do. As to crudity, wait and see. I don't want you to take the opera if it is bad, but if you approve of it, give it a chance."

In the end Mortimer promised, that if he approved of the libretto and music, he would try the piece at the end of the run of "Prince Carnival," but put "Eblis" in rehearsal, in case his forebodings of failure should be justified. When, however, the first act was finished and shown to him, he was graciously pleased to say there was good stuff in it, and began to be a little more hopeful as to its success. So Keith worked hard all day at his employment, and at night on his libretto, to which Ezra put bright, tuneful music. With the usual sanguine expectations of youth, they never dreamt of failure, and Keith wrote the most enthusiastic letters to his betrothed, announcing the gratifying fact that he had got his foot on the lowest rung of the ladder of fame.

As to his uncongenial employment at the pawnshop, he strove to conquer his repugnance to it, and succeeded in winning the approval of old Lazarus by his assiduous attention to business. He attended to the books, and, as time went on, the pawnbroker actually let him pay money into the bank, so great had his confidence in the young man become. He increased Keith's salary, and even then chuckled to himself over his cleverness in retaining such a clever servant at so low a price.

Though his business was ostensibly that of a pawnbroker, he was in the habit of conducting very much more delicate transactions. In his dingy little den at the back of the shop he sat like a great spider waiting for flies, and the flies generally came in at a little door which led from the room into a dirty yard, and there was a kind of narrow right-of-way which gave admittance to this yard from the street. By this humble way many well-known people came, particularly at night—the fast young man who had backed the wrong horse, the speculative sharebroker, and the spendthrift society lady, all came here in quest of money, which they always got, provided their security was good, and, of course, they paid an exorbitant percentage. Lazarus had dealings with all sorts and conditions of men and women, but he was as silent as the grave over their affairs, and no one knew what secrets that dirty old Hebrew carried in his breast. Of these nocturnal visitors Keith saw nothing, as he left at six o'clock, after which Isaiah shut up the shop, and the front of the house was left in profound darkness, while business went on in the little back room.

It was now a fortnight since the robbery, and the nine days' wonder having ceased to amuse, people were beginning to forget all about it. Keith still lived in East Melbourne with Ezra, and on going home one night was surprised to find a letter from the manager of the Hibernian Bank, which informed him that the sum of five hundred pounds had been placed to his credit. Stewart went next day to find out the name of his unknown benefactor, but the manager refused to tell him, as he had been pledged to secrecy. So Keith returned to Ezra in a state of great perplexity to talk over the affair. They sat in Ezra's sitting-room, and discussed the matter late at night with great assiduity, but were unable to come to any conclusion.

"You don't know any one who would do you a good turn?" asked Lazarus, when he heard this news.

"No—no one," replied Keith. "I haven't a single relative in the Colonies, and no friend rich enough to give me so much money—unless it were your father," with a sudden inspiration.

"He!" laughed Ezra scornfully; "he'd as soon part with his blood. Why, I asked him to give me some money so that I could marry, and he refused. What he wouldn't do for his son he certainly would not do for a stranger."

"It's very queer," observed Keith meditatively. "It can't be Caprice?"

"Not likely; she needs all her money herself," said Ezra. "Besides, I hear she's been rather hard up of late. I suppose Fenton will soon go broke, and then, *Le roi est mort, vive le roi*."

"What a pity she goes on like that," said Keith, regretfully. "I like her so much."

"Yes, and she likes you," retorted Ezra pointedly. "Don't you get entangled in the nets, or you'll forget all about the girl at Sandhurst. Does she know you're engaged?"

"No."

"I wouldn't tell her if I were you," said the Jew significantly, "or she'll withdraw the light of her countenance, and then it will be all up with our burlesque."

"Pooh, nonsense," replied Stewart, with an uneasy laugh. "I wonder who'll be Fenton's successor?"

"Yourself."

"Not I. I'm not far enough gone for that. Besides, I've no money."

"True, except your anonymous five hundred, which would be nothing to Caprice. So, as she wants money, I expect it will be old Meddlechip."

"But he's married."

"True, O Sir Galahad," retorted Ezra sarcastically; "but he's an unholy old man for all that—she'll ensnare him, and we'll see how long it will take her to break the richest man in the Colonies."

"Oh, the deuce take Kitty Marchurst and her affairs," said Keith impatiently. "I want to know who sent me this money?"

"Better not ask," murmured Ezra. "Curiosity is a vice. Remember Adam and Eve, Bluebeard's wife, etcetera. Take the goods the gods bestow, and don't try to find out where they come from; but now you are rich, you'll be giving up the shop."

"No, I'll stay on for a time till I find that the five hundred is really and truly mine. Who knows, some day it may take to itself wings and fly."

"It certainly would with some young men," said Ezra; "but I don't think you are that sort."

"You are right. I want to save up all my money for Eugénie."

"Ah! you are going to marry her?"

"When I get rich. Yes."

"You won't marry her if Caprice can help it."

"Why?" disbelievingly.

"Because she's fallen in love with you, and her love, like the gifts of the Danaes, is fatal.

"Rubbish. I'm not a child. Caprice will never take my heart from Eugénie."

"Hercules," remarked Ezra musingly, "was a strong man; yet he became the slave of a woman. Solomon was a wise man—same result. My friend, you are neither Hercules nor Solomon, therefore—"

Keith departed hurriedly.

X

Naball makes a Discovery

When Kilsip undertook to educate Naball in the business of a detective, he gave him an epigrammatical piece of advice: "Cultivate curiosity." This golden rule Naball constantly followed, and found it of infinite service to him in his difficult profession. He was always on the lookout for queer cases, and when he discovered one that piqued his curiosity, he never rested until he found out all about it. The Red Indian follows the trail of his enemy by noting the most trivial signs, which to others with a less highly cultivated instinct would appear worthless. And Naball was a social Red Indian, following up the trail of a mystery by a constant attention to surrounding events. A casual observation, a fleeting expression, a scrap of paper—these were the sign-posts which led him to a satisfactory conclusion, and he never neglected any opportunity of exercising his faculties. By this constant practice he sharpened his senses in a wonderful degree, and cultivated to the highest extent the unerring instinct which he possessed in discovering crimes.

Consequently, when he found there was no legal authority to be given him in unravelling the mystery of the diamond robbery, he determined to investigate it on his own account, in order to satisfy his curiosity. To a casual spectator, it appeared to be a mere vulgar burglary, in which the thieves had got off with their plunder, and until his interview with Caprice the detective had supposed it to be so. But when he went over in his own mind the peculiar circumstances of that interview, he saw there was a complicated criminal case to be investigated, so he set himself to work to unravel the mystery, and gratify his inquiring mind.

In the first place, he drew up a statement of the case pure and simple, and then, deducing different theories from the circumstances, he tried to get a point from whence to start. He placed his ideas in the form of questions and answers, as follows:—

Q: Was Villiers outside on the verandah when Caprice mentioned where her diamonds were kept?
A: To all appearances he was.

Q: Had he any inducement to steal the diamonds?

A: Undoubtedly. He was poor, and wanted money, proved by his calling on Caprice and asking for some. He said he would be revenged because she did not give him more than a sovereign, and there would be no sweeter revenge than to steal her diamonds, as it would punish her, and benefit himself.

Q: Did he know the room where the diamonds were kept?

A: Yes. Caprice said her bedroom, and as Villiers had been several times to the house before, he knew where it was.

Q: Did Caprice know Villiers had stolen her jewels?

A: Extremely probably, hence her refusal to prosecute, as he was the husband of Madame Midas, whom she had treated so basely. The refusal to prosecute Villiers might be, in Caprice's opinion, an act of expiation.

When he had got thus far, Naball paused. After all, this was pure theory. He had not a single well authenticated fact to go on, but all the circumstances of the case seemed to point to Villiers, so he determined to go on the trail of Villiers, and find out what he was doing.

Mr. Villiers had of late been under the espionage of the police, owing to some shady transactions with which he was connected, so Naball knew exactly where to find him, and, putting on an overcoat, he sallied forth in the direction of the slums in Little Bourke Street, with the intention of calling on a Chinaman named Ah Goon, who kept an opium den in that unsavoury locality.

To his drinking habits Villiers now added that of being a confirmed opium smoker, and was on terms of intimacy with Ah Goon, in whose den he was accustomed to pass his evenings. Naball therefore intended to watch for Villiers, and find out, if possible, when, owing to drink and opium combined, he was not master of himself, what he had done on the night of the robbery after leaving Caprice.

He soon entered Little Bourke Street, and plunged into the labyrinth of slums, which he knew thoroughly. It was a clear, starry night, but the cool, fresh air was tainted in this locality by the foul miasma which pervaded the neighbourhood, and even the detective, accustomed as he was to the place, felt disgusted with the sickly odours that permeated the atmosphere.

Ah Goon's house was in a narrow right-of-way off one of the larger alleys, and there was a faint candle burning in the window to attract customers. Pausing at the door a moment, Naball listened to hear if there was any European within. The monotonous chant of a Chinese beggar could be heard coming down the alley, and every now and then the screams of two women fighting, while occasionally a number of noisy larrikins would come tramping heavily along, forming a strong contrast to the silent, soft-footed Orientals.

Pushing open the door, Naball entered the den, a small, low-ceilinged room, which was filled with a dull, smoky atmosphere. At the end was a gaudy-looking shrine, all yellow, red, and green, with tinsel flowers, and long red bills with fantastic Chinese letters on them in long rows. Candles were burning in front of this, and cast a feeble light around—on a pile of bamboo canes and baskets heaped up against the wall; on strange-looking Chinese stools of cane-work; on *bizarre* ivory carvings set on shelves; and on a low raised platform at the end of the room, whereon the opium-smokers reclined. Above this ground-floor were two or three other broad, shallow shelves, in each of which a Chinaman was lying, sunk deep in an opium slumber; there was also a kerosene lamp on the lower floor, beside which Ah Goon was reclining, and deftly preparing a pipe of opium for a fat, stolid-looking Chinaman, who watched the process with silent apathy.

Ah Goon looked up as the detective entered, and a bland smile spread over his face as he nodded to him, and went on preparing his pipe, while Naball stood watching the queer operation. There was an oil lamp with a clear flame in front of Ah Goon, who was holding a kind of darning-needle. Dipping this into a thick, brown, sticky-looking substance, contained in a small pot, he twirled the needle rapidly, spinning round the glutinous mass like treacle. Then he placed it in the flame of the lamp, and turned it slowly round and round for a short time until it was ready; then, having placed it in the small hole of the opium pipe, which he held ready in his other hand, he gave it to his countryman, who received it with a grunt of satisfaction, and, lying back, took the long stem between his lips and inhaled the smoke with long, steady breaths. When his pipe was done, which was accomplished in three or four whiffs, he devoted himself to preparing another, while Ah Goon arose to his feet to speak to Naball.

He was a tall man, with a thin, yellow-skinned, emaciated face, cunning, oblong eyes, and flattish nose. His pigtail, of course—black hair craftily lengthened by thick twisted silk—was coiled on top of his head; and his dress, consisting of a dull blue blouse, wide trousers of the same colour, and thick, white-soled Chinese slippers, by no means added to his personal beauty. Standing before Naball, with an unctuous smile on his face, and his long, slender hands clasped in front of him, Ah Goon waited for the detective to speak.

Naball glanced rapidly round the apartment, and not seeing Villiers, addressed himself to the stolid Celestial, who was looking slyly at him.

"Ah Goon, where is the white man who comes here every night?"

"Plenty he come allee muchee night—me no have seen," replied Ah Goon, blinking his black eyes.

"Yes, I know that," retorted Naball quickly; "but this one is short—black hair and whiskers—smokes opium—drinks a lot—is called Villiers."

Whether Ah Goon recognised the gentleman thus elegantly described was doubtful; at all events, he put on a stolid air.

"Me no sabee," he answered.

Naball held out a half-a crown, upon which Ah Goon fixed his eyes lovingly.

"Where is he?"

The money was too much for Ah Goon's cupidity, so he gave in.

"Him playee fan-tan-ayah!" he answered, in a sing-song voice, "allee same."

"Oh!"

Mr. Naball did not waste any words, but threw the half-crown to the expectant Ah Goon, and turned towards the door. Just as he reached it there was a noise of hurried footsteps outside, and Villiers' voice, husky and savage, was heard,—

"Ah Goon, you yellow devil, where are you?" and there came a heavy kick at the door.

In a moment Naball drew back into a shadowy corner, and placed his finger on his lips to ensure silence, a pantomime which the intelligent Ah Goon understood at once.

Villiers opened the door and lurched noisily into the room, stopping for a minute on the threshold, dazed by the yellow, smoky glare.

"Here, you, Ah Goon," he cried, catching sight of the Chinaman, "I want some money—more money."

"Ah Goon no have," murmured that individual, clutching his half-crown.

"I've lost all I had on that infernal fan-tan of yours," shrieked Villiers, not heeding him; "but my luck must change—give me another fiver."

"Ah Goon no have," reiterated the Chinaman, edging away from the excited Villiers.

"Curse your no have," he said fiercely; "why, I've only had twenty pounds from you, and those diamonds were worth fifty."

Diamonds! Naball pricked up his ears at this. He was winning after all. Kitty did not steal her jewels, but this was the thief, or perhaps an accomplice.

"Give me more money," cried Villiers, lurching forward, and would have laid his hand on the shoulder of the shrinking Chinaman, when Naball stepped out of his corner.

"What's the matter?" he asked, in his silky voice.

Villiers turned on the new-comer with a sudden start, and stared suspiciously at him; but the detective being muffled up in a heavy ulster, with his hat pulled over his eyes, he did not recognise him.

"What do you want?" he said ungraciously.

"Nothing," replied Naball quickly. "I'm only strolling round the Chinese quarter out of curiosity, and heard you rowing this poor devil."

"Poor devil!" sneered Villiers, with a glance of fury at Ah Goon, who had complacently resumed his occupation of preparing an opium pipe; "he's rich enough."

"Indeed," said the detective, carelessly—"to lend money?"

"What's that to you?" growled Villiers, with a snarl. "I s'pose I can borrow money if I like."

"Certainly, if you've got good security to give."

Villiers glared angrily at the young man.

"Don't know what you're talking about," he said sulkily.

"Security," explained Naball smoothly; means "borrowing money on land, clothes, or—or diamonds."

Villiers gave a sudden start, and was about to reply, when the door opened violently, and a bold, handsome woman, dressed in a bright green silk, dashed into the room and swooped down on Ah Goon.

"Well, my dear," she said effusively, "'ere I am; bin to the theatre, and 'ere you are preparing that pisin of yours. Oh, I must 'ave one pipe to-night, just one, and—Who the blazes are you?" catching sight of the two strangers.

"Shut up," said Villiers, and made a step towards her, for just on the bosom of her dress sparkled a small crescent of diamonds set in silver. The woman's eyes caught his covetous glance, and she put her hand over the ornament.

"No, you don't," she said scowling. "Lay a finger on me and I'll—ah!"

She ended with a stifled cry, for without warning, Villiers had sprung on her, and his hands were round her throat. Ah Goon and another Chinaman jumped up and threw themselves on the two, trying to separate them. The woman got Villiers' hands off her, and started to sing out freely, so Naball began to think of retreating, as the noise would bring all the undesirable bullies of the neighbourhood into the unsavoury den.

While thus hesitating, the woman flung the diamond ornament away from her with an oath, and it fell at Naball's feet. In a moment the detective had picked it up and slipped in into his pocket.

Villiers, seeing the ornament was gone, flung the woman from him with a howl of fury, and turned to look for it, when the door was burst violently open, and a crowd of Chinese, all chattering in their high shrill voices like magpies, surged into the room. Ah Goon, with many gesticulations, began to explain, Villiers to swear, and the woman to shriek, so in the midst of this pandemonium Naball slipped away, and was soon walking swiftly down Little Bourke Street, with the diamond ornament safe in his pocket.

"I believe this is one of the stolen jewels," he muttered exultingly, "and Villiers was the thief after all. Humph! I'm not so sure of that. Well, I'll find out the truth when I see how she looks on being shown this little bit of evidence."

XI

WHAT NABALL OVERHEARD

It is said that "Counsel comes in the silence of the night," so next morning Mr. Naball, having been thinking deeply about his curious discovery, decided upon his plan of action. It was evidently no good to go straight to Caprice and show her the diamond crescent, as, judging from her general conduct with regard to the robbery, she would deny that the jewel belonged to her.

The detective therefore determined to ascertain from some independent person whether the jewel was really the property of Caprice, and after some consideration came to the conclusion that Fenton would be the most likely individual to supply the necessary information.

"He's her lover," argued Naball to himself as he walked along the street, "so he ought to know what jewellery she's got. I dare say he gave her a lot himself; but, hang it," he went on disconsolately, "I don't know why I'm bothering about this affair; nothing will come of it; for some reason best known to herself, Caprice won't let me follow up the case. I can't make it out; either she stole the jewels herself, or Villiers did, and she won't prosecute him. Ah! women are rum things," concluded the detective with a regretful sigh.

He had by this time arrived at The Never-say-die Insurance Office, and on entering the door found himself in a large, lofty apartment, with a long shiny counter at one end, and a long shiny clerk behind it. This individual, who looked as if he were rubbed all over with fresh butter, so glistening was his skin, received him with a stereotyped smile, and asked, in a soft oily voice, what he was pleased to want?

"Take my card up to Mr. Fenton," said Naball, producing his pasteboard from an elegant card-case, "and tell him I want to see him for a few minutes."

The oleaginous clerk disappeared, and several other clerks looked up from their writing at the detective with idle curiosity. Naball glanced sharply at their faces, and smiled blandly to himself as he recognised several whom he had seen in very equivocal places. Little did the clerks know that this apparently indolent young man knew a good deal about their private lives, and was anticipating coming into contact with several of them in a professional manner.

Presently the oily clerk returned with a request to Mr. Naball to walk into the manager's office, which that gentleman did in a leisurely manner; and the shiny clerk, closing the door softly, returned to his position behind the shiny counter.

Mr. Fenton sat at a handsome writing-table, which was piled up with disorderly papers, and looked sharply at the detective as he took a seat.

"Well, Naball," he said, in his strident voice, "what is the matter? Can't give you more than five minutes—time's money here. Yes, sir."

"Five minutes will do," replied the detective, tapping his varnished boots with his cane. "It's about that robbery."

"Oh, indeed!" Mr. Fenton laid down his pen, and, leaning back in his chair, prepared to listen.

"Yes! I've been looking after Villiers."

"Quite right," said the American. "That's the man I suspect—fixed up anything, eh?"

"Not yet, but I was down Little Bourke Street last night in an opium den, to which Villiers goes, and I found this."

Fenton took the diamond crescent, which Naball held out to him, and looked at it closely.

"Humph!—set in silver—rather toney," he said; "well, is this part of the swag?"

"That's what I want to find out," said Naball quickly. "You know the peculiar way in which Caprice has treated this robbery."

"I know she's a fool," retorted Fenton politely. "She ought to go right along in this matter; but for some silly reason, she won't."

"No; and that's why I've come to you. I'm going down to see her when I leave here, and it's likely she'll deny that this belongs to her. Now, I want your evidence to put against her denial. Is this the property of Caprice?"

Fenton examined the jewel again and nodded.

"Yes, sir," he replied, with a nasal drawl, "guess I gave her this."

"I thought you'd recognise it," said Naball, replacing the jewel in his pocket; "so now I'll go and see her, in order to find out how Villiers got hold of it."

"Stole it, I reckon?"

"I'm not so sure of that," replied the detective coolly. "I don't believe Caprice cares two straws about Villiers being the husband of Madame Midas. If he stole the diamonds, she'd lag him as sure as fate; no, as

I told you before, she's got a finger in this pie herself, and Villiers is helping her."

"But the diamonds were stolen on that night," objected the American.

"I know that—don't you remember you told me that Caprice had an interview in the supper room with Villiers? Well, I believe she went upstairs, took the diamonds, and gave them to Villiers to dispose of."

"For what reason?"

"That's what I'd like to find out," retorted Naball. "She evidently wanted a sum of money for something; now, are you aware that she wanted money?"

"Why, she's always wanting money."

"No doubt—but this must have been a specially large sum?"

Fenton glanced keenly at Naball's impassive face, drummed impatiently with his fingers on the table, then evidently made up his mind.

"Tell you what," he said rapidly, "she did want a large sum of money—fact is, a friend of hers got into a fix, and his wife went howling to her, so she said she would replace the money, and I've no doubt sold her diamonds to do so."

"I thought it was something like that," said Naball coolly; "but why the deuce couldn't she sell her diamonds openly without all this row?"

"Guess you'd better ask her," said Fenton, rising to his feet; "she won't let me meddle with the affair, so I can't do anything—if she's fool enough to lose or sell five thousand pounds' worth of diamonds, I can't help it: and now, sir, the five minutes—" glancing at his watch.

"Are up long ago," replied Naball, rising to his feet. "Well, I'm curious about this case, and I'm going to get at it somehow, so at present I'm off down to see Caprice about this," and he tapped his breast-pocket, where the jewel was placed.

"You won't get anything out of her," said Fenton yawning, "if all you surmise is true."

"I don't care what she says," observed Naball, going to the door. "I can discover all I want from the expression of her face when she knows what I've got, and where I got it."

With this Naball disappeared, and Fenton, returning to his desk, flung himself back in his chair.

"Why the devil won't she prosecute?" he muttered savagely to himself. "Guess she knows more about this robbery than she says, but even then—confound it, I'm mixed."

Having come to this unsatisfactory conclusion, Mr. Fenton went on with his work, and dismissed all thoughts of the diamond robbery from his mind.

Meanwhile, Naball was on his way down to Toorak, meditating over the revelation made to him by Fenton about Caprice's sudden fit of generosity.

"I didn't think she was so tender-hearted," murmured Naball, full of perplexity; "she must have had some strong reason for selling her diamonds. I wonder who the man is?—and the wife called. Humph! this is quite a new game for Caprice."

When he left the station, and walked to the house, instead of ringing the front-door bell, he strolled round the corner to the verandah, on which the drawing-room windows looked out. He did this because—wondering if Villiers was concerned in the robbery—he wanted to see the window by which he entered the dining-room on the night of the robbery. Soft-footed and stealthy in his motions, the detective made no noise, and was just pausing on the edge of the verandah, wondering whether he would go forward or return to the front door, when he heard Kitty's voice in the drawing-room raised in a tone of surprise.

"Mrs. Malton!"

"Hullo!" said Naball to himself, "that's the name of Fenton's assistant manager. Now, I wonder what his wife is calling here about? I'll wait and hear."

So the detective, filled with curiosity, took up his position close to one of the windows, so that he could hear every word that was said, but, of course, was unable to see anything going on inside. He commenced to listen, out of mere curiosity, but soon the conversation took a turn which interested him greatly, and, to his mind, threw a great deal of light on the diamond robbery.

"Why have you called to see me again?" asked Kitty, in a cold tone.

"Because I want to thank you for saving my husband," replied Mrs. Malton. "They told me you were busy, but I have waited in the next room for half-an-hour to see you. My husband is safe."

"I congratulate you—and him," answered Caprice, in an ironical tone. "It is to be hoped Mr. Evan Malton won't embezzle any more money."

Naball, outside, could hardly refrain from giving a low whistle. So this was the man mentioned by Fenton—his own familiar friend—and Kitty Marchurst had helped him. In Heaven's name, why?

"It is due to your kindness that he is safe," said Mrs. Malton, in a faltering tone; "you replaced the money."

"Not at all," said Caprice; "I never replaced a sixpence."

"But you did, you did!" said Mrs. Malton vehemently, falling on her knees before Kitty; "every penny of the money has been paid back, and only you could have done it."

"I did not pay a penny, I tell you," said Caprice; "still, I have had something to do with it."

"I knew it! I knew it!" cried the poor wife, kissing the hand of the actress. "May God bless you for doing this good action."

"I wouldn't have done it had it not been for the sake of your child," said Kitty coldly.

"Wonderful," thought the listener; "Kitty Marchurst has a heart."

"Good-bye, good-bye!" said Mrs. Malton, rising to her feet. "I may never see you again."

"I've no doubt of that," replied Caprice, with a cynical laugh; "you've got all you wanted, so now you leave me."

"No, no!" cried the other woman vehemently. "I am not ungrateful. I will visit you if you will let me. I am sorry for you. I pity you."

"Keep your pity and your visits for some one else—I want neither."

"But your heart?"

"My heart is stone; it was hardened long, long ago. Leave me—I have done all I can for you—now go."

Mrs. Malton made a step forward, and, catching Kitty in her arms, kissed her.

"God bless you!" she cried, in a low voice, and as she kissed her she felt a hot tear fall on her hand. It was Caprice who wept, but, with a stifled sigh, she pushed Mrs. Malton away.

"You are a good woman," she said hoarsely. "Go! go! and if you ever think of me, let it be as one who, however bad her life, did at least one good action."

She sank back into a chair, covering her face with her hands, while Mrs. Malton, with a look of pity on her face, and a low "God bless you," left the room.

Meanwhile, the detective outside was smitten with a kind of remorse at having overheard this pathetic scene.

"I've found out what Caprice wanted the money for," he muttered; "but I'm sorry for her—very sorry. I never knew before she was a woman—I thought she was a fiend."

Kitty, drying her eyes, arose from her seat and dragged herself slowly across the room to the window near which the detective was standing. He heard her coming and tried to escape, and in another moment Kitty had opened the window, and they were face to face.

"Mr. Naball," she cried, with a sudden, angry light in her eyes, "you have heard—"

"Every word," said Naball, looking straight at her wrathful face.

XII

Naball tells a Story

Kitty looked at him in silence with flashing eyes, and then laughed bitterly.

"And how long is it since you added the spy business to your usual work?" she asked, with a sneer on her colourless face.

"Since a few moments ago," replied Naball coolly. "I came to see you on business, and, hearing you in conversation with a lady, did not like to interrupt till you were disengaged."

"I'm very much obliged to you for your courtesy," said Caprice scornfully; "but now you have satisfied your curiosity. M. le Mouchard, I'll trouble you to take yourself off."

"Certainly, after I've had a few moments' conversation with you."

"I decline to listen," said Kitty haughtily.

"I think you had better," observed Naball significantly, "as it's about the robbery of your jewels."

"I forbade you to go on any further with that matter."

"You did; but I disobeyed your injunction."

"So I understand," replied Kitty indignantly; "and may I ask if you have discovered anything?"

"Yes—this!" and he showed the diamond crescent to Caprice. She started violently, and her pale face flushed a deep red.

"Where did you get it?" she asked.

"From Randolph Villiers."

"Villiers!" she echoed in surprise. "How did it come into his possession?"

"That is what I want to discover."

"Then you may save yourself the trouble, for you will never know."

"I understand that," said Naball quietly; "nothing can be done unless you permit me to go on."

"I forbid you to go on," she retorted angrily.

Naball bowed.

"Very well," he said quietly, "then there is nothing for me but to leave."

"No, I don't think there is," assented Kitty coldly, turning to re-enter the house.

"But, before I go," went on the detective, playing his great card, "I will leave your jewel with you."

"That," said Kitty, glancing over her shoulder at the crescent—"that is not mine."

"Mr. Fenton says it is."

"Mr. Fenton!" echoed Caprice jeeringly; "and how does Mr. Fenton know?"

"I should think he was the best person to know," retorted Naball, nettled at her mockery.

"A good many people think the same way," said Kitty disdainfully, "but in this case Mr. Fenton is wrong—I never saw those diamonds before."

"Then how did it come into Mr. Villiers' possession?"

"I don't know, not being in Mr. Villiers' confidence."

"Oh!" said Naball significantly, "you are quite certain you are not?"

"I don't understand you," replied Kitty coldly; "explain yourself."

"Certainly, if you wish it," said the detective smoothly. "I will tell it in the form of a little story—have I your permission to be seated?"

She nodded carelessly, whereupon Naball sat down on one of the lounging chairs, and, crossing his legs, settled himself composedly, while Kitty, standing near him with loosely-clasped hands, looked idly at the green lawn, with its brilliant border of many-coloured flowers.

"There was once a woman called Folly, who lived—let us say—in Cloudland—" began Naball airily.

"Rubbish!" said Kitty angrily.

"Nothing of the sort," retorted Naball coolly, "it is truth in disguise. I have been to school—I have read Spenser's 'Faery Queen'—if you please, we will consider this story, though not in verse, as one of the lost cantos of the poem."

Kitty shrugged her shoulders with contempt. "I think you're mad," she said coldly. "Perhaps I am," retorted Naball sharply, "but there's method in my madness, as you will soon find out—so, to go on with the lost canto of the 'Faery Queen.' This woman, Folly, was reputed to have a hard heart—no doubt she had, but there was one soft spot in it—love for her child. Many men loved this charming Folly, and paid dearly for the privilege. One man, misnamed Strength, loved her madly, and gave her many jewels. Strength had a friend, called Weakness, and though they were so dissimilar in character, they worked together. Weakness also loved Folly, though he had a wife, and, to gain Folly's love, he stole a lot of money. His wife discovered this, and going to Folly, implored her to help Weakness, but in vain, till at last she gained her point by appealing to the one soft spot in Folly's heart—love for her child. She was successful, and Folly promised to save the husband by replacing the money, which she could do through the agency of Strength, who was her lover.

"Folly, however, did not know where to get the money, so, in despair, determined to part with her jewels. She dared not do so openly, lest the inhabitants of Cloudland should find out what Weakness had done, so she enlisted the services of a man called Vice. Here," said Naball gaily, "we will leave the narrative style, and finish the story dramatically."

Kitty, who had grown pale, made no sign, so Naball resumed.

"Scene, a supper-room, with a window open—time, night—supper ended—guests away—enter Vice through open window—helps himself to champagne. Folly, informed of presence of Vice, enters the room and orders him out—he refuses to leave till he gets money—she refuses to give it to him. Suddenly an idea strikes her, and she tells Vice she will give him money if he sells her jewels for her secretly—Vice consents. Folly goes up to her room, gets jewels, gives them to Vice, who goes away and breaks down shrubs under window, which is opened by Folly to show every one that a burglar has stolen the jewels. Rumours of the theft get about—Bloodhound goes on the track—traces Vice to his den—finds one jewel—comes to show it to Folly—overhears wife of Weakness thanking Folly for replacing money stolen by her husband—exit wife of Weakness—enter Bloodhound to Folly, who denies having ever seen jewel before. Bloodhound tells a story to Folly, which Folly—"

"Denies, yes, denies!" broke in Kitty angrily; "your story is wrong."

"Pardon me," said Naball, rising, "allegorical."

"I can understand what you mean," said Kitty, after a pause; "but it's all wrong. I never paid this money for Malton."

"Pardon me,—Weakness," said Naball politely.

"Bah! why keep up this transparent deception? Your story is excellent, and I understand all about Folly, Vice, and Strength, but you are wrong—that jewel is not mine. I never paid the money, and I don't know anything about Malton's business, so you can leave me at once, and never show your face again."

"But the jewel?" said the detective, holding it out.

Kitty snatched it out of his hand, and flung it across the lawn. It flashed brilliantly in the sunlight, and fell just on the verge of the flower-bed.

"You can follow it,—Bloodhound," she said disdainfully, and, entering the house, closed the window after her.

Naball stood for a moment smiling in a gratified manner to himself, then, sauntering slowly across the lawn, picked up the jewel and replaced it in his pocket.

"I knew I was right," he murmured quietly, as he strolled to the gate; "she stole the diamonds to pay Malton's debt, and Villiers got this for payment as an accomplice. I wish I could get on with the case, but she won't let me—what a pity; dear, dear, what a pity!"

He had by this time reached the gate, and was passing through it, when a hansom drove up, from out which Fenton jumped.

"Well?" he asked, when he saw Naball.

"Well," said Naball, dusting his varnished boots with a silk handkerchief.

"What does she say?" asked Fenton inquiringly

"What a woman generally does say—everything but the truth. Going to see her?"

"Yes," said Fenton, paying his cab fare; "can I do anything?"

"Two things," observed Naball quietly: "in the first place, let me have your cab; and in the second, give this to Caprice with my compliments," and he handed the crescent of diamonds to Fenton.

"Why didn't you give it to her yourself?" asked Fenton, taking it.

"Because she said it wasn't hers," replied Naball, getting into the cab. "I can't do anything more in the matter; it's a beautiful case spoiled."

"Why spoiled?" asked Fenton, pausing at the gate.

"Because there's a woman in it," replied Naball; "good-bye!" and the cab drove off in a cloud of dust, leaving Fenton at the gate looking in a puzzled manner at the diamond crescent.

"Why the deuce did she deny this being hers?" he asked himself as he opened the gate. "I know it well—I ought to, considering I paid for it—there's some game in this."

He rang the bell, which was answered by Bliggings, who, in reply to his question as to whether Kitty was at home, burst out into a volley of language.

"Oh, gracious an' good 'eavens, missus 'ave bin talkin' to a lady this mornin', and is that upset as never was—chalk is black to her complexing, and penny hices 'ot to the chill of her feets."

"Humph!" said Fenton, entering the house and leisurely taking off his hat, "just tell your mistress I want to see her."

"Oh, gracious an' good 'eavens!" cried Bliggings, "she's a-lyin' down in company with a linseed poultase an' a cup of tea, both bein' good for removin' 'eadaches."

"Great Scot!" said Fenton impatiently, pushing the voluble Bliggings aside, "I'll go and see her straight off myself."

He went upstairs and knocked at the sitting-room door. Hearing a faint voice telling him to come in, he entered the room, which he found in semi-darkness, with the pungent aroma of *eau de cologne* pervading the atmosphere.

"What do you want?" asked Kitty fretfully, thinking it was the servant.

"To see you," replied Fenton gruffly.

"Oh, it's you!" cried Caprice, sitting up on the sofa, looking pale and wan in her white dress. "I'm glad of that—I've just seen that Naball, and he's been accusing me of stealing my own jewels."

"Well, did you?" asked Fenton complacently.

"Of course I didn't," she retorted angrily; "why should I? Naball thinks I did it to replace the money Malton stole."

"How did he find out that?" asked Fenton, who knew quite well he had told him about it himself.

"He overheard Mrs. Malton thanking me," retorted Kitty impatiently; "the money has been replaced, so I suppose, you did it."

"Yes, I did," said Fenton boldly, "for your sake."

"You're a good fellow, Fenton," said Kitty, in a softened tone. "I'm glad you did what I asked you—now, go away, for I must get a sleep, or I'll never be able to act to-night."

"But what about this jewel?" asked Fenton, taking the crescent out of his pocket. "Naball said you denied it being yours."

"So I did," replied Caprice pettishly.

"But why? I gave it to you."

"Well, you can give it to me again," she said coolly. "Put it on the table, and go away."

Fenton thought a moment, then, going over to the table, placed the jewel thereon, and turned once more to Caprice.

"Look here, Kitty," he said slowly, "did you do anything with those diamonds?"

"Perhaps I did, and perhaps I didn't," replied Caprice enigmatically; "at all events, I'm not going to have any more fuss made over them."

"Well, good-bye at present," said Fenton carelessly. "I say, you might give me a kiss, after fixing up Malton's affair."

"So I will—at the theatre to-night. Do leave me, my head is so bad."

"Not so bad as you are, you little devil," murmured Fenton, closing the sitting-room door softly after him. "Well, I guess there'll be no more trouble about those diamonds, at all events."

XIII

The Gossip of Clubs

It was called "The Skylarks' Club," because, like those tuneful birds, the members were up very early in the morning. Not that the aforesaid members were early risers by any means—but because they never went to bed till three or four o'clock. To put it plainly, they stayed up nearly all night, and it seemed to be a point of honour with them that, as long as a quorum were on the premises, the club should be kept open.

Most of the members were dissipated and led fast lives, drank a good deal, gambled away large sums, betted freely, and, to all appearances, were going to the dogs as fast as they possibly could. The code of morality was not very strict, and the "Skylarks" generally viewed each other's good or bad luck in a cynical manner. Occasionally a member disappeared from his accustomed place, and it was generally understood he had "gone under," or, in other words, was vegetating on some up-country station, doubtless cursing the "Skylarks" freely as the cause of his ruin.

Other clubs in Melbourne were fast—not a doubt about that—but every one declared that the "Skylarks" overstepped all bounds of decency. Whatever devilment was to be done, they would do it, and, as they had no characters to lose, they generally amused themselves by trying to destroy other people's good name, and generally succeeded.

It was a Bohemian club, and among its members were stock-brokers, musicians, journalists, and actors, so that, whatever the moral tone of the place, the conversation was generally brilliant, albeit rather malicious. One way and another, there was a good deal of money floating about, for if the members worked hard at business during the day, they also worked hard at pleasure during the night, so, systematically, burned the candle at both ends. "*Fay ce que vouldras*" was their motto, and they certainly carried it out to the very last letter.

Keith Stewart was a member of this delectable fraternity, having been introduced by Ezra Lazarus, and, thanks to his mysterious five hundred pounds, was able to cut a very decent figure among the members. He was still in the pawnbroker's office, although he very much wanted to leave it, but, having passed his word to old Lazarus to stay six months, he was determined to do so.

It was now about three months since the diamond robbery, and, after being a nine days' wonder, it had passed out of the minds of every one. Nothing more was heard of the theft, and, after a great number of surmises, more or less wrong, the matter was allowed to drop, as a new divorce case of a novel character now engrossed the public mind.

"Prince Carnival" had been withdrawn after a very successful run, and Kitty Marchurst was now appearing in "Eblis," which, as she expected, had turned out a failure. Under these circumstances, "Prince Carnival" was revived, pending the production of "Faust Upset," a new burlesque by Messrs. Stewart and Lazarus.

Both these young men had worked hard at the piece, and Mortimer, having approved of the first act, had determined to put the play on the stage: first, because he saw it was by no means a bad piece, and secondly, he had nothing else handy to bring forward. If he could have obtained a new and successful opera-bouffe from London, "Faust Upset" would have been ignominiously shelved, but, luckily for Keith and his friends, all the late opera-bouffes had been failures, so Mortimer made a virtue of necessity, and gave them a chance.

It was about eleven o'clock at night, and the smoking-room of the "Skylarks" was full. Some of the members had been there for some hours, others had dropped in after the theatres were closed, and here and there could be seen a reporter scribbling his notes for publication next day.

A luxurious apartment it was, with lounging chairs covered with crimson plush, plenty of mirrors, and a number of marble-topped tables, which were now covered with various beverages. Every one was talking loudly, and the waiters were flitting about actively employed in ministering to the creature comforts of the patrons of the club. What with the dusky atmosphere caused by the smoking, the babel of voices, the jingle of glasses, and the constant moving about of the restless crowd, it looked like some fantastic nightmare.

Keith was seated in a corner smoking a cigarette and waiting for Ezra, who had promised to meet him there, and in the meantime was idly watching the crowd of his friends, and listening to their gossip. Malton was also lounging about the room, chatting to his friends on current topics.

"Anything going on in the House?" asked Pelk, a theatrical critic, of Slingsby, who had just entered.

That gentleman shrugged his shoulders.

"A slanging match, as usual," he replied, taking a seat and ringing the bell. "Some members have got an idea that abuse is wit. I don't think much of the Victorian Parliament."

"It's better than the New South Wales one, at all events," said Keith, smiling.

"That's not saying much," retorted Slingsby, lighting a cigar. "The Sydney men are more like fractious children than anything else, though to be sure that's only proper, seeing our Parliaments are nurseries for sucking politicians."

"That's severe."

"But true—the truth is always disagreeable."

"Perhaps that's the reason so few people speak it."

"Exactly—truth is a sour old maid whom nobody wants."

"Not you, at all events, Slingsby"

"No—it's a matter of choice—*Video meliora proboque deteriora sequor.*"

"Don't be classical—it's out of place here."

"Not a bit," retorted Slingsby smoothly, looking round at the circle of grinning faces, "it's out of the dictionary, you know, foreign words and affixes."

Every one roared at this candid confession.

"No wonder *The Penny Whistle* flourishes when there's such men as you on the staff," said Toltby, with a sneer.

"You've no cause to complain," replied Slingsby; "they've been kind enough to you."

"Yes; they recognise good acting."

Slingsby looked at him queerly.

"Dear boy, I prefer the stage of the House to that of the theatre—the actors are much more amusing."

At this moment Felix Rolleston, now looking much older since the Hansom Cab murder case, but as lively as ever, entered the room and danced up to the coterie.

"Well, gentlemen," he said gaily, "what is the news?"

"Good news, bad news, and such news as you've never heard of," quoted Keith lazily.

"Thank you, my local Gratiano," replied Felix, quickly recognising the quotation as from the "Merchant of Venice." "By the way, there's a letter for you outside."

"Oh, thanks," said Stewart rising, "I'll go and get it," and he sauntered out lazily.

"Humph!" exclaimed Felix, looking after him, "our friend is the author of 'Faust Upset,' I understand?"

"Yes," replied Toltby; "deuced good piece."

"That means you've got an excellent part," struck in Slingsby mercilessly.

"Quite right," retorted Toltby complacently; "all the parts are good— especially Caprice's."

"Oh, that goes without saying," said Pelk, with a grin; "our friend is rather sweet there."

"So is she," said Felix significantly; "case of reciprocity, dear boy!"

"She's given Fenton the go-by."

"Yes, and Meddlechip is elevated to the vacancy. Wonder how long it will be before she breaks him?"

"Oh, even with her talents for squandering, Caprice can't burst up the richest man in Victoria," said Slingsby vulgarly; "when she does give him up, I suppose Stewart will succeed him."

"Not enough cash."

"Pooh! what is cash compared to love?"

"Eh! a good deal in this case, as Fenton found out."

"Speak of the devil," said Felix quickly; "here comes the gentleman in question."

Fenton, looking harassed and worn, entered the room, and glanced round. Seeing Rolleston, he came over to him and began to talk.

"Guess you look happy, boys," he said, in his nasal voice.

"It's more than you do," replied Rolleston, scanning him keenly.

"No; I've overworked myself," said Fenton coolly, "I need pulling up a bit."

"Go and see a doctor—try tonics."

"Ah, bah! glass of champagne will fix me straight. Here, waiter, bring in a bottle of Heidsieck. Any of you boys join?"

All the boys assenting to the hospitable proposition, Fenton ordered two bottles, and lighted a huge cigar. When the waiter came back with the wine, Keith also entered, with a soft look on his face which puzzled Rolleston. He had put on his overcoat.

"Ah!" said that astute gentleman, "you look pleased—your letter was pleasant?"

"Yes, very," replied Keith laconically.

"Then it was from a woman," said Fenton.

"Humph! that's generally anything but pleasant," grunted Slingsby.

"No doubt, to such a Don Juan as you," said Pelk, amid a general laugh.

The waiter was opening the wine so slowly that Fenton lost patience, and snatched one bottle up from the table.

"Guess we had better fix those two up at once," he said. "Any one got a knife?"

Keith put his hand in his pocket, and produced therefrom Meg's present.

"Great Cæsar, what a pig-sticker," said Fenton, holding it up.

"What made you buy such a thing, Stewart?" asked Felix, laughing.

"I didn't buy it," replied Keith; "it's a present from a lady."

"A very young lady, I should say," said Slingsby drily; "not much idea of taste."

"Matter of opinion," said Keith serenely; "I like the knife for the sake of the donor—her name's on the handle."

Fenton by this time had opened the bottle, and laid the knife down on the table, from whence Felix picked it up and examined it.

"'From Meg,'" he read, in an amused tone; "gad, Stewart, I thought it was the mother, not the daughter."

Fenton shot a fiery glance at Keith, who laughed in rather an embarrassed manner.

"It was just the child's whim," he said, laughing. "I saved her from the tram-car, so she gave me this as a souvenir;" and, taking up the knife, he shut it with a sharp click, and slipped it into his overcoat pocket.

When they had all finished the wine, Fenton said he had to see Mortimer about some business.

"Half-past ten," he said, looking at his watch; "they'll just be about through."

"I've got to see Mortimer to-night," observed Keith, "and I'm waiting here for Lazarus."

"About the new play, I reckon," said Fenton; "well, you'd better walk up with me."

Keith shook his head.

"No, thanks; I must wait for Lazarus."

"Then come and have a game of billiards in the meantime," said Felix, rising; "take off your coat, you'll find it hot."

"All right," assented Keith readily "Here, Alfred," and, slipping off his coat, handed it to a waiter, who was just passing, "hang this up for me."

The waiter took the coat, threw it over his arm, and vanished; while Keith and Felix strolled leisurely away in the direction of the billiard-room.

"How the deuce does Stewart run it?" asked Fenton, looking after them; "he can't get much salary at old Lazarus' place."

"Case of God tempering the wind to the shorn lamb," said Slingsby ironically.

"Hang it, I don't think he ought to be a member of the Club, a confounded pawnbroker's clerk."

"It is rather a topsy-turvy business, ain't it; but you see, in the colonies Jack's as good as his master."

"And in some cases a deal better," said Pelk, referring to the relative positions of Malton and Fenton.

"Particularly when Jack's got a pretty wife," finished Toltby significantly.

Fenton knew this was a hint at his *penchant* for Mrs. Malton, but he did not very well see how he could take it to himself, particularly when he saw every one smiling, so he smiled back saturninely at the circle.

"You're devilish witty, boys," he said coldly; "guess the wine has sharpened your brains."

As he strolled away in his usual cool manner, Slingsby looked after him.

"Our friend's hard hit over Mrs. Malton," he said at length.

"Every one knows that," grinned Toltby, "except the husband."

"Yes, the husband is generally the last to find out these things," remarked Pelk drily; and the conversation ended.

Meanwhile Rolleston and Keith were playing their game of billiards, a pastime in which the former was an adept, and soon defeated Keith, who threw down his cue in half anger.

"You always win," he said pettishly; "it's no use playing with you."

"Oh, yes, it is," said Felix cheerfully. "I know I'm a good player, so if you play with me it will improve you very much—that remark sounds conceited, but it's true—come and have another game."

"Not to-night," replied Keith; "I've got to keep my appointment with Mortimer—it's no use waiting for Lazarus."

"Oh, yes, it is," cried a new voice, and Lazarus made his appearance at the door of the billiard-room. "I'm sorry for having kept you waiting, but it was unavoidable. I'll tell you all about it as we walk up."

"All right," replied Keith, and turned to go, followed by Ezra, who nodded to Rolleston.

"Good-night," cried that gentleman, making a cannon. "Good luck be with you."

"Amen," responded Keith laughing, and disappeared with Ezra.

XIV

A Struggle for Fame

The two young men walked slowly up the street in the direction of the Bon-Bon Theatre, passing into Swanston Street just as the Town Hall clock struck eleven. It was a beautiful moonlight night, but no breeze was blowing, and the heat which the earth had drawn to her bosom during the day was now exhaled from the warm ground in a faint humid vapour. Crowds of people were in the streets sauntering idly along, evidently unwilling to go to bed. The great buildings stood up white and spectral-like on the one side of the street, while on the other they loomed out black against the clear sky. The garish flare of the innumerable street lamps seemed out of place under the serene splendour of the heavens, and the frequent cries of the street boys, and noisy rattling of passing cabs, jarred on the ear. At least Keith thought so, for, after walking in silence for some time, he turned with a gesture of irritation to his companion.

"Isn't this noise disagreeable?" he said impatiently; "under such a perfect sky the city ought to lie dead like a fantastic dream of the Arabian Nights, but the gas lamps and incessant restlessness of Melbourne vulgarises the whole thing."

"Poetical, certainly," replied Ezra, rousing himself from his abstraction; "but I should not care to inhabit an enchanted city. To me there is something grand in this restless crowd of people, all instinct with life and ambition—the gas lamps jar on your dream, but they are evidences of civilisation, and the hoarse murmur of the mob is like the mutterings of a distant storm, or white waves breaking on a lonely coast. No, my friend, leave the enchanted cities to dreamland, and live the busy life of the nineteenth century."

"Your ideas and wishes are singularly at variance," said Keith smiling. "The city suggests poetical thoughts to you, but you reject them and lower yourself to the narrow things of everyday."

"I am a man, and must live as one," replied the Jew, with a sigh; "it's hard enough to do so—Heaven knows!—without creating Paradises at whose doors we must ever stand like lost Peris."

"What's the matter with you to-night?" asked Keith abruptly.

"Nothing particular; only I've had a quarrel with my father."

"Is that all? My dear Lazarus, your father lives in an atmosphere of quarrelling—it's bread and meat to him—so you needn't fret over a few words. What was the quarrel about?"

"Money."

"Humph!—generally a fruitful cause of dissension. Tell me all about it."

"You know how I love Rachel?" said Lazarus quietly. "Well, I am anxious to marry her and have a home of my own. It's weary work living in tents like a Bedouin. I get a good salary, it's true; but I asked my father to give me a sufficient sum of ready money to buy a piece of land and a house. I might have saved myself the trouble—he refused, and we had angry words, so parted in anger."

"I wouldn't bother about it, if I were you," said Keith consolingly. "Words break no bones—besides, this burlesque may bring us a lot of money, and then you can marry Rachel when you please."

"I don't expect much money out of it," replied the Jew, with a frown. "It's our first piece, and Mortimer will drive a hard bargain with us—but you seem very hopeful to-night."

"I have cause to. Eugénie has written me a letter, in which she says she is coming to Melbourne."

"That's good news, indeed. Is she going to stay?"

"I think so," said Keith gaily. "I told you she was a governess, so she has replied to an advertisement in the *Argus*, and hopes to get the situation."

"I trust she will," observed Ezra, smiling at Keith's delight. "She will do you a lot of good by her presence, and guard you from the spells of Armida."

"*Alias* Caprice. Thanks for the warning, but I've not been ensnared by the fair enchantress yet, and never mean to; but here we are at the theatre. I hope we get good terms from Mortimer."

"So do I, for Rachel's sake."

"We are both *preux chevaliers*, anxious to gain for our lady-loves not fame, but money. Oh, base desire!"

"It may be base, but it's very necessary," replied the prudent Jew, and they both entered the stage-door of the theatre.

Mortimer's sanctum was a very well-furnished room, displaying considerable taste on the part of the occupant, for the manager of the "Bon-Bon" was sybaritic in his ideas. The floor was covered with a heavy velvet carpet, and the walls adorned with excellent pictures, while the furniture was all chosen for comfort as well as for ornament. Mortimer was seated at his desk with a confused mass of papers before him, and leaning back in a chair near him was Caprice, who looked rather pale and worn.

There was a lamp on the table with a heavy shade, which concentrated all the light into a circle, and Kitty's pale face, with its aureole of fair hair seen in the powerful radiance, appeared strange and unreal. Dark circles under her heavy eyes, faint lines round the small mouth, and the weary look now habitual to her, all combined to give her face a wan and spiritual look which made even Mortimer shiver as he looked at her.

"Hang it, Kitty," he said roughly, "don't look so dismal. You ought to see a doctor."

"What for?" she asked listlessly. "I'm quite well."

"Humph! I don't think so. You've been going down the hill steadily the last few months. Look how thin you are—a bag of bones."

"So was Rachel," replied Caprice, with a faint smile.

"Well, she didn't live very long. Besides, you ain't Rachel," growled Mortimer, "and I don't want you to get ill just now."

"No, you could hardly supply my place," said Caprice, with a sneer. "Don't you bother yourself, Mortimer, I'm not going to die yet. When I do I sha'n't be sorry; life hasn't been so pleasant to me that I should wish to live."

"I don't know what you want," grumbled the manager; "you've got all Melbourne at your feet."

"I can't say much for Melbourne's morality, then," retorted Caprice bitterly; "circumstances have made me what I am, but I'm getting tired of the cakes and ale business. If I could only secure the future of my child, I'd turn religious."

"Mary Magdalen!"

"Yes, a case of history repeating itself, isn't it?" she replied, with a harsh laugh.

"Strange!" said Mortimer, scrutinising her narrowly; "the worse a woman is in her youth, the more devout she becomes in her old age."

"On the authority of M. de la Rochefoucauld, I suppose," answered Caprice; "old age gives good advice when it no longer can give bad example."

"Who told you that?"

"A man you never knew—Vandeloup."

"I don't know that my not being acquainted with him was much to be regretted."

"No, I don't think it was," replied Caprice coolly; "he had twice your brains—to know him was a liberal education."

"In cheap cynicism, gad, you've been an apt pupil."

Kitty laughed, and, rising from her seat, began to walk to and fro.

"I wish those boys would come," she said restlessly; "I want to go home."

"Then go," said Mortimer; "you needn't stay."

"Oh, yes, I need," she replied; "I want to see that they get good terms for their play."

"I'll give them a fair price," said Mortimer; "but I'm not going to be so liberal as you expect."

"I've no doubt of that."

"I believe you're sweet on that Stewart."

"Perhaps I am!"

"Meddlechip won't like that,"

"Pish! I don't care two straws for Meddlechip."

"No; but you do for his money."

"Of course; that goes without saying."

"You're a hardened little devil, Caprice."

"God knows I've had enough to make me hard," she replied bitterly, throwing herself down in her chair, with a frown.

There was a knock at the door at this moment, and, in reply to Mortimer's invitation to "come in," Ezra and Keith appeared.

"Well, you two are late," said Mortimer, glancing at his watch; "a quarter-past eleven."

"I'm very sorry," said Ezra quietly; "but it was my fault. I was telling Stewart about some business."

"Well, we won't take long to settle this affair," remarked Mortimer, looking over his papers. "Be seated, gentlemen."

Keith took off his overcoat and threw it over the back of a chair, on which Kitty's fur-lined mantle was already resting.

Caprice, who had flushed up on the advance of Stewart, leaned back in her chair, while Keith sat down near her, and Ezra took a position opposite, close to Mortimer.

"Now then, gentlemen," said Mortimer, playing with a paper-cutter, "about this burlesque—what is your opinion?"

"That's rather a curious question to ask an author," replied Keith gaily. "We naturally think it excellent."

"I hope the public will think the same," observed Mortimer drily; "but I don't mean that. I want to know your terms."

"Of course," said Ezra, smoothly; "but just tell us what you are prepared to give."

"I'm buyer, gentlemen, you are sellers," replied the manager shrewdly; "I can't take up your position."

Kitty leaned back in her chair and bent over close to Keith's ear.

"Ask five pounds a night," she whispered.

Stewart glanced at Ezra, and seeing he was in doubt as to what to say, spoke out loudly.

"Speaking for myself and partner, I think we'll take five pounds a night."

"Yes, I'll agree to that," observed Ezra eagerly

"I've no doubt you will," rejoined Mortimer, raising his eyebrows; "that's thirty pounds a week, fifteen pounds apiece—a very nice sum, gentlemen—if you get it."

"Then what do you propose to give?" asked Keith.

"One pound for every performance."

Stewart laughed.

"Do you take us for born fools?" he asked angrily.

"No, I do not," replied Mortimer, catching his chin between finger and thumb, and looking critically at the two young men; "I take you for very clever boys who are just making a start, and I'm willing to help you—at my own price—which is one pound a night."

"The game's not worth the candle," said Ezra, in a disappointed tone.

"Oh, yes, it is," retorted Mortimer; "it gives you a chance. Now, look here, I've no desire to take advantage of my position, which, as you see, is a very strong one."

"In what way?" asked Caprice, elevating her eyebrows.

Mortimer explained in his slow voice as follows,—"I can write home to London and get successful plays with big reputations already made."

"Yes, and pay big prices for them."

"That may be," replied the manager imperturbably; "but if I give a good price I get a good article that is sure to recoup me for my outlay. I don't say that 'Faust Upset' isn't good, but at the same time it's an experiment. Australians don't like their own raw material."

"They never get the chance of seeing it," said Keith bitterly; "you of course look at it from a business point of view, as is only proper, but seeing that you draw all your money from Colonial pockets, why not give Colonial brains a chance?"

"Because Colonial brains don't pay, Colonial pockets do," said Mortimer coolly; "besides, I am giving you a chance, and that at considerable risk to myself. I will put on this burlesque in good style because Caprice is dead set on it; but business is business, and I can't afford to lose money on an untried production."

"Suppose it turns out a great success," said Ezra, "we, the authors, only make six pounds a week, while you take all the profits."

"Certainly," retorted Mortimer; "I've taken the risk."

"Then if we make a great success of this burlesque," said Keith, "you will give us better terms for the next thing we write?"

"Well, yes," said the manager, in a hesitating manner; "but, of course, though your position is improved, mine is still the same."

"I understand; as long as you have the run of the London market, you can treat Colonial playwrights as you choose?"

"You've stated the case exactly."

"It's an unfair advantage."

"No doubt, but business is business. I hold the trump card."

"It's a bad lookout for the literary and musical future of Australia when such men as you hold the cards," said Ezra gloomily; "but it's no use arguing the case. I've heard all this sort of thing before. The Australians are too busy making money to trouble about such a contemptible thing as literary work."

"I'll tell you what, Mortimer," broke in Caprice, "give them two pounds a night for the piece."

"Not I."

"Yes you will, or I don't show at the Bon-Bon."

"You forget your engagement, my dear," said Mortimer complacently.

"No, I don't," retorted Kitty, snapping her fingers; "that for my engagement. I don't care if I broke it to-morrow. You've got your remedy, no doubt; try it, and see what you'll make of it."

Mortimer looked uneasily at her. He knew he had the law on his side, but Caprice was so reckless that she cared for nothing, and would do what she pleased in spite of both him and the law. Besides, he could not afford to lose her, so he met her half way.

"Tell you what," he said genially, "I've no wish to be hard on you, boys—I'll give you one pound a night for a week, and if the burlesque is a success, two pounds—there, that's fair."

"I suppose it's the best terms we can get," said Keith recklessly; "anything for the chance of having a play put on the stage. What do you say, Lazarus?"

"I accept," replied the Jew briefly.

"In that case," said Kitty, rising, "I needn't stay any longer. Mr. Lazarus, will you take me to my carriage?"

"Allow me," said Keith advancing.

Kitty recoiled, and an angry light flashed in her eyes.

"No, thank you," she said coldly, snatching up her cloak, "Mr. Lazarus will see me down," and without another word she swept out of the room, followed by Ezra, who was much astonished at the rebuff Keith had received.

"What's that for?" asked Mortimer looking up. "I thought you were the white boy there."

"I'm sure I don't know," said Keith, in a puzzled tone. "She has been rather cold to me for the last three months, but she never snubbed me till now."

"Oh, she's never the same two minutes together," said Mortimer, turning once more to his desk. "Have a drink?"

Keith nodded, whereupon Mortimer, who was the most hospitable of men, brought forth whisky and seltzer. As he was filling the glasses, Ezra re-entered with Keith's coat.

"Caprice carried this downstairs with her by mistake," he said, giving it to Keith, "and called me back to return it."

"Gad! she went off in such a whirlwind of passion I don't wonder she took it. I'm glad she left the chair," said Mortimer coolly. "Will you join us?"

"No, thanks," replied Ezra, putting on his hat. "I've got to go back to the office. Good-night. See you to-morrow, Keith; you can settle with Mortimer about the agreement," and thereupon he vanished.

Keith and Mortimer sat down, and the latter drafted out an agreement about the play which he promised to send to his lawyer, and then, if the young men approved of it, the whole affair could be settled right off.

This took a considerable time, and it was about half-past twelve when Keith, having said good-night to Mortimer, left the theatre. He walked down Collins Street, smoking his cigarette, and thinking about his good luck and Eugénie. How delighted she would be at his success. He would make lots of money, and then he could marry her. After wandering about for some considerable time, he turned homeward. Walking up Bourke Street, he entered Russell Street, and went on towards East Melbourne. Passing along in front of Lazarus' shop, he saw a man leaning against the door.

"What are you doing there?" asked Keith sharply, going up to him.

The man struck out feebly with his fists, and giving an indistinct growl, lurched heavily against Keith, who promptly knocked him down, and had a tussle with him. The moon was shining brightly, and, as the light fell on his face, Keith recognised him instantly—it was Randolph Villiers.

"You'd better go home, Villiers," he said quickly, raising him to his feet, "you'll be getting into trouble."

"Go to devil," said Mr. Villiers, in a husky voice, lurching into the centre of the street. "I'm out on business. I know what I know, and if you knew what I knew, you'd know a lot—eh! wouldn't you?" and he leered at Stewart.

"Pah, you're drunk," said Stewart in disgust, turning on his heel; "you'd better get home, or you'll get into some mischief."

"No, I won't," growled Villiers, "but I know some 'un as will."

"Who?"

"Oh, I know—I know," retorted Villiers, and went lurching down the street, setting the words to a popular tune,—

"I know a thing or two,
Yes I do—just a few."

Keith looked at the drunken man rolling heavily down the street—a black, misshapen figure in the moonlight—and then, turning away with a laugh, walked thence to East Melbourne thinking of Eugénie.

XV

The Russell Street Crime

The next morning a rumour crept through the city that a murder had been committed in a house in Russell Street, and many people proceeded to the spot indicated to find out if it were true. They discovered that for once rumour had not lied, and Lazarus, the pawnbroker, one of the best known characters in the city, had been found dead in his bed with his throat cut. The house being guarded by the police, who were very reticent, no distinct information could be gained, and it was not until *The Penny Whistle* came out at four o'clock that the true facts of the crime were ascertained. A general rush was made by the public for copies of the paper, and by nightfall nothing was talked of throughout Melbourne but the Russell Street crime. The version given by *The Penny Whistle*, which was written by a highly imaginative reporter, was as follows, and headed by attractive titles:—

Terrible Crime in Russell Street
Lazarus has passed in his Checks.
An Unknown Assassin
is
In Our Midst.

It is often said that truth is stranger than fiction, and we have now an excellent illustration of this proverb. A crime has been committed before which the marvellous romances of Gaboriau sink into insignificance, and the guilty wretch who has stained his soul with murder is still at large. The bare facts of the case are as follows:—

Early this morning it was noticed by a policeman that the shop of Lazarus, a well-known pawnbroker, was not opened, and knowing the methodical habits of the old man, the policeman was much surprised. However, thinking that Lazarus might have overslept himself, he passed on, and had gone but a few yards when a boy called Isaiah Jacobs rushed into the street from an alley which led to the back of the house. The lad was much terrified, and it was with considerable difficulty that the policeman elicited from him the following story:—

He had come to his work as usual at eight o'clock, and went round to the back door in order to get into the house. This door was generally open, and Lazarus waiting for him, but on this morning it was closed, and although the boy knocked several times, no response was made. He then noticed that the window which is on the left-hand side of the door going in, was wide open, and becoming impatient, he climbed up to it, and looked in to see if the old man was asleep. To his consternation he saw Lazarus lying on the floor in a pool of blood, and, seized with a sudden terror, he dropped from the window and rushed into the street.

On hearing this, the policeman sent him for Sergeant Mansard, who soon arrived on the scene, with several other members of the force. They went round to the back and found the door closed and the window open as the boy had described. Having tried the door and found it locked, the police burst it open, and entered the house to view a scene which baffles description.

The murdered man was lying nearly nude in the middle of the room in a pool of blood. His throat was cut from ear to ear, and, judging from the bruises and cuts on his hands and arms, there must have been a terrible struggle before the murderer accomplished his act. The bed-clothes, all stained with blood, were lying half on the bed and half on the floor, so that it is surmised that the deceased must have been attacked while asleep, and woke suddenly to fight for his life.

A large iron safe which stood near the head of the bed was wide open, the keys being in the lock, and all the drawers pulled out. A lot of papers which had evidently been in the safe were lying on the floor, but in spite of a rigid examination, no money could be found, so it is presumed that the murder was effected for the sake of robbery. On one sheet of the bed were several stains of blood, as if the assassin had wiped his hands thereon, but the weapon with which the crime was committed cannot be found. A door looking into the shop was closed and bolted, so the murderer must have made his entry through the window, and, departing the same way, forgot to close it.

The body of the deceased has been removed to the Morgue, and an inquest will be held to-day. The case has been placed in the hands of Detective Naball, who is now on the spot taking such notes as he deems necessary for the elucidation of this terrible mystery.

Hereunder will be found a plan of the room in which the murder was committed, and also the alley leading to the street. We wish our readers to take particular note of this, as we wish to give our theory as to the way in which the murderer went about his diabolical work.

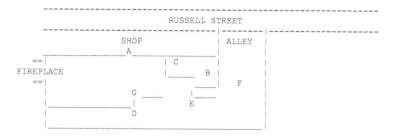

A. Door leading into shop—found bolted.

B. Bed with clothes in disorder.

C. Safe found open, with all valuables abstracted.

D. Window found open by which assassin probably entered.

E. Door leading to alley—found locked.

F. Alley leading to street, by which entrance was gained to back of house.

G. Place where body of murdered man was discovered.

In the first place, there is no doubt that the motive of the crime was robbery, as is proved by the open safe rifled of its contents. The murderer evidently knew that Lazarus slept in the back room and had the keys of the safe—as we have since ascertained—under his pillow. He must also have known the position of the safe and bed, for had he groped about for them, he would have awakened the old man, who would have instantly have given the alarm.

The window D is about five feet from the ground, and was fastened with an ordinary catch, as it never seemed to have entered the old man's head that an attempt would be made to rob him.

Our theory is that the murderer is a man who knew the deceased, and had been frequently in the back room, so as to assure himself of the position of things. Last night he must have entered the alley—at what hour we are not prepared to say, as the time of the murder can only be determined by medical evidence—and opened the window by slipping the blade of his knife between the upper and lower parts, and pushing back the latch.

He then climbed softly into the room, and going straight to the bed, found the deceased asleep. Very likely he did not intend to kill him had he slept on, but in trying to abstract the keys from under the pillow, Lazarus must have sprung up and tried to give the alarm. Instantly the murderer's clutch was on his throat; but the old man, struggling off the bed, fought with terrible strength for his life. The struggle took them into the centre of the room, and there Lazarus, becoming exhausted, must have fallen, and the murderer, with diabolical coolness, must have cut his throat, so as to effectually silence him.

Then, taking the keys from under the pillow, he must have opened the safe, taken what he wished, and made his escape through the window, and from thence into the street. Probably no one was about, and he could slink away unperceived, for, had he met any one, his clothes, spotted with the blood of his victim, would have attracted attention.

We conclude he must have had a dark lantern in order to see the contents of the safe, but, as none has been found, he must have taken it with him, together with the knife with which the crime was committed.

This is all we can learn at the present time, but whether any sounds of a struggle were heard, can only be discovered from the witnesses at the inquest to-morrow.

Of one thing we are certain, the murderer cannot escape, as his blood-stained clothes must necessarily have been noticed by even the most casual observer.

We will issue a special edition of *The Penny Whistle* to-morrow, with a full account of the inquest and the witnesses examined thereat.

XVI

THE INQUEST

There was naturally a great deal of excitement over the murder, as, apart from the magnitude of the crime, Lazarus was a well-known character in Melbourne. He knew more secrets than any priest, and many a person of apparently spotless character felt a sensation of relief when they heard that the old Jew was dead. Lazarus was not the sort of man to keep a diary, so to many people it was fortunate that he had died unexpectedly, and carried a number of disagreeable secrets with him to the grave.

The report of the inquest was followed with great interest, for though it was generally thought that robbing was the motive for the crime, yet some hinted that, considering the character of the old man, there might be more cogent reasons for the committal of the murder. One of these sceptics was Naball, in whose hands the case had been placed for elucidation.

"I don't believe it was robbery," he said to a brother detective. "Old Lazarus knew a good many dangerous secrets, and I wouldn't be a bit surprised to find that the murderer was some poor devil whom he had in his power."

"But the open safe?" said the detective.

"Pish! that can easily be accounted for; there may have been papers implicating the murderer, or the robbery might have been a blind, or—oh, there's dozens of reasons—however, we'll find it all out at the inquest."

In opening the proceedings, the Coroner mentioned all the circumstances in connection with the murder which had come to the knowledge of the police, and said that as yet no clue had been found likely to lead to the detection of the assassin, but without doubt the evidence of the witnesses about to be examined would afford some starting point.

The first witness called was the policeman who had found the body, and he deposed to the circumstances which led to the discovery. He was succeeded by Dr. Chisholm, who had examined the body of the deceased, and, having been sworn in the usual manner, deposed as follows:—

"I am a duly qualified medical practitioner. I have examined the body of the deceased. It is that of an old man—I should say about seventy years of age—very badly nourished; I found hardly any food in the stomach. There were many bruises and excoriations on the body, which, I have no doubt, are due to the struggle between the murderer and his victim. I examined the neck, back, and limbs, but could find no fractures. The throat was cut evidently by some very sharp instrument, as the windpipe was completely severed. I examined the body about nine o'clock in the morning,—it was then warm, and, according to my belief, the deceased must have been dead eight or nine hours."

CORONER: "Are you certain of that?"

DR. CHISHOLM: "Not absolutely. It is a very difficult thing to tell exactly, by the temperature of the body, what length of time has elapsed since death. After a sudden and violent death, the body often parts with its heat slowly, as I think it has done in this case. Besides, the night was very hot, which would be an additional reason for the body cooling slowly."

CORONER: "Was the body rigid when you examined it?"

DR. CHISHOLM: "Yes; *rigor mortis* had set in. It generally occurs within six hours of death, but it might occur earlier if there had been violent muscular exertion, as there was in this case. I think that the deceased was awakened from his sleep, and struggled with his murderer till he became exhausted; then the murderer cut his throat with a remarkably sharp knife."

CORONER: "And, according to your theory, death took place about midnight?"

DR. CHISHOLM: "Yes—I think so; but, as I said, before, it is very difficult to tell."

The next witness called was Isaiah Jacobs, who gave his evidence in an aggressively shrill voice, but the Coroner was unable to elicit more from him than had already been published in *The Penny Whistle*. After the echo of the young Israelite's shrill voice had died away, Keith Stewart was sworn, and deposed as follows:—

"I was clerk to the deceased, and had occupied the position for some months. On the day previous to the murder, I had received a hundred pounds, in twenty bank notes of five pounds each, which I gave to the deceased, and saw him place them in his safe. He always slept on the premises, and kept his keys under his pillow. He told me that he always had a loaded revolver on the table beside his bed. On the night, or rather morning, of the murder I was passing along Russell Street on my way home. I saw a man standing near the shop. I knew him as Randolph Villiers. I asked him what he was doing, but could get no very decided answer—he was quite intoxicated, and went off down the street."

CORONER: "About what time was this?"

STEWART: "Two o'clock."

CORONER: "You are certain?"

STEWART: "Quite—I heard it striking from the Town Hall tower."

CORONER: "Was Villiers' intoxication real or feigned?"

STEWART: "Real, as far as I could see."

CORONER: "It was a moonlight night, I believe?"

STEWART: "Yes; the moon was very bright."

CORONER: "Did you notice anything peculiar about Villiers? Was he confused? Were his clothes in disorder? Any marks of blood?"

STEWART: "No; I saw nothing extraordinary about him. He is generally more or less drunk, so I did not notice him particularly."

CORONER: "I believe, Mr. Stewart, you belong to the Skylarks' Club?"

STEWART: "I do."

CORONER: "And yet you are a clerk in a pawnbroker's office—aren't the two things rather incongruous?"

STEWART: "No doubt; but I am in a position to be a member of the Skylarks' Club, and as to being a clerk to Lazarus, it's merely a matter of honour. When he engaged me he stipulated that I should stay for six months, and though I unexpectedly came in for some money, I felt myself bound in honour to keep my agreement."

CORONER: "Thank you, that will do, Mr. Stewart. Call Mrs. Tibsey."

That lady, large, red-faced, and energetic, was sworn and gave her evidence in a voluble manner. She had evidently been drinking, as there was a strong odour of gin in the air, and kept curtseying to the Coroner every time she answered.

"My name's Tibsey, my lord—Maria Tibsey. I've bin married twice, my first being called Bliggings, and died of gunpowder—blowed up in a quarry explosion. My second, also dead, sir, 'ad no lungs, and a corf which tored him to bits. Only one child, sir, 'Tilda Bliggings, out in service, my lord."

CORONER: "Yes, yes, Mrs. Tibsey, we don't want to learn all these domestic affairs. Come to the point."

MRS. TIBSEY: "About Sating, sir?—I called 'im Sating, sir, 'cause he were a robber of the widder and orfin—me, sir, and my darter. I was a-talking to my darter on that night, your worships, she 'aving visited me. I lives near old Sating, as it was 'andy to drop in to pop anything, and about twelve I 'eard a scream—a 'orrid 'owl, as made my back h'open and shut, so I ses, ''Tilda,' ses I,' old Sating is 'avin' a time of it, e's boozin',' and that's all, sir."

CORONER: "You never went to see what it was?"

MRS. TIBSEY: "Me, my lord? no, your worship, it weren't my bisiniss. I didn't think it were murder."

CORONER: "You are quite sure it was twelve o'clock?"

MRS. TIBSEY: "I swears h'it." Miss Matilda Bliggings was then called, and deposed she also heard the scream, and that her mother had said it must be old Lazarus. It was twelve o'clock.

Ezra Lazarus was then called, but could give no material evidence. He said he had quarrelled with his father on the day preceding the murder, and had not seen him since.

The next witness called caused a sensation, as it was none other than Mr. Randolph Villiers, who stated:—

"My name is Villiers. I do nothing. I know old Lazarus. I was passing through Russell Street, and leaned up against the shop door—I was drunk—on my way to Little Bourke Street. I remember meeting Mr. Stewart—think it was two, but ain't sure."

CORONER: "Where were you before you met Mr. Stewart?"

VILLIERS: "About the town somewhere."

CORONER: "Alone?"

VILLIERS: "Sometimes I was, sometimes I wasn't."

This ended all the evidence procurable, and the Coroner summed up.

The crime had evidently been committed for the purpose of robbery, as the hundred pounds which Mr. Stewart swore had been placed in the safe by the deceased were gone; the knife with which the deed had been committed had not yet been found; in fact, all the evidence was of the barest character. According to Dr. Chisholm's evidence, the deceased had been murdered about midnight, and as Mrs. Tibsey and her daughter heard a scream also at that time, all the evidence seemed to point to that hour as having been the time of death. Mr. Stewart met Villiers at two o'clock, and Villiers stated that he had only been in Russell Street a few minutes before he met Mr. Stewart. The jury would be kind enough to bring in a verdict in accordance with the facts before them.

The jury had a long argument; some wanted to bring in a charge of murder against Villiers, as he certainly had not accounted for his presence in Russell Street; but the evidence altogether was so vague that they at length came to the conclusion it would be best to leave the matter to the police, and brought in a verdict that the deceased had met his death at the hands of some person or persons unknown.

Great dissatisfaction was expressed by the public at this verdict, as, in the opinion of most people, Villiers was the guilty man. A regular battle was fought in the newspapers over the whole affair; but one man said nothing.

That man was Naball!

XVII

A Council of Three

When the inquest was over, Naball went straight home, and carefully read all the notes he had taken of the evidence given. After doing so, he came to the conclusion that the person on whom most suspicion rested was Keith Stewart.

"In the first place," said Naball, thoughtfully eyeing his papers, "Stewart was the clerk of old Lazarus, and knew what was in the safe, and where the keys were kept; he is a member of an expensive club, which he can't possibly afford to pay for out of his salary as a clerk; as to his coming in for money, that's bosh!—if he had, agreement or no agreement, he wouldn't have remained with old Lazarus. He states that he left the theatre at half-past twelve, and the doctor says the death took place at midnight; but then he wasn't sure, and it might have taken place at half-past one, which would give Stewart time to commit the crime. He could not account for his time between leaving the theatre and seeing Villiers except by saying he had been walking, which is a very weak explanation. Humph! I think I'll see Mr. Stewart and ask him a few questions."

Mr. Naball glanced at himself in the mirror, arranged the set of his tie, dusted his varnished boots, and then sallied forth in search of Keith. Passing along Swanston Street, he went into a florist's, and purchased himself a smart buttonhole of white flowers, then held a short council of war with himself as to where to find Stewart.

"Wonder where he lives?" muttered the detective, in perplexity; "let me see, what's the time," glancing at his watch—"nearly five; he's a great friend of Mr. Lazarus, and I know Lazarus is sub-editor of *The Penny Whistle*; I'll go along and ask him—he's sure to be in just now."

He walked rapidly along to the newspaper office, and, being admitted to Ezra's room, found that young man just putting on his coat preparatory to going away, his labours for the day now being concluded.

"Well, Mr. Naball," asked Ezra, in his soft voice, "what can I do for you—anything about this unfortunate affair?"

"Yes," said Naball bluntly; "I want to see Mr. Stewart."

"Oh, you do!" broke in a new voice, and Stewart stepped out of an adjoining room, where he had been waiting for his friend; "what is the matter?"

"Nothing much," observed Naball, in a frank voice; "but as this case has been put into my hands, I want to ask you a few questions.'

"Am I in the way?" asked Lazarus, taking up his hat.

"By no means," replied Naball politely; "in fact, you may be of assistance."

"Well, fire away," said Keith, coolly lighting a cigarette. "I'm ready to answer anything."

Naball glanced keenly at both the young men before he began to talk, and noted their appearance. Keith had a rather haggard look, as though he had been leading a dissipated life; while Ezra's face looked careworn and pale.

"Cut up over his father's death, I guess," said Naball to himself; "poor chap!—but as for the other, it looks like late hours and drink. I must find out all about your private life, Mr. Stewart."

"I'm waiting," said Keith impatiently; "I wish you wouldn't keep me very long; I've got to meet a train from the country to-night."

Naball closed both doors of the room, and, resuming his seat, looked steadily at Keith, who, seated astride a chair, leaned his elbows on the back, and smoked nonchalantly.

"Are you aware," asked Naball deliberately, "if the late Mr. Lazarus had any enemies?"

"I can answer that question best," said Ezra quickly, before Keith could speak. "Yes, he had plenty; my father, as you know, was a moneylender as well as a pawnbroker, and, as he took advantage of his possession of money to extort high interest, I know it made a lot of people feel bitter against him."

"Considering that you are his son, sir," said Naball, in a tone of rebuke, "you do not speak very well of the dead."

"I have not much cause to," rejoined Ezra bitterly; "he was father to me in name only. But you need not make any comments—my duty to my father's memory is between myself and my conscience. I have answered your question—he had many enemies."

"So I believe also," said Keith slowly; "but I don't think any one was so hostile as to desire his death."

"As you don't think so," observed Naball sharply, "I myself believe that the murder was committed for the sake of robbery."

"That's easily seen," said Ezra calmly, "from the fact of the safe being open and the money gone."

"That might have been a blind," retorted Naball quickly, "but you talk of money being stolen; I think, Mr. Stewart, in your evidence to-day you said they were bank notes?"

"Yes; twenty ten-pound notes," replied Keith.

"Do you know the numbers of them?"

"No; I never thought of taking the numbers."

"And you handed them to Mr. Lazarus?"

"I did; at half-past five—he put them in his safe."

"Were there any other valuables in the safe?"

"I don't know," retorted Keith coldly; "I was not in the confidence of my employer."

"Do you know?" said Naball, turning to Ezra.

The young Jew smiled bitterly.

"I also was not in my father's confidence," he said, "so know nothing."

"There was some gold and silver money also in the safe," said Keith to Naball, knocking the ashes off his cigarette.

"Humph! that's not much guide," replied the detective; "it's the notes I want—if I could only find the numbers of those notes—where did they come from?"

"A man at Ballarat, called Forbes."

"Oh! I'll write to Mr. Forbes of Ballarat," said Naball, making a note, "but if those notes are put in circulation, do you know of any means by which I can identify them?"

Keith shook his head, then suddenly gave a cry.

"Yes; I can tell you how to identify one of the notes."

"That will be quite sufficient," said the detective eagerly. "How?"

"That boy, Isaiah," said Stewart, "he's great on backing horses, and frequently tells me about racing. When I was making up my cash on that night, the notes were lying on the desk, and as the door of Mr. Lazarus' room was open, Isaiah was afraid to speak aloud about his tip, so he wrote it down."

"But how can that identify the bank-note?" asked the perplexed detective.

"Because the young scamp wrote his tip, 'Back Flat-Iron,' on the back of a ten-pound note."

"In pencil?" asked Naball.

"No; in ink!"

"So one of the notes that were stolen has the inscription 'Back Flat-Iron' on the back of it?"

"Exactly!"

Naball scribbled a line or two in his pocket-book, and shut it with a snap.

"If that note goes into circulation," he said, in a satisfied tone, "I'll soon trace it to its original holder."

"And then?" asked Ezra.

"And then," reiterated Naball quietly, "I'll lay my hands on the man who killed your father. And now, Mr. Stewart, I want to ask you a few questions about yourself."

"Go on!" said Keith imperturbably; "I hope you don't think I killed Lazarus?"

"I think—nothing," replied Naball quietly; "I only want to find out as much as I can. You were at the Bon-Bon Theatre on that night?"

"Yes; talking to Mr. Mortimer."

"Any one else with you?"

"Yes," replied Ezra, "I was, and Caprice; we left about half-past eleven."

"And you, Mr. Stewart?"

"I left at half-past twelve."

"Where did you go then?"

"I was excited over some business I had done, and strolled about the city."

"Anywhere in particular?"

"No. I went along Collins Street, up William Street, round about the Law Courts, and then came down Bourke Street, on my way home."

"How long were you thus wandering about?"

"I think about an hour and a half, because as I turned into Russell Street the clock struck two."

"Why did you turn into Russell Street?"

"Why!" echoed Keith, in surprise, "because I wanted to go home. I went through Russell Street, down Flinders Street, and then walked to East Melbourne, past the Fitzroy Gardens."

"Oh! and you saw Villiers standing about the shop?"

"Yes; he was leaning against the door."

"Drunk?"

"Very!"

"What did you do?"

"I ordered him off."

"Did he go?"

"Yes; rolled down the street towards Bourke Street, singing some song."

"You noticed nothing peculiar about him?"

"No."

"Was the door of the alley leading to the back open or shut?"

"I don't know—I never noticed."

"After Villiers disappeared, you went home?"

"I did—straight home."

Naball pondered for a few moments. Stewart certainly told all he knew with perfect frankness, but then was he telling the truth?

"Do you want to ask me any more questions?" asked Keith, rising.

Naball made up his mind, and spoke out roughly,—

"I want to know how you, with a small salary, can afford to belong to an expensive club like the 'Skylarks?'"

Keith's face grew as black as thunder.

"Who the devil gave you permission to pry into my private affairs?"

"No one except myself," retorted Naball boldly, for, though inferior to Stewart in size, he by no means wanted pluck; "but I'm engaged in a serious case, and it will be best for you to speak out frankly.

"You surely don't suspect Stewart of the murder?" interposed Ezra warmly.

"I suspect nobody," retorted Naball. "I'm only asking him a question, and, if he's wise, he'll answer it."

Keith thought for a moment. He saw that, for some extraordinary reason or another, Naball suspected him, so, in order to be on the safe side, resolved to take the detective's advice and answer the question.

"It is, as you say, a serious matter," he observed quietly, "and I am the last person in the world not to give any assistance to the finding out of the criminal; ask what you please, and I will answer."

This reply somewhat staggered Naball, but, as he had strong suspicions about Stewart's innocence, he put down the apparent frankness of the answer to crafty diplomacy.

"I only want to know," he said mildly, "how a gentleman in your position can afford to belong to an expensive club."

"Because I can afford to do so," replied Keith calmly. "When I first came to Melbourne, I had no money, and was engaged by Mr. Lazarus as his clerk, with the understanding I should stay with him six months.

To this I agreed, but shortly afterwards a sum of five hundred pounds was placed to my credit, and afforded me a chance of living in good style. I wished to leave the pawnshop, but Mr. Lazarus reminded me of my position, and I had to stay. That is all."

"Who placed this five hundred to your credit?" asked Naball.

"I don't know."

"You don't know?" echoed Naball, in surprise. "Do you mean to say that a large sum like that was placed to your credit by a person whom you don't know?"

"I do."

"And I can substantiate that statement," said Ezra quietly.

Naball looked from one to the other in perplexity, puzzled what to ask next. Then he felt the only thing to be done was to go away and think the matter over. But he did not intend to lose sight of Keith, and this absurd statement about the five hundred only seemed to strengthen his suspicions, so he determined to have him shadowed.

"Thank you, Mr. Stewart," he said quietly. "I have nothing more to ask. What time did you say you were going to meet a country train?"

"I mentioned no time," replied Keith sharply.

Baffled by this answer, Naball tried another way.

"Will you kindly give me your address?" he asked, pulling out his pocket-book. "I may want to communicate with you."

"Vance's boarding-house, Powlett Street, East Melbourne."

Mr. Naball noted this in his book, and then, with a slight nod, took his leave.

"Damn him," cried Keith fiercely, "he suspects me of this crime."

"Pooh! that's nonsense," replied Ezra, as they went out, "you can easily prove an alibi."

"No, I can't," replied Keith, in a hard tone. "From half-past twelve o'clock till two I was by myself, and no one saw me. I say I was wandering about the streets, he thinks I was in Russell Street committing a murder."

"I don't think you need be a bit afraid of anyone suspecting you," said Ezra bitterly. "Why, they might as well think I killed my father."

"You!"

"Yes. I had a quarrel with him, and then he was murdered. Oh, I assure you they could get up an excellent case against me."

"But you could prove an alibi."

"That's just where it is," said Ezra coolly; "I can't."

"Why not?"

"Because, after leaving Kitty Marchurst, I went down the street to *The Penny Whistle* office, and found it closed. I then walked home along Collins Street, through the Fitzroy Gardens. It was a beautiful night, and, as I was thinking over my quarrel with my father, I sat down on one of the seats for a time, so I did not get home till two o'clock in the morning. No one saw me, and I've got quite as much difficulty in proving an alibi as you have."

"Do you think Naball suspects you?"

"No; nor do I think he suspects you, but I've got a suspicion that he suspects some one."

"And that some one—"

"Is called Randolph Villiers."

XVIII

Circumstantial Evidence

When Naball left the two young men, he went straight to the Detective Office in order to get some one to look after Keith Stewart, and see that he did not leave Melbourne. Naball did not believe that he was going to meet any one that night, and wanted to find out why he was going to the station.

"If he wanted to give me the slip," he thought, "he wouldn't have told me he was going to the railway station—humph! can't make out what he's up to."

The gentleman who was to act as Mr. Stewart's shadow was a short, red-nosed man with a humbled appearance and a chronic sniffle. He was sparing of words, and communicated with his fellow-man by a series of nods and winks which did duty with him for conversation.

"Tulch!" said Naball, when this extraordinary being appeared, "I want you to go to Vance's boarding-house, Powlett Street, East Melbourne, and keep your eye on a man called Keith Stewart."

An interrogatory sniff from Tulch.

"Ah, I forgot you don't know his personal appearance," said Naball thoughtfully; "he's tall, with fair hair, wears a suit of home-spun—humph;—that won't do, there are dozens of young men of that description. Here!—tell you what, I'll give you a note to deliver to him personally; muffle yourself up in an ulster when you deliver it, so that he won't know you—understand?"

Mr. Tulch sniffed in the affirmative.

"Follow him wherever he goes, and tell me what he's up to," said Naball, scribbling a note to Stewart and handing it to Tulch. "That's all—clear out."

A farewell sniffle, and Tulch was gone.

"Humph," muttered Naball to himself, "now I'd like to know the meaning of all this—I don't believe this cock-and-bull story about Stewart having money left him in this mysterious manner—people don't do that sort of thing now-a-days—I believe he's been robbing the old man for some time and was found out—so silenced him by using his knife. Knife," repeated Naball, "that's not been found yet—I must see about this—now there's Villiers—I wonder if he could help me? It was curious that he should have been about the shop at that special time—he's a bad lot—gad, I'll go and see what I can find out from him."

Knowing Mr. Villiers' habits, he had no difficulty in discovering his whereabouts. Ah Goon's was where Villiers generally dwelt, so, after Naball had partaken of a nice little dinner, he went off to Little Bourke Street.

It was now between seven and eight o'clock, which was the time Villiers generally dined, so, Naball not finding him at Ah Goon's, betook himself to a cook-shop in the neighbourhood, to which he was directed by a solid-looking Chinaman.

It was a low-roofed place, consisting of a series of apartments all opening one into the other by squat little door-ways. The atmosphere was dull and smoky, and the acrid smell of burning wood saluted Naball's nostrils when he entered. Near the door-way a Chinaman was rolling out rice bread to the thinness of paper; then, cutting it into little squares, he wrapped each round a kind of sausage meat, and placed the rolls thus prepared on a tray for cooking.

In the next apartment was a large boiler, with the lid off, filled with water, in which ten or twelve turkeys, skewered and trussed, were bobbing up and down amid the froth and scum of the boiling water. A crowd of Chinese, all chattering in their high shrill voices, were moving about half seen in the smoky atmosphere, through which candle and lamp light flamed feebly.

Villiers, in a kind of little cell apartment, was having his supper when the detective entered. Before him was a large bowl filled with soup, and in this were squares of thin rice bread, and portions of turkey and duck mixed up into a savoury mess, and flavoured with the dark brown fluid which the Chinese use instead of salt.

"Oh, it's you," growled Villiers, looking up with a scowl, "what do you want?"

"You, my friend," said Naball cheerfully, taking a seat.

"Oh, do you?" said Villiers, rubbing his bleared eyes, inflamed by the pungent smoke of the wood-fire. "I s'pose you think I killed old Lazarus?"

"No, I don't," retorted the detective, looking straight at him, "but I think you know more than you tell."

"He! he!" grinned the other sardonically. "Perhaps I do—perhaps I don't—it's my business."

"And mine also," said Naball, somewhat nettled. "You forget the case is in my hands."

"Don't care whose hands it's in," retorted Villiers, finishing his soup, "t'aint any trouble of mine."

The detective bit his lip at the impenetrable way in which Villiers met his advances. Suddenly a thought flashed across his mind, and he bent forward with a meaning smile.

"Got any more diamonds?"

Villiers pushed back his chair from the table, and stared at Naball.

"What diamonds?" he asked, in a husky voice.

"Come now," said Naball, with a wink, "we know all about that—eh? Ah Goon is a good pawnbroker, isn't he?"

"Ah Goon!" gasped Villiers, turning a little pale.

"Yes; though he did only lend twenty pounds on those diamonds."

"Look here, Mr. Jack-o'-Dandy," said Villiers, bringing his fist down on the table, "I don't want no beating about the bush, I don't. What do you mean, curse you?"

"I mean that I know all about your little games," replied Naball, leaning over the table.

"I know Caprice stole her own jewels for some purpose, and gave you some of the swag to shut your mouth, and I know that you're going to tell me all you know about this Russell Street business, or, by Jove, I'll have you arrested on suspicion."

Villiers gave a howl like a wild beast, and, flinging himself across the table, tried to grapple with the detective, but recoiled with a shriek of wrath and alarm as he saw the shining barrel of a revolver levelled at his head.

"Won't do, Villiers," said Naball smoothly; "try some other game."

Whereupon Villiers, seeing that the detective was too strong for him, sat down sulkily in his chair, and after invoking a blessing on Naball's eyes, invited him to speak out. The detective replaced the revolver in his pocket, whence it could be easily seized if necessary, and smiled complacently at his sullen-faced friend.

"Aha!" he said, producing a dainty cigarette, "this is much better. Have you a light?"

Villiers flung down a lucifer match with a husky curse, which Naball, quite disregarding, took up the match and lighted his cigarette. Watching the blue smoke curling from his lips for a few moments, he turned languidly to Villiers, and began to talk.

"You see, I know all about it," he said quietly; "you were too drunk to remember that night when you tried to take a diamond crescent off that woman, and I expect Ah Goon never told you!"

"It was you who took it, then," growled Villiers fiercely.

"In your own words, perhaps it was, perhaps it wasn't," replied Naball, in an irritating tone; "at all events, it's quite safe. You had better answer all my questions, because you bear too bad a character not to be suspected of the crime, particularly as you were about Russell Street on that night."

"Yes, I was," said Villiers angrily; "and who saw me—Keith Stewart—a mighty fine witness he is."

"Aha!" thought the astute Naball, "he does know something, then."

"I could put a spoke in Stewart's wheel," grumbled the other viciously.

"I don't think so," replied the detective, fingering his cigarette, "he is far above you—he's got money, is going to make a name by a successful play, and, if report speaks truly, Caprice loves him."

"I don't care a farthing whether she does or not," said Villiers loudly; "she'd love any one who has money. Stewart's got some, has he; where did he get it?"

"I'm sure I don't know."

"I do!"

"Indeed! where?"

"Never you mind," said Villiers suspiciously. "I know my own knowing."

"Remember what I said," observed Naball quietly, "and tell me all."

"If I tell you all, what will you do?" asked Villiers.

"I'll save your neck from the gallows," replied Naball smoothly.

"Not good enough."

"Oh, very well," said the detective rising, "I've no more to say. I'm off to the magistrate."

"What for?"

Naball fixed his keen eyes on the bloated face of the other.

"To get a warrant for your arrest."

"You can't do that."

"Can't I—you'll see."

"No; wait a bit," said Villiers in alarm; "I can easily prove myself innocent."

"Indeed; then you'd better do so now, before a warrant is out for your arrest."

"You won't give me any money?"

"Not a cent—it's not a question of money with you, but life or death."

Villiers deliberated for a moment, and then apparently made up his mind.

"Sit down," he said sullenly. "I'll tell you all I know."

Naball resumed his seat, lighted a fresh cigarette, and prepared to listen.

"I was rather drunk on the night of the murder," he said, "but not so bad as Stewart thought me. He saw me at the shop-door at two o'clock, but I was there a quarter of an hour before."

"Did you see anything?"

"I saw the gate which led into the alley open," replied Villiers. "No one was about, so I walked in."

"What for?" asked Naball, glancing at him keenly.

"Oh, nothing," replied Villiers indifferently; "the fact was, I saw a policeman coming along, and though I was pretty drunk, I'd sense enough to know I might be run in, so I went into the alley and closed the gate till he passed."

"And then you came out."

"No, I didn't. I walked to the back of the house just to see where it led to. I saw the window wide open, and looked in and saw—"

"The murdered man?"

Villiers nodded.

"Yes; the moonlight was streaming in at the window, and I could see quite plainly. I was in a fright, as I thought, seeing I had no business on the premises, I might be accused, so I got down from the window and went off, closing the gate of the alley after me."

"It wasn't wise of you to stay about the premises," said Naball.

"I know that," rejoined Villiers tartly; "but I couldn't get away, because I saw Stewart coming up the street just as I was wondering where to go; I then pretended to be drunk, so that I could get away without suspicion."

"Why didn't you run?" asked Naball.

"Because he was too close, and besides, he might have given chase, thinking I had been robbing the shop; then, with the open window and the murdered man, it would have been all up with me."

"I don't know if it isn't all up with you now," said Naball drily. "How do I know you are innocent!"

"Because I know who killed Lazarus."

"The deuce you do—who?"

"Stewart himself."

"Humph! that's what I thought; but what proof have you?"

Villiers put his hand in his pocket and brought out a large knife.

"I found this just under the window," he said, handing it to Naball. "You'll see there's blood on the handle, so I'm sure it was with it the crime was committed."

"But how do you know it's Stewart's knife?" asked Naball.

Villiers placed his finger on one side of the handle.

"Read that," he said briefly.

"From Meg," read Naball.

"Exactly," said Villiers. "Meg is Kitty Marchurst's child, and she gave it to Keith Stewart."

"By Jove, it looks suspicious," said Naball. "He is in possession of a large sum of money, and can't tell how he got it. He can't account for his time on the night of the murder, and this knife with his name on it is found close to the window through which the murderer entered—humph!—things look black against him."

"I suppose you'll arrest him at once?" said Villiers malignantly.

"Then you suppose wrong," retorted Naball. "I'll have him looked after so that he won't escape; but I'll hold my tongue about this, and so will you."

"Until when?"

"Until I find out more about Stewart. I must discover if the knife was in his possession on the night of the murder, and also if this story about his money is true; again, I want to wait till some of these stolen bank notes are in circulation, so as to get more evidence against him."

"But what am I to do?" asked Villiers sulkily.

"You are to hold your tongue," said Naball, rising to his feet, "or else I may make things unpleasant for you—it's a good thing for your own sake you have told me all."

"Told you all," muttered Villiers, as Naball took his departure. "I'm not so sure about that."

XIX

A Lovers' Meeting

It is a great blessing that the future is hidden from our anxious eyes, otherwise, to use a familiar expression, we would go out in a coach and four to meet our troubles. If Keith Stewart had only known that the detective suspected him of the murder of Lazarus, and was surely but slowly finding out strong evidence in favour of such a presumption, he, no doubt, would have been much troubled. But he thought that Naball's hints at the interview were not worth thinking about, for, strong in the belief of his own innocence, such an idea of his being accused of the crime never entered his mind.

In spite of the disagreeable event which had occurred, Keith felt very happy on this night. He was young, he had a good sum of money in the bank, the gift of some beneficent fairy, he was going to make his *début* as a dramatic author, and, above all, he was going to see Eugénie again. Therefore, as he sat at dinner, his heart was merry, and to him the future looked bright and cheerful. Things seemed so pleasant that, with the sanguine expectations of youth, he began to build castles in the air.

"If this burlesque's a success," he thought, "I'll write a novel, and save every penny I make; then I'll go to London, after marrying Eugénie, and see if I can't make a name there—with perseverance I'm bound to do it."

Poor youth, he did not know the difficulty of making a name in London; he was quite unaware that the literary market was overstocked, and that many criticisms depend on the state of the critic's liver. He did not know any of these things, so he went on eating his dinner and building castles in the air, all of which buildings were inhabited by Eugénie.

From these pleasant dreams he was aroused by the entrance of the housemaid, a fat young person, who breathed hard, and rolled up to Keith, puffing and panting like a locomotive.

"If you please," said the young lady, "the man."

"What man?" asked Keith sharply.

"He's waiting to see you," returned the housemaid stolidly.

From experience Keith knew it was useless to expect sense from the housemaid, so he got up from the table and went out to the front-door, where a bundle, with a head at one end and a pair of boots at the other, held out a letter.

"For me?" asked Keith, taking it.

The bundle sniffed in an affirmative manner, so Stewart opened the letter and read it quickly. It only contained a line from Naball that if he heard of any new development of the case he would let Keith know, so that young gentleman, wondering why the detective took the trouble to write to him slipped the letter in his pocket, and nodded to the bundle.

"All right," he said quickly; "no answer," and he shut the door in the bundle's face, whereupon the bundle sniffed.

"I know him now," said Mr. Tulch to himself in a husky voice, as he walked away. "I'd know 'im if he was dooplicated twice h'over." Having come to this satisfactory conclusion, Mr. Tulch took up his position a short distance away, and began his dreary task of watching the house.

And it was dreary work. The long hot day was over, and the long hot night had begun. It was just a quarter past seven, and the sky was a cloudless expanse of darkish blue, blazing with stars; a soft wind was whispering among the leaves of the trees, and making little whirls of white dust in the road. Every now and then a gay party of men and women on their way to some amusement would pass the spy, but he remained passively at his post, watching the sun-blistered varnished door of Vance's boarding-house. At last his patience was rewarded, for, somewhere about half-past seven, Keith came hurriedly out, and sped rapidly down the street.

"What's he arter?" sniffed Mr. Tulch, stretching his cramped limbs. "I'll 'ave to ketch 'im h'up," and he rolled as quickly as he was able after the tall figure of the young man.

A tram came along, and, without stopping it, Keith jumped on the dummy—the spy, breathless with running, sprang on the step of the end car and got inside, keeping his eye on Keith. The tram car went rapidly along Flinders Street, stopping every now and then to pick up or drop passengers, at which Keith seemed impatient. At last Spencer Street station was reached, and Keith sprang out; so did Tulch, keeping close to his heels.

Stewart walked impatiently up and down one of the long platforms, which shortly began to fill with people expecting their friends. The shrill whistle of an approaching engine was heard, a red light suddenly appeared, advancing rapidly, and presently the long train, with its lighted carriages, drew up inside the station.

Such a hurry-scurry; people jumping out of the train to meet those pressing forward on the platform, porters calling to one another, boxes, rugs, portmanteaus, bundles, all strewing the ground—a babel of voices, and at intervals the shrill whistle of a departing train.

Amid all this confusion Tulch missed Keith, and was in a terrible state, for he knew what Naball would say. He dived hither and thither among the crowd with surprising activity, and at last came in sight of Stewart putting a young lady into a cab, in front of which was the luggage. He tried to hear the address given the cabman, but was unsuccessful, so he rapidly jumped into another cab and told him to follow. The cabby obeyed at once, and whipping up his horse, which was a remarkably good one, he easily kept the first cab in sight.

The front cab drove up Collins Street as far as the Treasury Buildings, and then turned off to the left, going towards Fitzroy. It stopped at the Buttercup Hotel, in Gertrude Street, and, Stewart alighting, helped the young lady out; then the luggage was taken care of by the porter of the hotel, and Keith, with his charge, vanished through the swing doors of the private entrance.

On seeing this, Tulch dismissed his cab, went into the bar of an hotel on the opposite side of the street, and, ordering a pint of beer, sat watching the door of the Buttercup Hotel.

Meanwhile Keith and Eugénie had been shown into a private room, and the landlady, a stout, buxom woman, in a silk dress and lace cap, made her appearance.

"Miss Rainsford?" she said interrogatively, advancing towards the girl.

"Yes," replied Eugénie brightly. "You are Mrs. Scarth, I suppose. Did you get Mrs. Proggins' letter?"

"Oh, yes, that's all right," replied the landlady, nodding. "Your room is ready, and I will do anything I can for you. Mrs. Proggins is an old friend of mine, and I'm only too happy to oblige her."

"Thank you," said Eugénie, taking off her hat. "Let me introduce Mr. Stewart to you; he kindly came to the station to meet me."

Mrs. Scarth nodded with a smile, for Mrs. Proggins had informed her of the relationship between the two young people, then observing she would go and order some tea for Eugénie, sailed majestically out of the room.

"Why did you introduce me to that old thing?" asked Keith, in a discontented tone.

"Policy, my dear," replied Eugénie mildly. "Mrs. Proggins wrote to her to look after me, and I'm very glad, otherwise a young lady with you as escort would hardly have found shelter for the night in this place. I always like to be in favour with the powers that be."

Eugénie Rainsford was a tall, dark-complexioned girl, with clearly cut features and coils of black hair twisted round the top of her well-shaped head. She was dressed in a blue serge costume, with a red ribbon round her throat, and another round her waist. A handsome girl with a pleasant smile, and there was a look in her flashing dark eyes which showed that she had a will of her own. Keith stood beside her, as fair as she was dark, and a handsomer couple could not have been found in Melbourne.

"Well, here I am at last. Keith," said Eugénie, slipping her arm through his. "Aren't you pleased to see me?"

"Very," replied Stewart emphatically; "let me look at you—ah, you are more beautiful than ever."

"What delightful stories you do tell," said Eugénie with a blush. "I wish I could believe them; now, my friend, let me return the compliment by looking at you."

She took his face between her hands and looked at it keenly beneath the searching glare of the gas, then shook her head.

"You are much paler than you used to be," she said critically. "There are dark circles under your eyes, deep lines down the side of your mouth, and your face looks haggard. Is it work, or—or the other thing?"

"Do you mean dissipation, Eugénie?" said Keith, with a smile, taking a seat. "Well, I expect I have been rather dissipated, but now you are here I'll be a good boy."

"Have you been worried?" asked Miss Rainsford.

Keith sighed.

"Yes; very much worried over this terrible case. I suppose you've seen all about it?"

Eugénie nodded.

"Yes; I've read all about it in the papers. Now I suppose you've nothing to do?"

"No—not that I care much—you see I've got this burlesque coming off, and then there's that money."

"The five hundred pounds," said Miss Rainsford reflectively. "Have you found out who sent you that?"

"No; I can't imagine who did so, unless it was Caprice."

"Caprice!"

"Yes," replied Keith hurriedly, flushing a little; "the actress I told you about, who is going to play the principal part in 'Faust Upset.'"

"Oh!"

It was all the comment Miss Rainsford made, but there was a world of meaning in the ejaculation.

"From what I've heard of the lady, I don't think it's likely," she said quietly.

"Well, at all events, I suppose I'd better use the money."

"Yes; I suppose so."

"You're not very encouraging, Eugénie," said her lover angrily.

"Well," observed the girl deliberately, "if you think this money came from Caprice, I certainly would not touch it. Why don't you ask her?"

"I can't; she's been so disagreeable to me lately."

"Oh!"

Eugénie Rainsford was of a very jealous temperament, and she began to feel vaguely jealous of this actress whom Keith seemed to know so well. She remained silent for a few moments, during which Keith felt somewhat awkward. He was not in love with Kitty, nor, as far as he knew, was she in love with him, yet he saw that some instinct had warned Eugénie against this woman.

"Come, Eugénie," said Keith, putting his arm round her slender waist; "you mustn't be angry with me the first night we meet."

"I'm not angry," said the girl, turning her face towards him; "but I'd like to see this Caprice."

"So you shall, dear—on the stage."

"Why not in private?"

Keith frowned, and pulled his moustache in a perplexed manner.

"Well, she's hardly a fit person for a girl to see."

"Pshaw!" replied Eugénie impatiently; "I'm not a girl, but a woman, and am not afraid of anything like that, and besides—besides," with hesitation, "I'm going to see her."

"What do you mean?" asked Keith, abruptly withdrawing his arm.

"Nothing; only I saw an advertisement in the paper wanting a governess for a little girl. I answered it, and found it was Miss Marchurst who wanted a governess. She engaged me, and I'm going there to-morrow."

"No, no," cried Keith vehemently; "you must not—you shall not go."

Eugénie raised her eyes to his.

"Have you any reason for wishing me not to go?"

"Yes, every reason—she's a bad lot."

"I thought you knew her?"

"So I do, but men may know women of that class, and women like you may not."

"I don't agree with you," said Eugénie, rising; "what is sauce for the goose is sauce for the gander, and if you persist in wishing me not to go, I'll begin to think you've some reason."

"I have none except what I've stated," said Keith doggedly.

"Then I'll go to-morrow," replied Eugénie quietly; "at all events, I've got the right to have a personal interview, whether I take the situation or not."

"You must not see her."

"That decides it," said Eugénie composedly; "I will."

"Eugénie, don't go, or I'll begin to think you don't trust me."

"Yes, I do, but—but you've been so much with this Caprice lately, that I want to see her."

"I don't care two straws about her."

"I know that, but I wish to see her."

"You intend to go?"

"I do."

Keith snatched up his hat and stick.

"Then I'll say good-bye," he said angrily; "if you disregard my wishes so much, you can't love me."

"Yes, I can!"

"You are jealous of this confounded woman."

"Perhaps I am."

Keith looked at her angrily for a moment—then dashed out of the room, whereon Eugénie burst out laughing.

"What a dear old boy he is," she said to herself; "he thinks I'm jealous. Well," with a frown, "perhaps I am. I wonder, if he knew that I gave him the five hundred pounds, what he'd say? He doesn't know that I'm a rich woman now, so I can test his love for me. I'm sure he's as true as steel."

She picked up her hat, and, going over to the mirror, leaned her elbows on the mantelpiece, looked searchingly at her beautiful face.

"Are you jealous, you foolish woman?" she said, with a laugh. "Yes, my dear, you are; at all events, you'll see your rival to-morrow. I'm afraid

I'll make Keith a dreadful wife," she said, with a sigh, turning away. "For I think every woman is in love with him. Poor Keith, how angry he was!"

She burst out laughing, and left the room.

XX

The Rivals

Eugénie Rainsford was a very clever young woman, much too clever to pass her life in the up-country wilds of Australia, and no doubt she would have left her solitude in some way even had not fortune favoured her. Luckily, however, fortune did favour her and in a rather curious way, for a rich sharebroker having seen her, fell in love with her, and wanted to marry her; she however refused, telling him that she was engaged to marry Keith Stewart, whereupon he made inquiries, and she told him the whole story.

He was so delighted with her fidelity to a poor man, that he made his will in her favour, feeling sure that, as he had no relations, she would be the most deserving person to leave it to. A carriage accident killed him six months afterwards, and Eugénie found herself a very rich woman, with as many thousands as she had pence before.

She took her good fortune very calmly, telling no one about it, not even her employers; but, after consultation with the lawyer, she sent five hundred pounds to Keith, with instructions to the bank that he was not to know where it came from. Then she set herself to work out a little scheme she had in her head, to find out if he were true to her.

In many of the letters he had written, she had been struck with the frequent mention of one name, Caprice, and on making inquiries, found out all about the actress. She bought a photograph of her, and was struck with the pathetic face of a woman who was said to lead so vile a life. Dreading lest Keith should have fallen in love with this divinity of the stage, she determined to go down to Melbourne and see for herself.

By chance, however, she found in a newspaper an advertisement that Kitty Marchurst wanted a governess for her little girl, and seeing at once an excellent opportunity of finding out if her suspicions were correct, wrote offering herself for the situation.

Kitty on her side remembered the name of Eugénie Rainsford as that of the girl to whom Keith told her he was engaged, so, curious to see what she was like, engaged her for a governess at once. Eugénie was delighted when she received this letter, and, still in the character of a poor and friendless girl, she left Mr. Chine, the lawyer, to manage her property, after binding him to secrecy, and came down to take the situation.

Keith's evident desire that she should not accept the situation made her all the more determined to do so, and twelve o'clock the next day found her in the drawing-room of Caprice's house, waiting for the entrance of her future mistress.

When Kitty entered the room she could not help admiring the handsome woman before her, and on her part Eugénie was astonished to see the bright vivacity of the melancholy face, for Caprice's features were sad only when in repose.

The two women stood opposite to one another for a moment, mentally making up their minds about each other. Kitty was the first to speak.

"Miss Rainsford, I believe?"

"Yes; I came to see you about—about the situation."

"Governess for my little girl," said Kitty, nodding her head. "Yes, I want some one whom I can trust."

"I hope you will be able to trust me."

Caprice looked keenly at her, and then burst out into a torrent of words.

"Yes, I think I can trust you—but the question is, will you take care of my child—I mean will you accept the trust? You have come from the country—you don't know who I am?"

"Yes, I do—Miss Marchurst."

"No! not Miss Marchurst—Caprice!"

She waited for a moment to see what effect this notorious name would have on her visitor, but, to her surprise, Eugénie simply bowed.

"Yes, I know," she replied.

Caprice arose and advanced towards her.

"You know," she exclaimed vehemently, "and yet can sit down in the same room with a woman of my character. Are you not afraid I'll contaminate you—do you not shrink from a pariah like me—no—you do not—great heavens!" with a bitter laugh, sitting down again; "and I thought the age of miracles was past—ah, bah! But you are only a girl, my dear, and don't understand."

Eugénie arose and crossed over to her.

"I do understand; I am a woman, and feel for a woman."

Kitty caught her hand and gave a gasping cry. "God bless you!" she whispered, in a husky voice.

Then in a moment she had dashed the tears away from her eyes, and sat up again in her bright, resolute manner.

"No woman has spoken so kindly as you have for many years," she said quickly; "and I thank you. I can give you my child, and you will take care of her for me when I am far away."

"What do you mean?" asked Eugénie, puzzled.

"Mean—that I am not fit to live with my child, that I am going to send her to England with you, that she may forget she ever had a mother."

"But why do this," said Eugénie in a pitying tone, "when you can keep her with you?"

"I cannot let her grow up in the atmosphere of sin I live in."

"Then why not leave this sinful life, and go to England with your child?"

Kitty shook her head with a dreary smile.

"Impossible—to leave off this life would kill me; besides, I saw a doctor some time ago, and he told me I had not very long to live; there is something wrong with my heart. I don't care if I do die so long as my child is safe—you will look after her?"

"Yes," replied Eugénie firmly; "I will look after her."

Kitty approached her timidly.

"May I kiss you?" she said faintly, and seeing her answer in the girl's eyes, she bent down and kissed her forehead.

"Now I must introduce you to your new pupil," she said, cheerfully overcoming her momentary weakness.

"Wait a moment," said Eugénie, as Caprice went to the bell-pull. "I want to ask you about Mr. Stewart."

Caprice turned round quickly.

"Yes—what—about him?"

"Does he love you?"

Caprice came over to the fire and looked closely at her.

"You are the girl he is engaged to?"

"Yes."

"Then, make your mind easy, my dear, he loves no one but you."

Eugénie gave a sigh of relief, at which Kitty smiled a little scornfully.

"Ah! you love him so much as that?" she said half pathetically; "it's a pity, my dear, he's not worth it."

"What do you mean?"

"Don't be angry, Miss Rainsford," said Kitty, quietly; "I don't mean that he loves any one else, but he's not the man I took him for."

"I don't understand."

"I wouldn't try to, if I were you," replied Kitty significantly. "I helped him when I first met him, because he saved my child's life. He came down here, and I liked him still more."

"You loved him?"

"No; love and I parted company long ago. I liked him, but though I do my best to help him, I don't care for him so much as I did, my dear: he's not worthy of you."

"That's all very well, but I don't see the reason."

"Of course not, what woman in love ever does see reason; however, make your mind easy, things are all right. I will tell you the reason some day."

"But I want to know now."

"Curiosity is a woman's vice," said Kitty lightly "Don't worry yourself, Miss Rainsford, whatever I know of Keith Stewart won't alter him in your eyes—now, don't say anything more about it. I'll ring for Meg."

Eugénie tried to get a more explicit answer out of her, but Kitty only laughed.

"It can't be anything so very bad," she said to herself, "or this woman would not laugh at it."

Meg came in quietly, a demure, pensive-faced little child, and after Kitty had kissed her she presented her to Eugénie.

"This is your new governess, Meg," she said, smoothing the child's hair, "and I want you to love her very much."

Meg hung back for a few moments, with the awkward timidity of a child, but Eugénie's soft voice and caressing manner soon gained her confidence.

"I like you very much," she said at length, nestling to Eugénie's side.

"As much as mumsey, Meg?" said Kitty, with a sad smile.

"Oh, never—never as much as mumsey," cried Meg, leaving her new-found friend for her mother, "There's no one so good and kind as mumsey."

Kitty kissed the child vehemently, and then bit her lips to stop the tears coming to her eyes.

"Mumsey," said Meg at length, "can I tell the lady a secret?"

"Yes, dear," replied Kitty smiling. Thereupon Meg slipped off Kitty's lap and ran to Eugénie.

"What is this great secret?" asked Eugénie, bending down with a laugh.

Meg put her mouth to Eugénie's ear, and whispered,—

"When I grow up I'm going to marry Keith."

"You see," said Kitty, overhearing the whisper, "my daughter is your rival."

"And a very dangerous one," replied Eugénie with a sigh, touching the auburn hair.

Meg was sent off after this, and then Kitty arranged all about the salary with Eugénie, after which she accompanied her to the door to say good-bye.

"I'm sorry I put any distrust into your heart about Mr. Stewart," she said; "but don't trouble, my dear, get him to give up his dissipated habits, and you'll no doubt find he'll make an excellent husband."

"Ah!" said Eugénie to herself as she walked to the station, "it was only dissipation she meant—as if anything like that could hurt Keith in my eyes."

Then she began to think of the strange woman she had left—with her sudden changes of temperament from laughter to tears—with her extraordinary nature, half-vice half-virtue, of the love she bore for her child, and the strong will that could send that child away for ever from her lonely life.

XXI

A First Night at the Bon-Bon

"Faust Upset" had been put into rehearsal at once, and three weeks after the murder of Lazarus it was to be produced. Mortimer had hurried on the production of the burlesque with the uttermost speed, as "Prince Carnival" was now playing to empty houses. The Bon-Bon company were kept hard at work, and, what with rehearsals during the day, the performance of the opera-bouffe in the evening, and rehearsals afterwards till two in the morning, they were all pretty well worn-out.

In spite of Kitty's indomitable spirit, she was looking haggard and ill, for the incessant work was beginning to tell on her system. The doctor told her plainly that she was killing herself, and that absolute rest was what she required; but in spite of those warnings she never gave herself a moment's peace.

"I don't care two straws if I die," she said recklessly to Dr. Chinston; "I've made arrangements for the future of my child, and there's nothing else for me to live for."

She was determined to make the burlesque a success, and worked hard at rehearsals getting the author and composer to alter some things, and cut out others, making several valuable suggestions as to stage-management, and in every way doing her best. But though friendly towards Keith, yet he was conscious of a kind of reserve in her manner towards him, and thought it was due to the knowledge that he was engaged to Eugénie.

He had become reconciled to his sweetheart, and she went down every day to teach Meg at Toorak. It had been arranged that in three months she was to go to England with Meg, and Kitty guaranteed to pay a certain sum annually for the salary of the governess and the maintenance of the child. Of course Eugénie never meant to take any money, as she had become strongly attached to Meg, but still kept up her semblance of poverty till such time as she judged it fit to tell Keith. Meanwhile, in spite of Keith's opposition, she lived with Caprice, and led a very quiet life, for what with the state of her health and constant rehearsals, Kitty gave no Sunday receptions.

But while Stewart fumed and fretted over the fact of his sweetheart staying with a woman of bad character like Caprice, and attended to all the rehearsals of the burlesque, Naball was silently winding his net round him. The detective had made inquiries at the Skylarks' Club, and found that Keith had been there on that night, in the company of Fenton. On discovering this, he went to Fenton and discovered that Stewart had lent the American the knife with which the crime had been committed, to cut the wires of a champagne bottle, and afterwards slipped it into his coat pocket. From the club he went to the Bon-Bon Theatre, and, as the detective knew from Keith's own admission, had left there at half-past twelve.

"And then," said Naball to himself, "he told me he wandered about the streets till two o'clock, and then saw Villiers—rubbish—he went straight to Russell Street and committed the crime."

It had taken Naball some time to collect the necessary evidence, and it was only on the day previous to the production of "Faust Upset" that he was able to get a warrant for Keith's arrest, so he determined to let the performance take place before he arrested him.

"If it's a success," said Naball to himself, as he slipped the warrant in his pocket, "he'll have had one jolly hour to himself, and if it's a failure—well, he'll be glad enough to go to gaol." So, with this philosophical conclusion, Mr. Naball settled in his own mind that he would go to the theatre.

Keith wanted Eugénie to go to a box with him in order to see the play, but she said she would rather go to the stalls by herself, in order to judge of the effect the burlesque had on the audience. After a good deal of argument, Stewart gave way; so on the momentous night she took her seat in the stalls, eager to see the first bid her lover made for fame.

Tulch had been recalled from his task of watching Stewart, as Naball judged that the vanity of an author seeing his work on the stage would be enough to keep the young man in Melbourne; but Tulch, true to his instincts of finishing a job properly, took his place in the gallery and kept his eye on Keith, who sat with Ezra in a private box. The Jew was calm and placid, as having succeeded to his father's fortune, he had not staked everything, like Keith, on the burlesque being a success; still, for his partner's sake as well as his own, he was anxious that it should go well.

Such a crowded house as it was—everybody in Melbourne was there—for a new play by a colonial author was a rare thing, and a burlesque by a colonial author, with original music by a colonial composer, was almost unheard of.

The critics who were present felt an unwonted sense of responsibility to-night, for as this was the first production of the piece on any stage, they had to give an opinion on their own responsibility. Hitherto the generality of plays produced in Melbourne had their good and bad points settled long before by London critics, so it was comparatively easy to give a verdict; but to-night it was quite a different thing, therefore the gentlemen of the press intended to be extra careful in their remarks.

Although "Faust Upset" was called a burlesque, it was more of an opera-bouffe, as there was an absence of puns and rhyme about the dialogue, besides which, the lyrics were really cleverly written, and the music brisk and sparkling. Keith had taken the old mediæval legend of Faust, and reversed it entirely—all the male characters of the story he made female, and *vice versa*. There was a good deal of satire in the piece about the higher education of women, and the devotion of young men to athletics, to the exclusion of brain work. In fact, the libretto was of a decidedly Gilbertian flavour, albeit rather more frivolous, while the music was entirely of the Offenbachian school, light, tuneful and rapid.

After a medley overture, containing a number of taking melodies in the piece, the curtain rose on the study of Miss Faust, a blue-stocking of the deepest dye, who, after devoting her life to acquiring knowledge, finds herself, at the age of fifty, an old maid with no one to care for her. The character was played by Toltby, who was a genuine humorist; and he succeeded in making a great deal out of the part, without ever condescending to vulgarity. His appearance as a lank, long maiden, in a dingy sage-green gown, with wan face and tousled hair, was ludicrous in the extreme.

The opening chorus was sung by a number of pretty girls, in caps and gowns, and on their going out to meet their lovers, Miss Faust, overcome with loneliness, summons to her aid the powers of evil, and in response "Miss Mephistopheles" appears.

Kitty looked charming as she stood in the centre of the red limelight. She was arrayed in the traditional dress of red, but as a female demon wore a petticoat, and her face was also left untouched. Miss Faust fainted in her chair, and Miss Mephistopheles, with a bright light in her eyes, and a reckless devil may-care look on her expressive face, whirled down to the footlights, and dashed into a rattling galop song, "Yes, this is I," which melody ran all through the opera.

With the assistance of various cosmetics, new dress, and sundry other articles of feminine toilet, which were brought in by a number of small imps, Miss Mephistopheles succeeds in making Miss Faust young; shows her a vision of Mr. Marguerite, a young athlete; and finally changes the scene to the market-place, where there was a chorus of young men in praise of athletic sports.

It would be useless to give the plot in detail, as Keith followed the lines of the legend pretty closely. Miss Faust meets Mr. Marguerite, who is beloved by Miss Siebel, a sporting young woman. There was the garden scene, with a lawn tennis ground; a vision on the Brocken, of the future of women, with grotesque ballets and fantastic dresses; the scene of the duel, which was a quarrel scene between Mrs. Valentine and Miss Faust, after the style of Madame Angot; then Miss Mephistopheles runs off with Mr. Marguerite, having fallen in love with him; the lovers are followed and thrown into a prison, which is changed by the magic power of Miss Mephistopheles to a race-course, in which scene there is a bewildering array of betting men, pugilists, pretty girls, and fortune-tellers. Miss Mephistopheles then resigns Mr. Marguerite to Miss Siebel, and wants to carry off Miss Faust to the nether regions, when a flaw is discovered in the deed, and everything is settled amicably, the whole play ending with the galop chorus of the first number.

When the curtain fell on the first act, the audience were somewhat bewildered; it was such an entirely new departure from the story of Faust, that they almost resented it. But as the piece progressed, they saw the real cleverness of the satire, and when the curtain came down they called loudly for the author and composer, who came forward and bowed their acknowledgments.

When Mortimer heard the eulogies lavished on the piece, he drew a long breath of relief.

"Jove! I thought it was going to fail," he said, "and I believe it would have, if Caprice hadn't pulled it out of the fire."

And, indeed, Caprice, with her wonderful spirits and reckless *abandon*, had carried the whole play with her, and saved it at the most critical moment, A young man sitting near Eugénie summed up his idea of the piece in a few words.

"It's a deuced clever play," he said; "but Caprice makes it go—if any one else plays her part, the theatre will be empty."

Eugénie turned angrily to look for the author of this remark, but could not see him. Just as she was turning away, a shrill voice near her said,—

"Ain't Caprice a stunner! I've seen 'er lots of times at old Lazarus's."

The speaker was a small, white-faced Jewish youth, being none other than Isaiah.

Miss Rainsford pondered over these words as she walked out of the theatre.

"Goes to old Lazarus's," she said to herself; "that was the old man who was killed. I wonder why she went there."

There was a crowd in the vestibule of the theatre, and she saw Keith standing in the corner, looking as pale as death, talking to a man.

She went up to congratulate him on the success of the performance, but something in his face made her afraid.

"What's the matter, Keith?" she asked, touching him.

"Hush!" he said in a hoarse whisper, "don't say a word—I'm arrested."

"Arrested! What for?" she gasped.

The man standing next to Keith interposed.

"For the murder of Jacob Lazarus," he said in a low voice.

Eugénie closed her eyes with a sensation of horror, and caught hold of the wall for support. When she opened her eyes again, Keith and the detective had both vanished.

"Arrested for the murder of Lazarus!" she muttered. "My God! it can't be true!"

XXII

Eugénie v. Naball

As a rule first performances in Melbourne take place on Saturday night, consequently the criticisms on "Faust Upset" were in Monday's papers. Simultaneously with the notices of the burlesque, there appeared an announcement that the author of the piece had been arrested for the murder of Jacob Lazarus.

Keith was very little known in Melbourne, so his arrest personally caused little talk; but the fact that a successful author and a murderer were one and the same person caused a great sensation.

The criticisms on the burlesque were, as a rule, good, and though some of the papers picked out faults, yet it was generally agreed that the piece had been a wonderful success; but the sensation of a successful colonial production having taken place was merged in the greater sensation of the discovery of the Russell Street murderer.

Keith Stewart, protesting his innocence of the charge, had immediately been taken off to gaol, and Eugénie was unable to see him until she got the permission of the proper authorities; but feeling certain that he had not committed the crime, she called on Ezra at *The Penny Whistle* early on Monday morning.

On sending up her card, she was shown into Ezra's room, and there found that Naball was present. The detective, who was fully convinced of Keith's guilt, had called in order to find out for certain from Ezra all about the prisoner's movements on the night in question.

When Eugénie entered the room, Ezra, who looked pale and careworn, arose and greeted her warmly. He then introduced her to Naball, who looked keenly at the sad face of the woman who was engaged to the man he had hunted down.

"Mr. Naball," said Ezra, indicating the detective, "has called upon me to find out about Stewart's movements on the night my father was murdered."

"Yes; that's so," replied Naball, with a shrewd glance at the Jew.

"Well," said Eugénie impatiently, "surely you can explain them, for Keith told me you were with him all the time."

Ezra looked dismal.

"No, I wasn't with him all the time; I only met him at the Bon-Bon, and I left before he did."

"Yes," interposed the detective smoothly; "and, according to Mr. Mortimer, Stewart left there about half-past twelve o'clock."

"And then, I presume," said Eugénie, with fine disdain, "you think he went and murdered Lazarus right off?"

"Well," observed Naball, deliberately smoothing his gloves, "according to the doctor's evidence, the crime was committed about twelve o'clock, or a little later. Now Stewart can't say where he was between the time he left the theatre and the time he met Villiers."

"He was wandering about the streets," explained Eugénie.

Naball smiled cynically.

"Yes; so he says."

"And so every one else says who knows Keith Stewart," retorted the girl. "He is incapable of such an act."

Naball shrugged his shoulders as much as to say that he had nothing to urge against such an eminently feminine argument.

Eugénie looked angrily at the detective, and then turned in despair to the Jew.

"You don't believe him guilty?" she asked.

"No, on my soul, I do not," he replied fervently; "still appearances look black against him."

Miss Rainsford thought for a few moments, and at last bluntly asked Naball the same question.

"Do you believe him guilty?"

"As far as my experience goes," said the detective coolly, "I do."

"Why?"

Naball produced a little pocket-knife, and began to trim his nails.

"The evidence is circumstantial," he said, shrugging his shoulders, "but the evidence is conclusive."

"Would you mind telling me what the evidence is?"

The detective shut his knife with a sharp click, slipped it into his waistcoat pocket, and, leaning over the table, looked steadily at Eugénie.

"Miss Rainsford," he said gravely, "I admire you very much for the way you stand up for Stewart, but, believe me, that though I would gladly see him free, yet the proofs are too strong to suppose him innocent."

Eugénie bent her head coldly. "Would you mind telling me the evidence?" she reiterated.

Naball, rather perplexed, looked at Ezra. "Yes, tell her all you know," said that gentleman. "I think, myself, Stewart is innocent, and perhaps Miss Rainsford may throw some light on the mystery."

"I don't call it a mystery," retorted Naball impatiently; "it's as clear as day. I'm willing to tell all I know; but as to Miss Rainsford throwing any light on the subject, it's absurd."

Eugénie questioned him for the third time in the same words.

"Would you mind telling me the evidence?"

"Certainly," said Naball sharply. "Stewart was in employment of the deceased as his clerk. He came to Melbourne with no money, and, according to his own account, given in this very room, and in the presence of this gentleman, he becomes possessed of a sum of five hundred pounds, which was mysteriously placed to his credit at the Hibernian Bank. I went to the bank, and discovered from the manager that such a sum had been placed to the prisoner's credit, but he refused to tell me by whom, so, as was only natural, I concluded that Stewart had robbed his employer of the money, and under a feigned name placed it to his credit. My reasons for such a belief are this—he had full command of all the books, and could cook the accounts as he liked. He did so, and obtained this money. Lazarus, however, who I know was a very sharp man, had suspicions, and determined to examine the books; this, of course, meant ruin to Stewart, so he made up his mind to kill his master. He was at the Skylarks' Club on the night of the murder, and gave Mr. Fenton, the manager of The Never-say-die Insurance Company, his knife to open a champagne bottle; that knife was one given to him by the child of Kitty Marchurst, and has on it an inscription, 'From Meg.' On receiving it back, he placed it in the pocket of his overcoat, and walked to the Bon-Bon. After an interview with Mr. Mortimer, he left the Bon-Bon at half-past twelve o'clock, went up to Russell Street, and entering by the back window (the position of which he knew thoroughly), killed the old man; then he took the keys from under the pillow, and robbed the safe of various things, including bank-notes to the amount of one hundred pounds, which he knew were placed therein; while leaving the place, he dropped his knife outside the window; he then wanders about the streets, perhaps goes home, but horror-struck with the dread of being found out, returns to the scene of his crime, and there sees Villiers, whom he questions, but getting no response from him, thinks Villiers is drunk. Villiers, however, was only shamming, and tells me some time afterwards that he picked up a knife under the open window, and was cognisant of the murder. I obtain the knife, and it is the one Stewart had in the club, with the inscription on it. I think, therefore, the evidence is very clear."

"In what way?" asked Eugénie quietly.

The detective became a little exasperated.

"Good heavens!" he said in an annoyed tone of voice, "there are three strong proofs: first, he is possessed of a large sum of money he can't account for; second, he is unable to prove an *alibi*; and third, his knife, covered with blood, is found on the scene of the crime."

"So far so good," said Eugénie ironically; "your reasoning is excellent, Mr. Naball, but untrue."

"Untrue?"

"I repeat untrue," she replied. "With regard to the five hundred pounds—I paid that into his credit."

"You," said Ezra, while Naball stared at her thunder-struck, "a poor girl."

"I'm not a poor girl," said Miss Rainsford coolly. "On the contrary, I'm worth fifty thousand pounds left to me by a sharebroker in Sandhurst. I did not tell Keith of my fortune as I wanted him to love me for myself. But as I knew he was poor, I placed to his credit the sum of five hundred pounds; so that settles your first proof, Mr. Naball."

"Well, it's certainly very curious," said Naball, after a pause. "I hardly know what to think—what about my second proof?"

"Oh! that's more difficult to prove," said Eugénie; "but I quite believe he did wander about. He's rather absent-minded, I know."

"Your answer to my second proof is weak," replied Naball sardonically. "And the third—"

"About the knife? Well," said Miss Rainsford, knitting her brows, "he had it at the club, you say, and slipped it into his overcoat pocket."

"Exactly."

"Then he went to the Bon-Bon."

"He did."

"And what happened to his overcoat there?' asked Eugénie.

"I can tell you," replied Ezra. "He took it off, and in mistake Caprice carried it downstairs with her fur mantle."

"Oh, did she take it away with her?" asked Naball quickly.

"No," said Ezra quietly, "she found out she had it when she was putting on her mantle in the carriage, and called me back to return it. I took it upstairs again, and gave it to Keith, who put it on."

"And the knife was still in the pocket?" said Eugénie.

"I suppose so," replied Ezra, rather confused. "I didn't even know the knife was there."

"What do you think?" asked Miss Rainsford, turning to Naball.

That astute young man wrinkled his brows.

"I see what you are driving at," he said rapidly. "You think that Caprice took the knife out of the pocket, saw the whole chance in a flash, and committed the crime."

"No! no!" cried Eugénie, horror struck. "I'm sure I don't believe she could be guilty of a crime."

"Humph! I don't know so much about that," said Naball disbelievingly.

"What nonsense," broke in Ezra angrily; "she could not have done such a thing—she had no motive."

Naball did not reply to this remark, but rising from his seat, walked hurriedly up and down the room in a state of great excitement. He had been fully convinced of the guilt of Stewart, but the conversation of Eugénie had shaken his belief, and he began to puzzle over the new aspect of the case.

"I wonder if Caprice ever had any dealings with Lazarus?" he said to himself, thinking of the diamond robbery.

"Yes," broke in Eugénie sharply, "she had—at least," in answer to Naball's questioning look, "when I was at the theatre on Saturday night a boy near me said he had seen her at Lazarus's place."

"A boy," asked Ezra sharply, "what boy?"

"I don't know," she replied; "a thin, pale-faced Jewish-looking boy, with a shrill voice."

"Isaiah," said Naball and Ezra with one voice, and then looked at one another, amazed at this new discovery.

"By Jove!" said the detective, "this is becoming exciting. You are sure you heard the boy say that?"

"Yes, I'm sure—quite sure," answered Eugénie firmly; "but I don't think that could prove Caprice guilty. Much as I wish to serve Keith, I don't want to ruin her."

Naball glanced at her keenly, then turned to Ezra.

"Send for the boy," he said sharply, "and we'll find out all about Caprice's visits to your father's place."

"It mightn't have anything to do with the murder," said Ezra, ringing the bell for the messenger.

"True," replied Naball, "but, on the other hand, it might have a good deal to do with the diamond robbery."

XXIII

The Cypher

When the messenger had been despatched, Naball drew his seat up to the table, and began to make some notes, after which he turned to Eugénie.

"I was firmly convinced of Stewart's guilt," he said quietly; "but what you have told me throws a new light on the subject. I said you could not do that—I beg your pardon—you can."

Eugénie bowed her head in acknowledgment of the apology, and asked him a question in a hesitating manner.

"You don't think Caprice is guilty?"

"I think nothing at present," he replied evasively; "not even that Stewart is innocent. When I see the boy, I'll tell you what I think."

They talked on together for a few minutes, and then there came a knock at the door. In reply to Ezra's permission to enter, the door opened, and Isaiah appeared on the threshold, holding some papers in his hand.

"Oh, you've come," said Ezra, as the boy shut the door after him.

"Yes; did you want me?" demanded Isaiah in a jerky manner, "'cos I never knowed you did."

"Didn't you meet a messenger?" asked Naball, turning his head round.

Isaiah deposited the papers he carried on Ezra's desk, and shook his head.

"No, I never met any one, I didn't," he answered. "Mr. Ezra asked me to bring all letters that came to the old 'un, so as these came, I did."

"That's right," said Lazarus, looking through the letters. "By-the-way, Isaiah, this gentleman wants to ask you a few questions."

"What, Mr. Naball?" said Isaiah in alarm. "Oh, sir, I never had nothing to do with it."

Naball smiled.

"No! no! that's all right," he said good-naturedly. "It would take a bigger man than a sprat like you to commit such a crime; but, tell me, do you know Caprice?"

Isaiah leered significantly.

"I've seen her on the stage, that's all."

"Never off?"

"Drivin' about the streets."

"Anywhere else?"

Isaiah glanced uneasily at Ezra, who laughed.

"Go on, Isaiah; it's all right."

"Well, I've seen her at the old 'un's place."

"Oh, indeed," said Naball quickly. "Often?"

"Yes—lots of times—at night—came to do business, I s'pose."

"When did you see her last?"

"Oh, not for a long time," replied Isaiah; "but do you remember the week them diamonds were stolen?"

"Yes, yes," said Naball eagerly.

Isaiah nodded.

"Well, she came to see the old 'un, then."

Naball suppressed his exultation with difficulty, and asked Isaiah another question.

"I say—those bank-notes that were stolen—"

"I never stole 'em."

"No one said you did," retorted Naball tartly; "but you wrote something on the back of one of 'em."

Isaiah turned scarlet, and shifted from one leg to the other.

"Well, you see," he murmured apologetically, "Mr. Stewart wanted to know a good 'un to back for the Cup, so I was afraid of the old 'un hearing, and as there wasn't no paper, I wrote on the back of one of 'em, 'Back Flat-Iron.'"

"In pencil?"

"No, in ink. Mr. Stewart, he laughs and nods, then puts the notes in the cash box, and puts 'em in the safe."

"That's all right," said Naball, dismissing him; "you can go."

Isaiah put on his hat, put his hands in his pockets, and departed, whistling a tune. When the door closed on him, Naball turned to his two companions with an exulting light in his eyes.

"What do you think now, Mr. Naball?" asked Eugénie.

"Think. I think as I've done all along," he replied. "Caprice stole those jewels herself, and sold them to old Lazarus."

"But what's that got to do with the death of my father?" asked Ezra.

"Perhaps nothing—perhaps a lot," said the detective. "I don't know but that boy's evidence has given me a clue. Suppose—I'm only supposing, mind you—Caprice stole her own diamonds, with Villiers as an accomplice. Suppose she took them to old Lazarus and sold 'em. Suppose Villiers, thinking the old man has them in his safe, goes to rob him, and commits the murder to do so. Suppose all that—I should think there would be a very pretty case against Villiers."

"Yes; but Keith's knife?" said Eugénie.

"Ah, now you have me," answered Naball, puzzled. "I don't know, unless Villiers managed to get it while Stewart was fighting with him on that night, and covered it in blood in order to throw suspicion on him."

"All your ideas are theoretical," said Ezra drily. "Perhaps Caprice never stole her own jewels, or sold them to my father."

"Yes, she did, I'll swear," retorted Naball decisively. "Why wouldn't she prosecute? why did I find Villiers with one of the jewels? You bet, she stole them for some freak, and I daresay Villiers committed the murder to get them back."

"I don't think my father would have kept such valuable jewels as that about the premises."

"No; he'd put 'em in the bank."

"No, he wouldn't," retorted Ezra; "he sent all his jewels to Amsterdam. And here," holding up a letter, "is an envelope with the Dutch postmark."

"By Jove!" exclaimed Naball, under his breath, "what a queer thing if it should turn out to be those diamonds of Caprice's. Open the letter."

"Suppose it does turn out to be the diamonds," said Ezra, slowly tearing the envelope.

"Well"—Naball drew a long breath—"it will be the beginning of the end."

"I hope it will end in Keith's being released," said Eugénie, looking at Ezra with intense anxiety.

That gentleman took out the letter, and glancing at it for a moment, gave vent to an ejaculation of disgust.

"What's the matter?" asked Eugénie and Naball together.

"The letter is in cypher," said Lazarus, tossing it over to the detective. "I don't think we'll be able to read it."

"Oh, we'll have a try," said Naball, quickly spreading oat the letter. "Let's have a look at it."

The letter was as follows:—

Dsidanmo seaf utnes teh ssteon ryiks sgenlil gto teher
tdhnoaus sgennid it lses teher hduenrd bneiertns.

"What the deuce does it mean?" asked Naball in a puzzled tone.

"It's a cypher, evidently, of which my father alone possesses the key," said Ezra. "I'll have a look among his papers, and if I find it, it will soon make sense of this jumble of words."

"It's like a Chinese puzzle," observed Naball, glancing at it. "I never could find out these things."

"Let me look," said Eugénie, taking the letter. "I used to be rather good at puzzles."

"We'll find this one out," said Naball significantly, "and you'll do some good for Stewart."

"You think it's about Caprice's diamonds?" she asked.

"I think it's about Caprice's diamonds," he replied.

"I think the words have been written backwards," said Ezra, looking over her shoulder.

Eugénie shook her head.

"I don't think so," she replied, scanning the letter closely. "If so, the word 'it' would have been written 'ti.'"

"Try a word of three letters, if there's one," suggested Naball, "and you can see how the letters are placed."

"Here's one spelt 'g-t-o.' What word can be made out of that."

"Got," said Ezra eagerly.

"Well, if so, in the cypher it reads, the first letter 'g,' the last, letter 't,' and the middle letter at the end."

"What do you think of that?" asked Naball bluntly.

"That the sender of this has taken the first and last letters of a word, and written them in rotation."

"I don't understand," said Naball in a puzzled tone.

"I think I do," said Eugénie quickly. "Let us take another word, and instead of guessing it, try my idea, Here is a word, 'teher.' Now, Mr. Naball, take a sheet of paper and write down what I say."

Naball got some paper and a pencil.

"Now," said Eugénie, "this word 'teher.' The first letter is 't,' now the second letter, which, I think, is the end one of the proper word, is 'e'— place that at the end."

Naball wrote "t—e."

"The third letter of the cypher, and the second of the proper word, is 'h'—put that next the 't;' and the fourth letter of the cypher, and third of the proper word, is 'e'—place that at the end also."

Naball added two letters as instructed, "t,h—e,e."

"Now," said Eugénie, "there's only one letter left, which must naturally be in the middle."

Naball finished his writing thus: t-h-r-e-e.

"That is three," he said, with a cry of triumph. "By Jove! Miss Rainsford, you are clever; let's make certain, by trying another letter."

"Take 's-s-t-e-o-n,'" suggested Ezra.

Naball wrote the letters as follows:—

$$s — s$$
$$t — e$$
$$o — n$$

Then he wrote them in a line, down the first column and up the second, which made the word "stones."

"Glad we've got it right, after all," he said delightedly, and then the whole three of them went to work on the same system, with the result that the letter read thus:—

Diamonds safe, unset the stones, risky selling, got three thousand, sending it less three hundred, bernstein.

"Ah!" said Naball when he read this, "wasn't I right?"

"So I think," said Ezra sadly; "my father evidently bought the jewels from her, and sent them to Amsterdam to be sold."

"Still," said Eugénie impatiently, "this does not clear up the mystery of the murder."

"You don't think Caprice did it?" said Ezra.

"No," replied the detective; "but Villiers might have done it in order to recover the jewels. But I tell you what, there's only one thing to be done, we'll go down and see Caprice."

This was agreed to, and without losing a moment they started.

"I may be wrong, as I was before," said Naball when they were in the train, "but I'll lay any money that Villiers has seen Caprice since the murder."

"You don't think she's an accomplice?" cried Eugénie.

"I think nothing," retorted Naball, "till I see Caprice."

XXIV

What Kitty knew

The trio soon arrived at Kitty's house, and Ezra was just about to ring the front-door bell, when suddenly Naball touched his arm to stop him.

"Hist!" he said in a quick whisper; "listen."

A woman's voice, talking in a high key, and then the deep tones of a man's voice, like the growl of an angry beast.

"What did I tell you?" whispered Naball again. "Villiers and Caprice, both in the drawing-room; wait a moment, count twenty, and then ring the bell."

He stepped round the corner of the porch, stepped stealthily on to the verandah, and then stole softly towards one of the French windows in order to listen. He was correct in his surmise; the two speakers were Kitty Marchurst and Randolph Villiers.

"You'd better give me what I ask," growled Villiers in a threatening tone, "or I'll go straight and tell how you were at Lazarus's on the night of the murder."

"Perhaps you'll tell I killed him?" said Caprice, with a sneer.

"Perhaps I will," retorted Villiers; "there's no knowing."

"There's this much knowing," said Kitty deliberately, "that I won't give you a single penny. If I am called on to explain my movements, I can't do so; but it will be the worse for you, it will place—"

At this moment the bell rang, and Caprice started in alarm.

"Hush," she cried, advancing towards Villiers; "come to me again. I must not be seen talking with you here. Go away—not by the door," she said, with an angry stamp of her foot as Villiers went towards the door; "by the window—no one will see you."

Villiers moved towards the French window, opened it, and was just about to step out when Naball stepped forward.

"I'm afraid some one will," he said serenely, pushing Villiers back into the room, and closing the window.

"Naball!" cried Kitty and Villiers in a breath.

"Exactly," replied that gentleman, taking a chair. "I've come to have a talk with you both."

"How dare you force your way into my house?" cried Kitty angrily, while Villiers stood looking sullenly at the detective.

"It's about the diamond robbery," went on Naball, as if he never heard her.

"Leave the house," she cried, stamping her foot.

"And about the murder," he finished off, looking from one to the other.

Kitty glanced at Villiers, who looked at her with a scowl, and sank into a chair. Just as he did so, the drawing-room door opened, and Eugénie entered, followed by Ezra Lazarus.

"I don't understand the meaning of all this," said Caprice, with a sneer; "but you seem to have a good idea of dramatic effect."

"Perhaps so," replied Naball lazily. Kitty shrugged her shoulders and turned to Eugénie.

"Perhaps you can explain all this, Miss Rainsford?" she said coolly.

"Yes," answered Eugénie slowly; "it's about Mr. Stewart. You know he has been arrested for this murder?"

"Know," repeated Kitty impatiently, "of course, I know. I'm sure I ought to—morn, noon and night I've heard nothing else. I don't know how it will affect the piece, I'm sure."

"Never mind the piece," said Ezra, a trifle sternly. "I don't mind that, as long as I save my friend."

"I hope you will," said Caprice heartily. "I am certain he never committed the crime. What do you say?" turning to the detective.

"I'm beginning to be of your opinion," replied Naball candidly. "I did think him guilty once," fixing his eyes on Villiers, "but now I don't."

"What about the knife I gave you?" asked Villiers abruptly.

"Ah!" said Naball musingly, "what, indeed."

"I found it on the scene of the crime," said Villiers in a defiant manner.

"So you said."

"Don't you believe me?"

"Humph!"

At this ambiguous murmur Villiers gave a savage growl, and would have replied, but Kitty stopped him by waving her hand.

"It's no good talking like this," she said quickly. "There is some reason for you all coming here; what is it?"

"I'll tell you," said Naball in a sharp official tone. "Do you remember the diamond robbery at this place? Well, those diamonds were sold to old Lazarus, and he sent them to Amsterdam for sale. The person who stole those diamonds thought they were still in the safe of Jacob Lazarus; and the person who stole those diamonds murdered Jacob Lazarus to recover them."

He finished triumphantly, and then waited to see what effect his accusation would have on Kitty. To his astonishment, however, she never moved a muscle of her face, but asked calmly,—

"And who is the thief and the murderer?"

"That's what I want to find out."

"Naturally; but why come to me?"

"Because, you know."

"I!" she cried, rising to her feet in anger. "I know nothing."

"Yes, you do, and so does Villiers there," persisted Naball.

Villiers glanced strangely at Kitty, and growled sullenly.

"Now, look here Miss Marchurst," said Naball rapidly, "it's no use beating about the bush—I know more than you think. You denied that you stole your own jewels, but I know you did, in order to pay the money embezzled by Malton. Lazarus's boy saw you go to his place during the week of the robbery, late at night. You did so in order to dispose of the jewels. The crescent I took from Villiers down Bourke Street was given to him by you as an accomplice; and I listened at that window to-day and heard Villiers say you were on the Russell Street premises on the night of the murder. Now, what do you say?"

Kitty, still on her feet, was deadly pale, but looked rapidly at Naball.

"You have made up a very clever case," she said quietly; "but entirely wrong—yes, entirely. I did not take my own jewels, as I told you before, therefore I was unable to pay the money for Mr. Malton. I did go to see Lazarus one night during the week of the robbery, in order to get some money, but was unable to do so. I never gave the crescent to Villiers, as he will tell you; and lastly, as you overheard him state, I was at Lazarus's on the night of the murder, but did not think it necessary to state so. I went there after I left the Bon-Bon, and made no secret of my doing so, as my coachman can inform you. I found the door locked, and no light inside, so thinking the old man had gone to bed, I came away, and went home; so, you see, your very clever case means nothing."

"Is this true?" asked Naball, turning to Villiers.

"Is what true?" asked that gentleman angrily.

"What she says."

"Some of it. Well, yes, most of it."

"You'd better go a little further," said Kitty quietly, "and say all of it. Did I give you the diamond crescent?"

"No, you didn't."

"Then, who did?" asked Naball pertinaciously.

"I sha'n't tell you," growled Villiers.

"Oh, yes, you will," said the detective, "because if you know who stole the diamonds, you know the murderer of Lazarus."

"No, I don't," retorted Villiers savagely. "I tell you I saw her round about the place on that night, and I picked up the knife I gave you; that's all I know."

"Humph! we'll see about that."

"You are sure that the person who stole the diamonds committed the crime?" asked Caprice, with a strange smile on her pale lips.

"Well, I'm pretty sure; it looks uncommon like it."

"And you think I stole the diamonds?"

"Yes," retorted Naball bluntly; "I believe you did."

"In that case, by your own reasoning, I'm a murderess," said Caprice.

"I don't say that," said the detective; "but I believe you know who did it," looking significantly at Villiers.

"I'm afraid your reasonings and your assertions are at variance," said Kitty quietly. "I don't know who committed the murder, but I do know who stole my diamonds."

"Who?" asked Ezra, in an excited tone.

"Keith Stewart!"

"Keith Stewart!" echoed all; "impossible!"

Eugénie stepped forward with a frown on her pale face, and looked at Kitty.

"I don't believe it," she said, "and you are a wicked woman to say so."

"Unfortunately, it's true," replied Caprice, with a sigh. "I have kept the secret as long as I could, but now it's impossible to do so any longer. Keith Stewart was at my place on the night of the robbery, and heard me say where my diamonds were. He was coming to the drawing-room, and saw my child descending the stairs, having got out of bed. He picked her up, and put her in bed again. The temptation was too strong to resist, I suppose, and he opened the drawer of the mirror, and took the jewels. He then got out of the window, and came round by the front of the house so as to enter by the front-door. Meg was awake all the time, and told it to me in her childish way, how he had gone to the window and got out of it. I told her not to speak of it, and kept silence."

"Why did you keep silence?" asked Naball.

"Why," cried Kitty, her face flushing with anger, "because he saved my child from death. He might have stolen anything of mine, but I would have kept silent, nor would I have betrayed him now but that you accuse me of murder."

There was a dead silence in the room, as every one was touched by the way in which Kitty spoke. Then Villiers gave a coarse laugh.

"Ha! ha!" he said harshly; "you said, Naball, that the person who stole the diamonds committed the murder also, so you've got the right man in gaol."

Naball cast a look of commiseration at Eugénie, and said nothing.

"Wait a moment," cried Ezra, stepping forward, "we've got to find the stolen bank-notes first. I don't believe Keith Stewart committed such a base crime; he is no murderer."

"No," cried Eugénie, springing to her feet; "nor is he a thief. I will prove his innocence."

"I'm afraid that's difficult," said Naball reflectively; "things look black against him."

"Of course they do," said Villiers coarsely. "Who knows he is innocent?"

Eugénie stepped in front of the ruffian, and raised her hand to the ceiling.

"There is One who knows he is innocent—God."

XXV

The Evidence of a Bank-Note

All this time while his friends were trying to prove his innocence, Keith was mewed up in prison, having now been there a week. The disgrace of being arrested on such a charge had aged him considerably, and his face had changed from a healthy bronzed colour to a waxen paleness, while the circles under his eyes, and the deep lines furrowing his brow, showed how deeply he was affected by the position in which he found himself.

He steadily denied that he committed the crime imputed to him, and regarding the knife found by Villiers, could only say that, after putting it in his pocket at the club, he thought no more of it till next morning, when, having occasion to use it, he found it had disappeared.

Some time after the interview with Kitty, when she told how Keith had stolen the diamonds, Eugénie was admitted to the presence of her unfortunate lover. She had tried to see him before, but had always been refused; so when she did gain her object at last, and they stood face to face, both were so overcome with emotion that they could hardly speak. Keith held out his arms to her, with a smile on his wan face, and with an inarticulate cry she flung herself on his breast, weeping bitterly.

"Don't cry, dear," he said soothingly, making her sit down on the bed. "There! there!" and he quieted her as if she had been a little child.

"I can't help it," she said, drying her eyes; "it seems so terrible to see you here."

"No doubt," replied Keith quietly; "but I know I am innocent, and that robs the disgrace of a good deal of its sting."

"I know you are innocent," answered Eugénie, "but how to prove it; I thought things would have turned out all right; but when we saw Kitty Marchurst—"

"She said I had stolen her diamonds," finished Stewart, with a satirical laugh. "I've no doubt she fully believes it, and I thank her for having held her tongue so long; but she was never more mistaken in her life. I did put Meg back to bed, but I came down the stairs again, and did not leave the room by the window."

"But how is it the child saw you? Of course, you know—"

"I know everything. Yes. Naball told me all. Meg says she saw a man she thought was me getting out of the window. I've no doubt she did see a man, but not me."

"But why should she think it you?" asked Eugénie, puzzled.

"Simply in this way. I put her to bed when she was half-asleep, and she knew I was in the room with her. When I left, she fell asleep, and as her slumber was fitful, as I am sure it was, seeing she came downstairs, she no doubt woke up at the sound of the window being opened, and saw a man getting out. You know how an hour's sleep passes as a moment when one wakes, so I've no doubt Meg thought she'd just closed her eyes, and opened them again to see me getting out of the window."

"I understand," said Eugénie; "but who could it have been?"

"I believe it was Villiers," observed Keith thoughtfully. "He was about the house on that night; he was in want of money, so no doubt when Caprice left him in the supper-room, he walked upstairs to the bedroom, stole the diamonds, and left by the window. He could easily do this, as every one was in the drawing-room. Then Naball found that diamond clasp in his possession, or, at least, in the possession of the Chinaman to whom he sold it."

"But if he sold all those diamonds to old Lazarus, he must have got a good deal of money for them. Why did he not leave the country?"

Keith sighed.

"I'm sure I don't know. It seems all so mysterious," he said dismally. "What do you think should be done, Eugénie?"

"I think I'll see Naball again, or some other detective, and sift the whole affair to the bottom."

Keith looked at her with a pitying smile.

"My dear child, that will cost a lot of money, and you have not—"

Eugénie gave a laugh. She was not going to tell him just yet, so she gave an evasive answer.

"I've got my salary," she said gaily. "Some of it was paid to me the other day. See!" And taking out her purse, she emptied it into his hand.

"Oh! what a lot of money," said Keith smiling. "A five-pound note, three sovereigns, and two one-pound notes."

"Which makes exactly ten pounds," remarked Eugénie, with a smile; "and I'm going to pay it all away to Naball, to get you out of this trouble."

Stewart, kissed her, and smoothed out the notes one after the other.

"It's no use, Eugénie," he said, offering her the notes back; "it will take more than that to help me; besides, you forget I have five hundred pounds in the bank."

"Yes," she said, turning away her face; "five hundred."

"And you'll have it—if—if I die."

She turned to him, and threw her arms round his neck.

"Oh, my darling! my darling!" she cried vehemently, "why do you say such things? You will not die. You will live to be happy and famous."

"Famous!" he said bitterly, "no; I'm not famous yet, but notorious enough. There's only one chance of escape for me."

"And that is?"

"To trace those notes that were stolen—twenty five-pound notes like this," taking up the five-pound note.

"But you haven't got the numbers."

"No; but, as I told Naball, that boy wrote something on the back of one of them." Here Keith turned over the five-pound note; and then, giving a cry of surprise, sprang to his feet. "Eugénie, look, look!"

She snatched the note from him, and there on the back were traced in ink the words, "Back Flat-Iron."

"One of the notes," said Keith hoarsely. "One of the notes stolen on that night by the person who murdered Jacob Lazarus."

Eugénie had also risen to her feet and her face wore a look of horror. She looked at her lover, and he looked back again, with the same name in their thoughts.

"Kitty Marchurst!"

"Good God!" said Stewart, moistening his dry lips with his tongue, "can she be guilty, after all?"

"I can't believe it," said Eugénie determinedly, "though Naball says he thinks she did it. But I certainly got this note from her."

"She may have received it from some one else," cried Keith eagerly. "God knows, I don't want to die myself, but to put the rope round the neck of that unhappy woman—horrible," and he covered his face with his hands.

Eugénie put on her gloves, and then touched his arm.

"I'm going," she said in a quiet voice.

"Going?" he repeated, springing to his feet.

"Yes, to see Naball, and show him the note."

"But Kitty Marchurst!"

"Don't trouble about her," said Eugénie, a trifle coldly. "She is all right, and I've no doubt can explain where she got this note. Wherever it was, you can depend it was not from the dead man's safe. Good-bye, Keith," kissing him. "This note gives us the clue, and before many days are over you will be free, and the murderer of Jacob Lazarus will be in this cell."

XXVI

ON THE TRACK

When Eugénie left the prison, she went straight to Naball's office, and finding him in, told all about the wonderful discovery of the veritable five-pound note endorsed in Isaiah's writing. To say that Naball was astonished would be a mild way to state his feelings on receipt of this intelligence.

"It's an uncommon piece of luck," he said, looking at the note; "we might have searched for a twelvemonth, and never come across this piece of evidence. I think we'll get to the bottom of things this time. You got it from Kitty Marchurst?"

"Yes, I got it yesterday in payment of my salary"

Naball whistled softly.

"Things look uncommon black against that young woman," he observed thoughtfully. "I didn't half believe that story of hers about Stewart's stealing the diamonds, and now this note turning up in her possession—humph!"

"But you don't think she's guilty?" said Eugénie, clasping her hands.

"I don't say anything," replied Naball savagely, for the difficulties of this case were beginning to irritate him. "I only say things look black against Caprice—she's as deep as a well."

"What are you going to do now?" asked Miss Rainsford in a trembling voice, as she rose to go.

The detective placed his hat jauntily on one side of his head, drew on his gloves, then taking his cane, walked to the door of the office, which he he held open for Eugénie to pass through.

"What are you going to do now?" she repeated when they were standing in the street.

"I'm going down to Toorak," said Naball quietly, "to trace this note, beginning with Kitty Marchurst as the last holder of it; she'll tell lies, but whether she does or not, I'll get to the bottom of this affair. Good-day, Miss Rainsford," and taking off his hat with a flourish, he left her abruptly, and strolled leisurely down the street.

Eugénie watched him with eager eyes until he was out of sight, and then turned round to walk home.

"Oh, my dear! my dear!" she murmured, "if I can only save you from this terrible danger—but not at the cost of that poor woman's life—oh, not that!"

The detective, on his way down to Toorak, went over the case in his own mind, in order to see against whom the evidence was strongest. At last, after considerable cogitation, he came to the conclusion that, after all, Villiers must be the guilty man, and that Kitty knew more about the crime than she chose to tell.

"I can't get over Villiers having had that diamond crescent," he thought, looking out of the carriage windows. "She denied it was hers, and then Fenton told me he gave it to her. I wonder if he had anything to do with the affair—humph!—not likely. If she thought it was him, she'd tell at once. Perhaps she really thinks Stewart stole the diamonds. Pish! I don't believe it. She's had a finger in the pie, whoever did it, and this murder is the outcome of the robbery. Well, I'll see if she can account for her possession of this five-pound note— that's the main thing."

Kitty Marchurst was at home, and sent a message to the detective that she would see him in a few minutes, so Naball walked up and down the long drawing-room with some impatience.

"If she'll only tell the truth," he muttered restlessly; "but I'm getting to doubt her, so that I can't be sure. There's one thing, Keith Stewart's fate rests entirely with her now, so if he saved her child's life, as she says he did, this is the time to prove her gratitude."

At this moment the door opened, and Caprice entered. She looked pale and weary, for the trials of the last few months had not been endured without leaving some mark of their passage. Naball did not know whether this haggard-looking woman was guilty or innocent, but he could not help pitying her, so worn-out did she seem.

"You are not well," he said when she seated herself.

Kitty sighed wearily, and pushed the loose hair off her forehead.

"No," she replied listlessly. "I'm getting worn-out over this trouble. It's no good my telling you anything, because you don't believe me. What is the matter now? Have you got further proof of my guilt?"

"I don't know," said Naball, coolly producing the five-pound note; "unless you call this proof."

"A five-pound note," she said contemptuously. "Well?"

"It is a five-pound note," explained Naball smoothly; "but not an ordinary one—in fact, it is one of the notes stolen from Lazarus's safe."

"Oh, how do you know that? By a very curious thing. One of the notes placed in the safe on the night of the murder was endorsed by the office-boy with the words 'Back Flat-Iron,' and strange to say the endorsed note has turned up."

"And that is it?"

"Exactly. Now, do you understand?"

Kitty shrugged her shoulders.

"I understand that you have secured an excellent piece of evidence, nothing more. Where did you get the note?"

"From Miss Rainsford."

"From Miss Rainsford!" repeated Kitty in surprise; "but you surely don't suspect—"

"No, I don't," interposed the detective; "because she was able to tell me where she got the note from."

"Well, I presume she got it from me."

"Yes," replied Naball, rather surprised at this cool admission. "She received it yesterday from you."

"Oh! then, you think I'm guilty?"

"Not if you can tell me where you got the note from."

"Certainly I can—from Mortimer—paid to me the day before yesterday."

"Your salary?"

"Not exactly," answered Kitty; "if it had been, you'd never be able to trace the note further back. No; I was at the theatre in the morning, and found myself short of money, so I asked Mortimer for some. He gave me that five-pound note, and, as he took it, from his waistcoat pocket, I've no doubt he'll be able to recollect from whom he received it."

"Why?"

"Because Mortimer doesn't carry fivers in his waistcoat pocket generally," said Caprice impatiently, "so he must have put that note there for some special reason. You'd better go and ask him."

"Certainly," said Naball, and arose to his feet. "I'm very much obliged to you."

"Then you don't think me guilty?" asked Kitty, with a smile.

"Upon my word, I don't know what to think," said the detective dismally. "The whole case seems mixed up. I'll tell you when I find the man who can't account for the possession of this fiver."

Kitty smiled, and then Naball took his leave, going straight from Toorak to the Bon-Bon Theatre, where he found Mortimer in his sanctum, up to the ears in business, as usual.

"Well, Naball," said the manager, looking up sharply, "what's up? Look sharp, I'm awfully busy."

"I only want to know where you got this?" asked Naball, giving him the five-pound note.

Mortimer took it up, and looked perplexed.

"How the deuce should I know; I get so many. Why do you want to know?"

"Oh, nothing. I just want to trace the note. Caprice said you gave it to her the day before yesterday."

"Eh! did I?"

"Yes. You took it from your waistcoat pocket."

"Of course; to be sure, she wanted some money. Yes; I kept it apart because it was made money—won it off Malton at euchre."

"Malton!" repeated Naball in amazement; "are you sure?"

"Yes, quite. You know I'm generally unlucky at cards, and this is about the first fiver I've made, so I kept it just to bring me luck; but Caprice wanted money, so I handed over my luck to her. There's nothing wrong, eh?"

"Oh, dear, no," replied Naball; "not the slightest—only some professional business."

"Because I shouldn't like to get any poor devil into a row," said Mortimer. "Now, be off with you, I'm busy. Good-day."

"Good-day, good-day."

Naball departed, curiously perplexed in his feelings. He had never thought of Malton in the light of a possible criminal, and yet it was so very strange that this note should have been traced back to him. Then he remembered the conversation he had overheard between Mrs. Malton and Kitty concerning the embezzlement, when Kitty denied that she had paid the money.

"By Jove!" said Naball, a sudden thought striking him, "he was present at that supper, and was in a regular hole for want of money. I wouldn't be a bit surprised if he stole those diamonds to replace the money, and his wife's thanking Caprice was all a blind, and then this note—humph!—things look rather fishy, my friend."

When he arrived at the Never-say-die Insurance Company Office, he sent in his card to the assistant manager, and in a few minutes was shown into Malton's room, where that individual received him with visible uneasiness.

"Well, Naball, and what brings you here?" he asked, watching the detective's face stealthily.

"Only a little business, in which I want your help," said Naball, taking the note out of his pocket-book. "Can you tell me where you got that?"

Malton's pink-and-white complexion grew a little pale, but he laughed in a forced manner as he glanced at the note.

"Got this?" he said. "I can't tell you. Was it ever in my possession?"

"It was," asserted Naball. "You gave it to Mortimer the day before yesterday."

"Oh, yes, I remember now," said Malton quickly. "He won it off me at cards."

"Exactly. Where did you get the note?"

Malton shifted uneasily in his seat, and his nether lip twitched uneasily.

"I'm afraid I can hardly remember," he murmured, pushing back his chair.

Naball's suspicions were now rapidly ripening to certainties. If Malton were innocent, why these signs of agitation? He wriggled and twisted about like an eel, yet never once met the keen eye of the detective.

"You'd better remember," said Naball mercilessly, "or it will be the worse for you."

"Why?" asked Malton, trying to appear composed.

"Because," explained Naball, in a low voice, "that note is one of those stolen by the man who murdered Jacob Lazarus."

Malton, with a smothered exclamation, started to his feet, and then, shaking in every limb, sat down again.

"No, no," he stammered, "that's absurd. It can't be—I tell you, it can't be."

"Oh, but it can be, and it is. I tell you, the note is endorsed 'Back Flat-Iron,' which was done by the office-boy a few moments before the notes were put in the safe by Stewart. They were gone after the murder, so there is no doubt they were taken by the man who committed the crime. I got this note from Miss Rainsford, who received it from Caprice; she, in her turn, got it from Mortimer, and he has referred us to you. Now, where did you get it?"

Malton drummed nervously on the table.

"I can't tell you," he said in a tremulous voice.

"You must."

"It's impossible."

"I tell you what, sir," said Naball coolly, "if you don't tell, it means trouble for you and the other man."

"What other man?" asked Malton shakily.

"The man you got this note from."

Malton thought for a moment, and then apparently made up his mind.

"You saw I was taken aback?" he asked Naball curiously.

The detective nodded.

"It's because I'm sorry for what I have to tell you—the man I got the note from was Ezra Lazarus."

Naball jumped to his feet with a cry.

"The dead man's son?" he said.

"Yes; the dead man's son," replied Malton slowly.

Naball stood for a few minutes, then putting the note in his pocket-book, once more took up his hat, and moved to the door.

"Where are you going?" asked Malton, rising.

"To see Mr. Ezra Lazarus," said Naball, pausing a moment. "In the meantime, till I have certain proof of his guilt, you hold your tongue." And he walked out, leaving Malton standing at his desk as if turned into stone.

Naball, on his way to the newspaper office, rapidly ran over in his own mind all the details of the case against Ezra.

"His father wouldn't give him any money, and he wanted to get married to that girl; father and son had a quarrel on the day preceding the murder; he was at the Bon-Bon on that night, and took Caprice downstairs to her carriage; she gave him Stewart's coat to take back to him again; in that coat was the knife found by Villiers under the window; she left the theatre long before Stewart,—where did he go? to his office, or—good heavens! if it should turn out to be true—"

Ezra received him, looking rather knocked up, but his face, though pale, was quite placid, and Naball wondered how a man guilty of such a terrible crime as parricide could be so calm.

"You look tired," he said, taking a seat.

"I am tired," admitted Ezra wearily. "I've been busy with my father's affairs."

"Humph!" thought Naball; "counting his gains, I suppose."

"Any fresh development of the case?" asked Ezra.

"Yes," said Naball solemnly. "I received this note to-day, and traced it back to Malton; he says it was given to him by you."

Ezra examined the note with great interest, and on turning it over saw the fatal words endorsed. He looked up quickly to Naball.

"This is one of the notes that were stolen?" he asked.

"Yes," replied Naball; "and Malton said it was given to him by you."

"By me!" repeated Ezra in amazement. "How on earth could I come across this note?"

"That's what I want to find out," said Naball.

Ezra looked at him for a moment, then the whole situation seemed to burst on him, and with a stifled groan the unhappy young man fell back into his chair, burying his face in his hands.

"Good God!" he cried, "you don't suspect me of killing my father?"

"If you are innocent, you can explain where you got the note."

"I cannot—I cannot," cried Ezra feverishly. "I had to pay some money to Malton, and did so last week. There were some five-pound notes among that money, but I cannot tell where this particular one came from."

"Where did you get the money?" asked Naball.

"From the Hibernian Bank."

"Oh, but if you had to pay Malton money, why did you not do so by cheque?"

"Because I wanted some money myself, and did not care about drawing two cheques, so I drew one, covering what I owed to him and a little over."

"Humph!" Naball thought a moment. "You are sure of this?"

"Yes; it's the only way I can account for having the note. Whoever killed my father, must have paid it into the bank, and it came round to me by some fatality."

"Where were you on the night of the murder?"

"At the Bon-Bon Theatre."

"Afterwards?"

"At this office."

"You can prove an *alibi?*"

"I'm afraid I can't. I was all alone."

"Look here, Mr. Lazarus," said Naball in a kind tone, "I must say things look black against you; but I'm not satisfied yet about the real criminal. To-day is Saturday, so I'll go to the bank the first thing on Monday, and find out what I can. There's so many suspected of this business, that one more or less don't matter."

Ezra groaned.

"You don't think I'm guilty?" he asked imploringly.

Naball looked keenly at him.

"No; I believe you innocent," he replied abruptly.

XXVII

Meg proves Useful

The next day was Sunday, and Caprice, quite worn-out with the excitement of the week and the strain of the performances of "Faust Upset," was lying in bed. The burlesque had become a great success, but the papers, with their usual kindly generosity towards authors, declared that it was due not so much to the intrinsic merit of the work, as to the wonderfully clever acting of Caprice. Last night, however, she had acted badly, going through her part with mechanical precision, but without that dash which usually characterised her performance. The worry of this murder case, anxiety for the future of her child, and pity for the unfortunate young man now in prison, had all wrought on her nerves, so that she felt overcome with extreme lassitude, and lay supinely in bed, with half-closed eyes, incapable of the slightest exertion.

From this state of tranquillity she was aroused by the entrance of Eugénie, who was also looking pale and worn. She had learned all about the tracing of the five-pound note to Ezra, and had now come to tell Kitty about it.

The room was in a kind of semi-darkness, as all the blinds had been pulled down to keep out the dazzling sunlight, and the atmosphere was permeated by the smell of some pungent scent which Kitty had been using to bathe her aching head. Eugénie came straight to the bed, and bent over it, on which Kitty opened her eyes and smiled faintly.

"Oh, is it you, Miss Rainsford?" she said drowsily. "I did not expect you to-day."

"No!" replied Eugénie. "I came to tell you all about that five-pound note; but I'm sorry to find you so ill."

"I'm worn-out," said Kitty fretfully. "All the worry and trouble of my earlier years are beginning to tell on me, and the anxiety of this case is the climax. I believe I'll die soon, and I don't much care, for I have your promise about the child."

"You have!—my solemn promise."

"Thank you. I don't mind when I die. My life has been a very unhappy one. I've had more than my share of sorrow, and now I would like to go to sleep, and slumber on—on for ever."

She finished the sentence in a sleepy tone, then suddenly recollecting why Eugénie had come down, she opened her eyes wide, and spoke briskly.

"Well, what about this five-pound note? To whom did it originally belong?"

"I'd better go through the whole history," said Eugénie slowly. "I received it from you."

"Exactly," interrupted Caprice, raising herself on her elbow; "and I got it from Mortimer. Who gave it to him?"

"Mr. Malton, for a gambling debt."

"Malton," repeated Kitty vivaciously. "Why, is he—did they—"

"Suspect him of the murder. No; because he says he got the note from Ezra Lazarus, and he cannot tell from whom he received it."

Kitty was wide awake by this time, and sitting up in bed, pushed the fair curls off her forehead.

"But, my dear," she said rapidly, "surely they don't suspect that poor young man of murdering his father?"

"Not exactly suspect him," observed Eugénie; "but, you see, Mr. Lazarus cannot account for the possession of that particular note, so that makes things look bad against him."

"I don't see why," said Caprice impatiently. "I'm sure I couldn't account for every individual five-pound note I receive—it's absurd;—is that all the case they have against him?"

"I think so; but Mr. Naball says—"

"Says!" interrupted Kitty impatiently; "Naball's a fool. I often heard what a clever detective he was, but I'm afraid I can't see it. He's mismanaged the whole of this case shamefully. Why he suspects every one all round on the slightest suspicion: first he thought it was me, because I was at Lazarus's place on that night; then he swore it was Villiers, because he found the knife Meg gave Mr. Stewart; then poor Mr. Stewart is arrested simply because he cannot prove an alibi. I daresay, when he found Malton had the note, he suspected him, and now, I'll be bound, he has firmly settled in his own mind that Ezra Lazarus killed his own father—pish! My dear, I tell you again Naball's a fool."

"That may be," observed the other woman bitterly; "but he's a fool on whose folly Keith's life depends."

"Not a bit of it," said Caprice cheerfully; "we'll find some way to save him yet. The only evidence against him is that knife, and I don't believe it was in his possession at the Bon-Bon Theatre."

"Why not?"

"Because no one could have taken it out of his overcoat pocket there. I took the coat downstairs by mistake, but I'm sure I never abstracted the knife. Ezra Lazarus took it back, and I'll swear, in spite of Mr. Naball, he didn't take it. It's not likely Mortimer would go fiddling in another man's pockets, so I believe the knife was taken from the coat pocket, without his knowledge, at the club."

"But who took it, and how?" asked Eugénie, with great interest.

"My dear," replied Kitty, with a shrug, "how do I know. Perhaps, after receiving back the knife from Fenton, and putting it in his pocket, he hung his coat up again; in that case, anyone who saw him put the knife away could have stolen it."

"But who would do so?"

"That's what our clever Naball ought to find out," said Caprice, with a disdainful smile, "only he's such an idiot. I tell you whom I suspect—mind you, it's only suspicion—and yet appearances are quite as black against him as any one else."

"Who is it?"

"Malton."

"Malton!" repeated Eugénie, starting up.

"None other," said Kitty coolly. "He was at the club, and I know was hard up for money. His wife came to me one day, and told me he had embezzled a lot of money at his office. Then, after the crime, she came to me, and thanked me for paying it. I never did so. Fenton said he did, but I doubt it, as there isn't much of the philanthropist about him, so the only one who could have replaced the money was Malton himself. How? Well, easily enough. He was at the club—saw Keith's knife, and, knowing he was Lazarus's clerk, the idea flashed across his mind of murdering the old man with the knife, and dropping it about, so as to throw suspicion on Stewart. So, by some means, I don't know how, he obtains the knife before Stewart leaves the club, commits the crime, gets the money, circulates the notes, and when taxed with the possession of a marked one, says he got it from Ezra Lazarus—very weak, my dear, very weak indeed. Ezra says he paid him some money, so naturally doesn't know each individual note; so such a thing favours Mr. Malton's little plan. So there you are, my dear. I've made up a complete case against Malton, and quite as feasible as any of Naball's theories. Upon my word," said Kitty gaily, "I ought to have been a detective."

Eugénie was walking to and fro hurriedly.

"If this is so, he ought to be arrested," she said quickly.

"Then go and tell Naball, my dear," said Kitty in a mocking voice. "He'll arrest any one on suspicion. I wonder half the population of Melbourne aren't in jail, charged with the murder. Oh, Naball's a brilliant man! He says the man who committed the murder stole my diamonds—pish!"

"And you say Keith stole them," said Eugénie reproachfully, "therefore—"

"Therefore the lesser crime includes the greater," finished Kitty coolly. "No, my dear, I don't believe he is a murderer; but as to the diamonds, what am I to think after what Meg told me?"

"Meg! Meg!" said that young person, dancing into the room, holding a disreputable doll in her arms, "mumsey want Meg?"

"Yes," said Kitty, as Meg came to the bedside.

"Come up here, dear, and tell mumsey how you are."

"Meg is quite well, and so is Meg's daughter," holding out the doll for Kitty to kiss; "but, mumsey, why is the lady so sad?"

Eugénie, who had remained silent since Kitty's speech, now came forward and kissed the child.

"I'm not sad, dear," she said quietly, taking her seat by the bed, "only I want Meg to tell me something."

Meg nodded.

"A fairy tale?" she asked sedately.

Kitty laughed, though she looked anxious.

"No, my dear, not a fairy tale," she said, smoothing the child's hair; "mumsey wants you to tell the story of the man who got out of the window."

"My Mr. Keith," said Meg at once.

Kitty glanced at Eugénie, who sat with bowed head, gazing steadfastly at her hands.

"You see," she observed with a sigh, "the child says it was Mr. Keith."

Miss Rainsford re-echoed the sigh, then looked at Meg.

"Meg, dear," she said in her soft, persuasive voice, "come here, dear, and sit on my knee."

Meg, nothing loth, scrambled down off the bed, and soon established herself on Eugénie's lap, where she sat shaking her auburn curls. Kitty glanced affectionately at the serious little face, and picked up her doll, which was lying on the counterpane.

"Now, Meg," she said gaily, "you tell Miss Rainsford the story of the man and the window. I'll play with this."

"Meg's daughter," observed Meg reprovingly.

"Yes, Meg's daughter," repeated Kitty with a smile.

"Come, Meg," said Eugénie, smoothing the child's hair, "tell me all about the man."

"It was my Mr. Keith, you know," began Meg, resting her cheek against Eugénie's breast, "He took me upstairs—'cause I was so sleepy— an' he put me to bed, an' then I slept right off."

"And how long did you sleep, dear?" asked Eugénie.

"Oh, a minute," said Meg, "just a minute; then I didn't feel sleepy, and opened my eyes wide—quite wide—as wide as this," lifting up her face in confirmation, "and Mr. Keith, he was getting out of the window."

"How do you know it was Mr. Keith?" asked Eugénie quickly,

"'Cause he put me in bed," said Meg wisely, "and he was there all the time."

"He didn't speak to you when he was near the window?"

"No; he got out, and tumbled. I laughed when he tumbled," finished Meg triumphantly; "then I slept again, right off."

Eugénie put the girl down off her knee, and turned to Kitty.

"I believe Keith did put the child to bed," she said quietly, "but I think she must have slept for some time, and that the man she saw getting out of the window was some one else; of course, being awakened by the noise, she would only think she had slept a minute."

"A minute, a minute," repeated Meg, who had climbed back on to the bed, and was jumping the doll up and down.

"But who could the second man have been?" asked Kitty, perplexed.

"You know Naball's theory that the man who stole the diamonds committed the murder," said Eugénie. "You think Malton is guilty of the murder, why not of the robbery also? He was present at the supper-party, and knew where the jewels were kept."

Kitty drew her brows together and was about to speak, when Meg held up her doll for inspection.

"Look at the locket," she said triumphantly; "it's like Bliggings's locket—all gold."

Kitty smiled, and touched the so-called locket, which was in reality part of a gold sleeve-link, and was tied round the neck of the doll with a bit of cotton.

"Who gave you this?" she said. "Bliggings?"

"No; Meg found it herself, here, after the man had got out of the window."

Eugénie gave a cry, and started up, but Kitty in a moment had seized the doll, and wrenched off the gold link which Meg called the locket.

"When did you find this, Meg?" she asked the child in a tone of suppressed excitement.

"After the man went out of the window," said Meg proudly.

"In the dark?" asked her mother.

"No, when Meg was dressed, and the sun was shining," said Meg, trying to get back the locket.

"Wait a moment, dear," said Kitty, pushing the child away.

"Miss Rainsford, do you know what this link means?"

"I half guess," faltered Eugénie, clasping her hands.

"Then you guess right," cried Kitty, raising herself on her elbow. "It means that the man who stole the jewels dropped this link, and I know who he is, because I gave it to him myself."

"Keith?" said Eugénie faintly.

"Keith!" repeated Caprice in a tone of scorn. "No; not Keith, whom I have suspected wrongfully all these months, but my very good friend, Hiram J. Fenton."

"Fenton!" echoed Eugénie in surprise.

"Yes; he must have committed the crime," said Kitty in anger, grinding her teeth. "The coward, he knew I suspected Keith, and let another man bear the stigma of his crime. I spared Keith when I thought him guilty, because he saved my child's life; but I'll not spare Fenton now I know he is a thief."

"What will you do?" asked Eugénie quickly.

"What will I do!" cried Caprice, with a devilish light shining in her beautiful eyes. "I'll put him in prison—ring the bell for pen, ink, and paper—I'll write him to come down here to-night to see me; and when he comes, I'll have Naball waiting to arrest him."

"But Keith?" faltered Eugénie.

"As for Keith," said Caprice, throwing herself back in the bed, "I'm sure he'll soon be free, for it's my belief that Fenton stole the diamonds, but was too cowardly to commit a murder. No; he did not do it himself, but he got some one else to do it."

"And that some one?" cried Eugénie.

"Is Evan Malton," said Caprice solemnly.

XXVIII

Malton makes a Discovery

Evan Malton had a house in Carlton, not a very fashionable locality certainly, but the residence of the assistant manager was a comfortable one. His wife and child were invariably to be found at home, but Malton himself was always away—either at his club, the theatre, or at some dance. He was one of those weak men who can deny themselves nothing, and kept his wife and child stinted for money, while he spent his income on himself. But with such tastes as he possessed, his income did not go very far, so in a moment of weakness he embezzled money in order to gratify his desires.

When he told his wife what he had done, the news came like a thunder-clap on her. She knew her husband was weak, pleasure-loving and idle, but she never dreamt he could be a criminal. With the desire of a woman to find excuses for the conduct of a man she loved, Mrs. Malton thought that his crime was due to the evil influence of Kitty Marchurst; hence her visit and appeal to the actress. It seemed to have been successful, for the money had been replaced, though Kitty denied having paid it, and Mrs. Malton breathed freely.

Her husband loved her in a kind of a way; he did not mind being unfaithful himself, but he would have been bitterly angered had he found her following his example. This type of husband is not uncommon; he likes to be a butterfly abroad, to lead a man-of-the-world existence, neglecting his home; yet he always expects on his return to find a hearty welcome and a loving-wife.

Of course, as Mrs. Malton was a handsome woman, with a neglectful husband, the inevitable event happened, and Fenton, the bosom friend of the husband, fell in love with the solitary wife. She repelled his advances proudly, as she really loved her husband; but the effect of long months of neglect were beginning to tell on her, and she asked herself bitterly if it was worth while for her to remain faithful to a husband who neglected her.

On the Sunday afternoon following the interview Malton had with Naball, she sat down in her drawing-room, idly watching the child playing at her feet. Malton had come home in a fearful temper the night before, and had been in bed all Sunday. Dinner had been early, and she had left him in the dining-room, with a scowling face, evidently drinking more than was good for him.

"What is the use of trying to make his life happy?" she said to herself with a sneer. "He cares no more for me than he does for the child. If I were to allow his dearest friend to betray me, I don't believe he would care a fig about it."

While she was thus talking, the door opened, and her husband came into the room, with a sullen look on his face. He was, as she saw, in a temper, and ready for a domestic battle; but, determined not to give him a chance, she sat in her chair in silent disdain.

"Well," he said, throwing himself on the sofa, "haven't you got a word to say for yourself?"

"What can I say?" she replied listlessly.

"Anything! Don't sit there like a cursed sphynx. How do you expect a man to come home when he finds things so disagreeable?"

She looked at him scornfully.

"You find things disagreeable," she said slowly. "You, who have neglected me ever since our marriage; who have passed your time with actresses and betting men; you, who—"

"Go to the devil," said Malton sulkily, cutting short her catalogue of his vices. "I don't want you to preach. I'll go where I like, and do what I like."

"Yet you deny me the right to do the same."

"What do you mean?"

"Mean!" she cried, rising to her feet; "mean that I'm tired of this sordid way of living. I'm tired of seeing you at the beck and call of every woman except your wife. I have tried to do my duty by you and the child, yet you neglect me for others. You squander your honestly earned money, and then embezzle thousands of pounds. I tell you, I'm sick of this life, Evan Malton; and if you don't take care, I'll make a change."

He listened in amazement to this tirade coming from his meek wife, then, with a coarse laugh, flung himself back on the sofa.

"You'll make a change!" he said, with a sneer. "You—I suppose that means bolting with another man—you do, my lady, and I'll kill you and your lover as well."

"My lover, as you call him, could break your neck easily," she said contemptuously.

"Then you have a lover!" he cried, starting to his feet in a transport of fury. "You tell me *that*—you a wife and a mother—in the presence of our child."

Without a word, she touched the bell, and a maid-servant appeared. Mrs. Malton pointed to the child.

"Take her away," she said coldly, and when the door closed again, she turned once more to her husband. "Now that the child is away," she said calmly, "I do tell you I have a would-be lover. Stay," she cried, holding up her hand, "I said a would-be lover. Had I been as careless of your honour as you have been of mine, I would not now be living with you."

Evan Malton listened in dogged silence, and then burst out into a torrent of words.

"Ah! I knew it would be so—curse you! What woman was ever satisfied with a husband?"

"Yes, and such a husband as you have been," she said sarcastically.

He stepped forward, with an oath, to strike her, then restraining himself by an effort, said in a harsh voice,—

"Tell me his name."

Mrs. Malton walked over to a writing-desk, unlocked it, and taking from thence a bundle of letters, flung them on the floor before him.

"You'll find all about him there."

Malton bent down, picked up the letters, and staggered back, with a cry, as he recognised the writing.

"My God! Fenton!" he cried.

"Exactly," she said coolly. "Your dear friend Fenton, who came to me with words of love on his lips, and lies in his heart, to get me to elope with him—in the last letter, you see, he asked me to go with him to Valparaiso."

"Oh, did he?" muttered Malton vindictively; "and you were going, I suppose?"

"If I had been going," she replied, with grave scorn, "I would not now be here, for he leaves for Valparaiso to-night."

"To-night!"

"Yes. I presume he's followed your example, and embezzled money. At all events, I refused his offer, and left him as I now leave you, Evan Malton, with the hope that this discovery may teach you a lesson."

"Where are you going?" he cried hoarsely, as she moved towards the door.

She turned with a cold smile.

"I am going to our child; and you—"

"And I," he said vindictively, "I'm going to Hiram Fenton's house, to give him back those letters. He'll go to Valparaiso will he? No, he won't. To-night, the police shall know all."

"All what?" his wife cried in sudden terror.

"All about the diamond robbery and the Russell Street murder."

She shrank back from him with a cry; but he came straight to the door, and taking her by the arm, flung her brutally on the floor.

"You lie there," he hissed out. "I'll deal with him first, and afterwards with you."

She heard the door close, and knew that he had left the house: then, gathering herself up slowly and painfully, she went to the chamber of her child, and sank on her knees beside the cot.

Meanwhile, Malton, with his brain on fire, his heart beating with jealous rage, and the bundle of letters in his breast-pocket, was rapidly walking down the hill, intending to go to Fenton's rooms and tax him with his treachery. It was partly on this account that he wished to see him; but there was also a more serious cause, for in the event of Fenton bolting, as he intended to do, things would be very awkward for his assistant manager.

"Curse him!" muttered Malton as he hailed a hansom, and told the man to drive to East Melbourne. "Does he think I'm such a fool as to let him go now? No, no, my boy; we've floated together for a good time, and, by Jove! we'll sink together."

Like all weak men, he was unable to restrain his temper, and was now working himself up into a state of fury which boded ill for the peace of Mr. Fenton. Fast as the cab was rolling along, it seemed hours to the impatient man, and it was with a cry of joy that he jumped out at Fenton's door, keeping the hansom waiting in case he should find the American absent.

The woman who opened the door told him that Mr. Fenton had gone out about half-an-hour ago, with a black bag in his hand, and had told her he was going to see some friends.

"Curse the man," groaned Malton, who saw what this meant at once, "he's off; I must follow——but where? I don't suppose he'd leave his address in his room, but I'll see if I can find anything there."

"Can I give him any message, sir?" asked the woman, who was still holding the door open.

"Yes; that is, I'll write him a note; show me up to his sitting-room."

"Yes, sir," and in a few minutes Malton found himself alone in the room so lately occupied by his enemy. He sat down at the writing-table till the woman closed the door, then springing to his feet, began to examine the desk with feverish energy to see if Mr. Fenton had left any trace as to his whereabouts.

There was a newspaper lying on a small table near, and Malton, seizing this, looked at the shipping announcements to see by what boat Fenton intended to go to South America.

"He's certain to go there," he said, as he ran his finger eagerly down the column, "or he wouldn't have told my wife. Here, oh, here it is—The 'Don Pedro,' for Valparaiso, at eight, Monday morning. He's going by that boat, now," he went on, putting down the paper, and pulling out his watch; "it's about six o'clock—why did he leave to-night, eh? I suppose he means to go on board, so as to avoid suspicion by going so early in the morning. He can't have gone back to see my wife, or she would have told me, for I'll swear she's true. Confound him, where can he have gone?"

He turned over the papers on the desk in feverish eagerness, as if he expected to find an address left for him, when suddenly, slipped in between the sheets of the blotting-pad, he found a note in Caprice's handwriting asking Fenton to come down to Toorak on that night. Melton struck a blow on the desk with his fist when he read this.

"He's gone there, I'll swear," he cried, putting the letter in his pocket. "It was only because Caprice laughed at him that he made love to my wife. Now she's whistled him back, he'll try and get her to go off with him to Valparaiso. Ah, Hiram Fenton, you're not off yet, and never will be—sink or swim together, my boy—sink or swim together."

He called the woman, gave her a short note for Fenton, in order to avert suspicion, then getting into the cab once more, told the man to drive to Toorak as quickly as possible.

"If I don't find you there, my friend," he muttered angrily, "I'll go straight down to the 'Don Pedro' at Sandridge. You won't escape me—sink or swim together, sink or swim together."

The evening sky was overcast with gloomy clouds, between the rifts of which could be seen the sharp, clear light of the sky, and then it began to rain, a tropical downpour which flooded the streets and turned the gutters to miniature torrents; a vivid flash of lightning flare in the sky, and the white face of the man in the hansom could be seen for a moment; then sounded a deep roll of thunder, as if warning Hiram Fenton that his friend and victim was on his track.

XXIX

Light at Last

I t was certainly a remarkable thing that when Kitty had prepared her trap for Fenton just on the eve of his going away, by having Naball in hiding to arrest him, that Malton, the only man who could effectually accuse the American, should also have come down to Toorak in the nick of time. But, then, coincidences do happen in real life as well as in novels; and had Kitty carefully constructed the whole scene with an eye to dramatic effect, it could hardly have turned out better.

Eugénie sat with the actress in the drawing-room, waiting for the arrival of Fenton, and talking to Naball, who was seated near them. The detective had listened to all with the keenest interest, but, much to Kitty's disgust, seemed doubtful of the American's guilt.

"You were quick enough in accusing other people," she said angrily, "myself among the number, and now, when I show you plain proof, you disbelieve."

"I don't think the proof is strong enough, that's all," replied Naball drily. "We have only the word of a child that she picked up the link in the bedroom."

"Meg never tells falsehoods," interposed Eugénie quickly.

"I daresay not," he replied coolly. "However, Fenton may have lost this link before."

"No, he didn't," said Caprice decisively. "He had the links on when he was at supper. I saw them, and I ought to know, because I gave them to him myself."

"But why should Fenton steal your diamonds? He's got lots of money," argued Naball, who was rather annoyed at Kitty finding out more than he had.

"I don't know why he should," retorted the actress; "it's not my business or yours to discover motives—all I know is, he did it, and I'm going to have him arrested."

"Perhaps he'll be suspicious, and won't come."

"Oh yes, he will. He thinks I believe Stewart to be the thief, and as to coming, I can whistle him back at any moment. Hark!" as a ring came at the door. "There he is; get behind that screen. Miss Rainsford, you go into the next room till I call."

Naball promptly did as he was told, so did Eugénie, and when Fenton entered the room, he only found Kitty, calmly seated beside a little table, reading a book.

Fenton was looking wonderfully well, but with a watchful look on his face, as if he feared discovery. He had a good sum of money with him, his passage to Valparaiso, and never for a moment thought that he was on the edge of an abyss. Of course, Kitty did not know he was about to abscond, and never thought how near her prey had escaped. She received him quietly, with friendly interest, and Fenton, pulling a chair next to hers, began to talk eagerly, never dreaming that an officer of the law was listening to every word.

Not only that, but outside, crouching on the verandah, was a dark figure, with a livid face, listening to what the man inside was saying. Hiram Fenton, utterly unconscious, was surrounded on all sides by his enemies, and went on telling all his plans to Kitty, never thinking how near he was to the felon's dock from which he was flying.

"And what did you want to see me about!" asked Fenton, taking Caprice's hand.

"Nothing in particular," she replied carelessly; "the fact is, I haven't seen you for such a long time."

"Then you do care for me a little?"

Caprice shrugged her shoulders.

"As much as I do for any man; but I didn't ask you to come here to make love. I want to talk seriously about giving up the stage."

She was leading him on so that he should betray himself to the detective, and he walked straight into the trap.

"Oh, you're tired of acting," said Fenton thoughtfully.

"Yes; and of Melbourne. I want to go away."

Fenton started, and wondered if she knew he was going away also. He thought for a moment, and then replied,—

"Then, why not come with me?"

"With you!" cried Kitty derisively. "What about Mrs. Malton?"

"I tell you, I don't care two straws about Mrs. Malton," he rejoined angrily. "I was only amusing myself with her."

Amusing himself! The man outside ground his teeth together in anger, and clutched the packet of letters fiercely.

"And what about your dear friend—her husband?"

FERGUS HUME

"Oh, Malton," said Fenton carelessly. "I don't know, nor do I care; he was a very useful man to me for a time. But, now, I'm off."

"Off!—where?"

"To Valparaiso. Yes, I'm sick of Australia, so I sail to-morrow morning for South America. Will you come with me, Kitty?"

Kitty looked doubtful.

"I don't know. We have no money."

"I have plenty. I've arranged all that, and if there's a row, my dear friend Malton will have to bear it. But now, Kitty, I've told you all, you must come with me. We can live a delightful life in South America. I know it well, and some of the places are Paradises. Come, say you'll come to-night."

He put his arms round her, and pressed a kiss on her lips. She shuddered at the impure caress, then pushing him away, arose to her feet.

"Don't touch me," she said harshly, "you—you thief!"

In a moment Fenton was on his feet, with an apprehensive look on his face.

"Thief! thief!" he cried fiercely; "what do you mean?"

"Mean," she said, turning on him like a tiger, "that I know now who stole my diamonds, Mr. Hiram Fenton."

"Do you accuse me?" he asked, with a pale face, gripping her wrist.

"Yes, I do," said Kitty, wrenching her wrist away, "and I've got a proof—this broken sleeve-link, dropped by you in my room on the night of the robbery."

"It's a lie!"

"It's true! I accuse you of stealing my diamonds. Detective Naball, arrest that man."

Fenton started as Naball stepped out from behind the screen, and then folded his arms, with an evil smile.

"So!" he said coolly, "this is a trap, I see; but I'm not to be caught in it. You say I stole your diamonds?"

"I do," said Kitty boldly.

"And your proof is that you picked up a broken sleeve-link?"

"Yes."

"Then, Mr. Detective," said Fenton, holding out both his wrists to Naball, "if you examine these, you will see neither of the links are broken."

Naball, with an ejaculation of surprise, examined both the links, and found what he said was correct—neither of the sleeve-links were broken.

"Have you not made a mistake?" he said to Caprice.

"No, I have not," she replied coolly. "When he found he had lost a sleeve-link, he got another made, in order to avert suspicion. I say Hiram Fenton stole my diamonds, and I give him in charge."

Naball stepped forward, but the American, who was now uneasy at the turn affairs had taken, waved him back.

"Wait a moment," he said quickly; "I deny the charge, and will prove it false to-morrow."

Kitty laughed derisively.

"By which time you will be on your way to Valparaiso. No, I'm not going to let you go."

"Neither am I," said Naball decisively. "I arrest you on this charge of robbery now," and he laid his hand on the shoulder of the American.

In a moment Fenton twisted himself away, and dexterously throwing Naball on the ground, darted towards one of the French windows.

"Not so fast, my friend," he said sneeringly, while Naball, half-stunned, was picking himself up; "guess I'll beat you this time. I care nothing for you nor that she-devil there. You can prove nothing."

Naball made a bound forward, but with a mocking laugh Fenton was about to step lightly through the window, when he was dashed violently back into Naball's arms, and Malton, pale as death sprang into the room.

"Hold him," he cried, clutching Fenton, who was too much astonished to make any resistance. "Don't let him go. He's guilty—I can prove it."

Eugénie had hurried into the room, attracted by the noise, and Kitty was standing near her, the two women clinging together for protection. Naball held Fenton firmly, while Malton, in a frenzy of rage, spoke rapidly.

"He is guilty of the robbery," he shrieked, menacing Fenton with his fists. "He embezzled money with me, and had it been found out, we would both have been put in prison. He stole the diamonds on the night of the supper, by going upstairs to your room, and then leaving by the window, so as to make people think it was a burglary."

"A cursed lie!" growled Fenton, making an effort to shake Naball off.

"No, it isn't," cried Malton furiously. "Villiers can prove it. You met him as you were coming round the house, and gave him some diamonds to make him hold his tongue."

"Oh, the crescent!" cried Naball.

"Yes, yes; and then he sold the diamonds to old Lazarus, and afterwards murdered him. Yes, he killed Jacob Lazarus!"

Fenton's nostrils dilated, he drew a deep breath, and gave a cry of anger; but Malton went on speaking rapidly.

"I got that note not from Ezra Lazarus, but from Fenton, and lied to shield him; but now, when I find out he makes love to my wife, I'll do anything to hang him. See, these letters—your cursed letters," flinging them on the ground before Fenton. "You liar, thief, murderer, you're done for at last!"

"Not yet!" yelled Fenton, and with a sudden effort he flung Naball off, and dashed for the window, but Malton sprang on him like a wild cat, and they both rolled on the floor. Naball jumped up, and went to Malton's help, when suddenly the American, with a supreme effort, wrenched himself clear of them, and ran once more for the window.

Seeing this, Kitty, who had remained a passive spectator, tried to stop him, but with an oath he hurled her from him, and she, falling against a table, knocked it over, and fell senseless on the ground. Fenton, with a cry of anger, dashed through the window, and disappeared into the darkness. But, quick as he was, Malton was quicker; for seeing his enemy escape him, he also sprang through the window, and gave chase.

Naball, breathless, and covered in blood, was about to go also, when a cry from Eugénie stopped him. The girl was kneeling down beside Kitty, while the frightened servants crowded in at the door.

"Oh, she is dead! dead!" cried Eugénie, looking down at the still face. "No; she can't be. Brandy—bring some brandy!"

A servant entered with the brandy, and Eugénie, filling a glass, forced some of the liquid between Kitty's clenched teeth. Naball also took a glass, as he was worn-out with the struggle, then, hastily putting on his hat, went out, leaving Kitty lying, to all appearances dead, in Eugénie's arms.

Meanwhile, Malton was close on the heels of the American, who had cleared out by the gate, and was making for the railway station. There were few people about; but the spectacle of two men racing bare-headed soon brought a crowd around. Fenton, with deep curses, sped on through the driving rain, and at last flew on to the platform, followed by Malton, who gasped out,—

"Seize him! Murderer! murderer!"

The station-master, a porter, and some passengers who were waiting, all sprang forward at this; so Fenton, seeing himself surrounded, gave one yell of rage, and, jumping on the line, ran along.

"My God!" cried the station-master, "the train is coming down; he will be killed."

He tried to hold Malton, who was mad with anger at seeing his prey escape him, and, foaming with anger, wrenched himself away.

"You'll be killed!" cried the porter; but Malton, with a hoarse cry, sprang on to the line, and sped after Fenton through the driving rain.

It was pitch dark, and the rain swept along in slanting sheets, through which gleamed the red and green of the signals. Malton, only actuated by a mad desire to seize Fenton, staggered blindly over the sleepers, stumbling at every step.

Suddenly he heard the hard breathing of the man he was pursuing, and the foremost figure loomed up dark and misshapen in the thick night. They were now near the railway bridge which crosses the Yarra-Yarra at this point, and the steady sweep of the river could be heard as it flowed against the iron girders.

Fenton, hearing some one close behind him, made a bound forwards, then fell on the line, with a shriek of despair. In a moment Malton was on him, and the two men rolled on the line, fighting like devils.

"Curse you!" hissed Malton, putting his knee on Fenton's chest, "I'll kill you!—I'll kill you!" And he dashed Fenton's head against the iron rails.

The American, in despair, flung up his hands, and caught Malton round the neck. Once more they fought, wrapped in a deadly embrace, when suddenly they felt the bridge vibrate, and, even in their struggle, saw rapidly approaching, through the darkness the light of the down train.

Malton, with a cry of horror, tried to release himself from Fenton's grip, but the American held him tight, and in another moment the train, with a roar, was on the bridge, and over their bodies.

One hoarse yell, and all was over. Evan Malton and Hiram Fenton were torn to pieces under the cruel wheels.

XXX

Exit Kitty Marchurst

So this was the end of it all. The criminal, guilty of the two crimes which had agitated Melbourne for so many months, turned out to be the respected manager of The Never-say-die Insurance Company. After the discovery of his guilt, the affairs of the company were examined, and found to be in a terrible state of confusion. Fenton, aided by Malton, had embezzled large sums of money, and so carefully manipulated the accounts that their defalcations had never been noticed.

It was true that once they were on the verge of discovery unless some of the money was paid back, and this had been accomplished by the robbery of Kitty Marchurst's diamonds. As the two guilty men were dead, the only man who knew anything about the affair was Mr. Villiers, who soon found things made so warm for him that he confessed all he knew about the crime.

It appeared that, on the night of the supper, Fenton was in great straits for want of money to replace that embezzled by himself and Malton. Hearing Kitty state where she kept her diamonds, he determined to steal them if he could do so with safety. In going to the drawing-room, he saw Stewart descending the stairs, and, as the young man told him he had been in Kitty's room putting the child to bed, he thought he could steal the jewels on that night, and let Stewart bear the blame.

With this idea, he went upstairs, took the diamonds from their place, and, in order to make things doubly secure, should his idea of implicating Stewart fail, he got out of the window, and clambered down, so as to show that the house had been burglariously entered.

In stealing round to the front of the house, he met Villiers, who had seen all, and, in order to make him hold his tongue, had given him the small diamond crescent which Naball secured in Little Bourke Street. Of course, Kitty would not prosecute Keith, as he had saved her child's life; and it was his security in this belief that caused Fenton to urge on the detective.

About the murder, Villiers, as a matter of fact, knew very little; but when Naball said that the man who stole the diamonds also committed the crime, he went to Fenton, and taxed him with it. Fenton, at first, indignantly denied the accusation, but ultimately confessed to Villiers that he had done so. After giving back Keith his knife at the club, he had seen him hang up his coat, and dexterously extracted the weapon therefrom unknown to the owner. Then he went to Russell Street and committed the crime, in reality to gain possession of the diamonds, thinking they were in the safe, as he did not know that Lazarus had sent them to Amsterdam.

Therefore, the whole mystery was cleared up; and after making his confession, Villiers found public opinion so much against him, that he left the colony, and disappeared, no one knew where.

The dead bodies of the American and Malton were found on the railway line, and, after an inquiry had been made, were duly buried. Mrs. Malton went back to live with her father, and shortly afterwards married again.

Stewart was released from prison and became quite the hero of the hour, as every one sympathised with him for the way in which he had been treated. Eugénie told him all about her accession to fortune, and they agreed to get married and go to Europe. Ezra, also, now that he was wealthy, turned Benedict, and was united to Rachel a short time after his father's death.

"Faust Upset" ran for some time, but was ultimately withdrawn, as the part of Miss Mephistopheles was taken by another woman, and she failed to draw the public.

But Caprice?

Ah! poor woman, she was dying. In the struggle with Fenton, she had fallen in a perilous position, and had so injured her spine, that there was no hope of recovery.

It was on a Tuesday evening, and poor, wicked Kitty was lying in bed, with her weary eyes fixed on Meg, who was seated on Eugénie's lap, rather puzzled by the whole affair. Keith and Ezra were also present, in deference to Kitty's desire, as she wanted to formally give Meg over to Eugénie to bring her up. All the legal formalities had been gone through, and now they were waiting for the end—alas! it was not very far off.

"Do you feel easier, dear?" asked Eugénie, gently bending over the bed.

"Yes," replied Kitty in a slow, tired voice. "Better now; it will soon be over. You—you will look after my child?"

"I promise you, I will," said Eugénie fervently. "Would you like to see a minister?"

Kitty smiled with a touch of her old cynicism, and then her eyes filled with tears.

"A minister, yes," she said in a faltering voice. "God help me! and I was a minister's daughter. Look at me now, fallen and degraded, dying, with my life before me, and glad—yes, glad to die."

In obedience to a sign from Eugénie, Keith had slipped out of the room in order to bring the clergyman, and Kitty lay quiet, with the clear light of the evening shining on her pale face.

"Give me my child," she said at length, and then, as she took Meg to her breast and kissed her, she wept bitterly.

"God bless you, my darling," she sobbed; "think of me with pity. Eugénie, never—never let her know what I was. Let her believe me to have been a good woman. If I have sinned, see how I was tempted— see how I have suffered—let my child think her mother was a good woman."

Eugénie, crying bitterly, promised this, and then tried to take Meg away.

"Mumsey," said Meg, clinging to her mother, "why do you cry? Where are you going?"

"I'm dying, Meg, darling."

"Dying!" said Meg, to whom the word conveyed no idea, "dying!"

"Yes, dear; going away."

"I'll go, too."

"No, dear, no. You must stay here, and be a good girl. Mumsey is going far away—to the sky," finished poor Kitty, in a faltering voice.

"To the sky—then you'll see God," said Meg.

At this Kitty could bear no more, but burst into tears, and Meg was taken out of the room, being pacified with difficulty. Then Keith entered with the clergyman, who was left alone with the dying woman for some time.

When they all returned, they saw she was sinking rapidly, but she smiled faintly as Eugénie approached.

"I've told him all," she said in a low voice, "and he says God will forgive me."

"I'm sure He will, dear," said Eugénie in a faltering voice.

"Strange," said the dying woman, in a dreamy voice, "I, who never cared for religion, should want it now. I'm glad to die, for there was nothing to live for; but this terrible Death—I fear it. I don't know where I'm going—where am I going?" she asked piteously.

"To Heaven, dear," said Eugénie.

"Heaven!" repeated Kitty, her memory going back to her childhood; "that is where there is neither sun nor moon—the glory of God is there. Oh, I'll never go there—never—never!"

The room w T as now filled with floating shadows, and all present were kneeling by the bed. Meg, who had been brought back, and held by Eugénie, was beside her mother, awed by the solemnity of the scene. A pale shaft of clear light came through the window, and shone on the disordered white clothes of the bed and the still face of the dying woman.

No sound save the sighing of the wind outside, the sobs of Eugénie, and the grave tones of the clergyman's voice, reading the Sermon on the Mount, which in former days had been a great favourite with Kitty.

"*Blessed are the pure in heart, for they shall see God*."

Poor soul, she that had not been pure was now dying, and dreaded lest her impurity should be brought up against her.

"*Blessed are the merciful, for they shall obtain mercy*."

Ah, Kitty Marchurst, what mercy did you ever show? The inward voice came to her like an accusing spirit, and she shrank back in the bed. Then she opened her eyes.

"I would have been a good woman," she said pathetically; "but I—I was so young when I met Gaston."

Her voice became inarticulate, and with an effort she kissed her child, while the clergyman said the Lord's Prayer.

"*Our Father which art in Heaven*."

"Meg, Meg," she murmured, "Meg—God bless my little child!" And those were the last words of Kitty Marchurst, for when the prayer was ended she was lying back, with her pure, childlike face stilled in death.

So she went into the outer darkness laden with sins, but surely God in His mercy pardoned this woman, whose impurity was more the result of circumstances than anything else.

Let us not deny to others the mercy which we ourselves will need some day. Kitty was dead, with all her frailties and passions; and as the clergyman arose from his knees, he repeated reverently the words of his Master,—

"*He that is without sin among you, let him first cast a stone at her*."

FINIS

FERGUS HUME

A Note About the Author

Fergus Hume (1859–1932) was an English novelist. Born in Worcestershire, Hume was the son of a civil servant of Scottish descent. At the age of three, he moved with his family to Dunedin, New Zealand, where he attended Otago Boy's High School. In 1885, after graduating from the University of Otago with a degree in law, Hume was admitted to the New Zealand bar. He moved to Melbourne, Australia, where he worked as a clerk and embarked on his career as a writer with a series of plays. After struggling in vain to find success as a playwright, Hume turned to novels with *The Mystery of a Hansom Cab* (1886), a story of mystery and urban poverty that eventually became one of the most successful works of fiction of the Victorian era. Hume, who returned to England in 1888, would go on to publish over 100 novels and stories, earning a reputation as a leading writer of popular fiction and inspiring such figures as Arthur Conan Doyle, whose early detective novels were modeled after Hume's. Despite the resounding success of his debut work of fiction, Hume died in relative obscurity at a modest cottage in Thundersley.

A Note from the Publisher

Spanning many genres, from non-fiction essays to literature classics to children's books and lyric poetry, Mint Edition books showcase the master works of our time in a modern new package. The text is freshly typeset, is clean and easy to read, and features a new note about the author in each volume. Many books also include exclusive new introductory material. Every book boasts a striking new cover, which makes it as appropriate for collecting as it is for gift giving. Mint Edition books are only printed when a reader orders them, so natural resources are not wasted. We're proud that our books are never manufactured in excess and exist only in the exact quantity they need to be read and enjoyed.

bookfinity™

Discover more of your favorite classics with Bookfinity™.

- Track your reading with custom book lists.
- Get great book recommendations for your personalized Reader Type.
- Add reviews for your favorite books.
- AND MUCH MORE!

Visit **bookfinity.com** and take the fun Reader Type quiz to get started.

Enjoy our classic and modern companion pairings!